I0459557

Executive Dirt

Maria E. Schneider

Copyright: 2015 © Maria E. Schneider

Bear Mountain Books

A Bear Mountain Books Production
www.BearMountainBooks.com

Maria E. Schneider

Copyright November 2015 © Maria E. Schneider

Printing History:
POD printing August 2015

Cover Art: Elements of the cover from depositphotos.com

All Rights Reserved. No part of this publication may be reproduced in any form without prior written permission from the author.

This is a work of fiction. Names, characters, places and incidents are either the product of the author's imagination or are used fictitiously, and any resemblance to any person, living or dead, is entirely coincidental.

ISBN-10: 0692494170
ISBN-13: 978-0692494172

Acknowledgments

Thanks to Marissa and Renee for suggesting questions for the Borgot phone. Thanks to those on the Mobileread forum for always being willing to talk tech, answer questions and tear apart the newest technology—including the Pebble Smartwatch. Thank you, Frank Tuttle, for letting me use your name, and that of your cousin, Big Foot, in the book.

A shoutout goes to the usual helpful culprits who keep me going during the days of blank pages and writing frustrations: Elisabeth, April, Dee and all those writers whose books inspire. A special thanks to Joan and LeAnn. Big smiley face for you two! A hat tip to Kevin, Wendie, the dogs and, if I must say so, the snake. A very special thanks to Kovid for Calibre. The tools you envisioned and created have been a great boon to writers and readers alike. Krittika has added her own special touch to helping authors as well.

And to my husband who not only puts up with my rantings and ravings, he reads them too.

Chapter 1

Sometimes you're so busy climbing the corporate ladder, you forget whether there is an actual goal. Your original dream might have been to make enough money to travel the world, but then you buy the house and the car, and you keep climbing. Before you know it, your dream becomes climbing to the next rung on the ladder.

I thought I'd already witnessed the worst of ladder climbing, but it turns out the shoving and clawing at an established company was mere child's play. Ladder climbing at a startup had the usual politics, but there were flamboyant fools who created ladder rungs out of toothpicks in an inane attempt to crown themselves king.

I worked at the Borgot startup thanks to Mark Huntington. His brother Steve Huntington kept offering me dangerous undercover jobs that involved ferreting out company malfeasance. Mark decided to find me a well-paying computer job that didn't involve any investigating whatsoever. This new job kept Mark happy, and these days his happiness was tied pretty closely to mine.

I have to admit, Borgot paid well for my skills as a computer technician. There was no need to even consider any job Huntington might offer. Besides, I always ended up fired when I accepted the jobs Huntington arranged.

Borgot was very modern, with a goal of designing a multi-language product to compete with Apple's Siri, the automated personal assistant voice. The technology part I liked. What I didn't appreciate was the ultra-modern office space that consisted of six-foot cubicles. I'd always enjoyed being a lab rat, testing machines and then running the maze all over again to see if the results changed when equipment changed. But add a cubicle to the work conditions, and suddenly I was the rat in the maze, and it was my survival skills being tested instead of the machines.

I wasn't winning the race either. The noise and lack of privacy set my teeth on edge. Doll Baby on the other side of one wall took phone calls all day, flirting and giggling. When she wasn't in her cube, she was sashaying all over the company cooing into her cell phone.

A peal of laughter vibrated against the shared wall of our cubes. "Who can she possibly be flirting with at ten in the morning after five earlier calls?" I asked no one.

Doll Baby, otherwise known as Monique, wasn't the worst of my cube-mates. No, that prize went to the dork who had just walked in, late again. Joe Black plopped down at his desk across the cube "hallway" breathing as though he had run all the way inside. He heaved a few extra pants and then shouted, "Owhay, ayay oingday?"

Perhaps it was some sort of cattle roundup call, or maybe he was having a stroke. Either way, I was not interested.

"Did you hear me?" With ridiculous pride, he spread his arms as far as the cube walls allowed, which meant he nearly punched a hole through his computer monitor. "Igpay atinlay."

I didn't even bother with a grimace. Ignoring him was easier.

He clarified magnanimously, "Pig Latin. It's a sign of higher intelligence. I can speak it faster than I can type and actually understand it quicker than most people can translate to a second language. They hired me because I'm a language expert. The phrases I'm contributing to the phone assistant are groundbreaking."

Joe "Dork" was balding badly. He had compensated for this by allowing the small amount of hair around his ears and along the back of his skull to grow long. He did not contain it in a neat ponytail. It wisped about his person as if it too wished it could leave him.

His phone rang. Thank God for small miracles.

Of course, the conversation was still broadcast loudly enough that even the cockroaches, needing daytime sleep, were probably leaving the building.

"I moved out of my place, man. I couldn't leave her on her own. The old lady was having a hard time with things, and shit, going over to her place to do the laundry, up the stairs and down the stairs, it was a pain in the ass. I had to move back in."

Before I, or anyone else forced to listen, could begin to marvel at Joe Dork actually having a girlfriend or wife, he clarified. "But she's my mom! I couldn't leave her in the lurch. She was going crazy trying to figure out what time to cook for me, too." Another pause while he listened. Then suddenly he acted as though he had just realized half the place could hear the conversation.

"Man, not now. I mean, I know it's important, but she's my mom. She isn't going to spout anything even if she notices. Ottagay ebay arefulcay."

My sorry brain translated without any explicit commands from me. "Gotta be careful?" I did not want to know what Dork had to be careful of. His mother killing him? I would wear earplugs tomorrow whether or not they stuck out my ears and made me look funny.

Joe glanced down at his geek watch as though he had a pressing meeting. "Okay, okay. I won't take it home with me. She'll never see it. Onay usinessbay atyay omehay."

He wouldn't take his business home with him? Of course he wouldn't. He didn't *do* any actual work. He was chronically late. He mostly showed up at meetings to crack bad jokes.

Dork's chair squeaked loudly in protest as he swiveled. His too obvious search for listeners was a tad on the desperate side.

Doll Baby sashayed past our cube openings. She actually wore those very words across the back of her pink hot-pants. Right across her butt. Her other favorite tights had a smiley face, one of those big yellow internet smileys, only hers was winking, of course.

I glued my eyes determinedly to my computer screen.

Joe Dork's next Pig Latin phrase was something about giving it back next week.

I continued to concentrate on my test report, but as soon as Joe hung up, he kicked the drawer of his desk as if that would somehow solve whatever problem had called him on the phone. He checked the time on his watch again, but caught the glare I shot in his direction.

"What?" he asked on an escaped belch.

A snarl escaped my lips. "Could you be quiet, already?"

He dropped his arm and pulled his sleeve down. "A man has to take care of his business."

I snorted in disgust.

He rolled his chair back warily as I stood and stalked past on the way to the break room.

Why couldn't he be just an ordinary, brilliant geek? Why did I have to sit next to a geek wannabe? Real geeks had talent. He had nothing but inane phrases and gadgets from a dime store, nothing he had created himself.

In the break room, I snatched up a kolache and a chocolate milk. The only reason management provided free food was to keep us here as many hours as possible. If they could have, the company would have brought in cots so that we could catch an hour or two of sleep before hitting the workload again.

I returned to my cubicle, heaving a sigh of relief when I saw that Joe Dork was no longer in his cube. Thank God. I hoped the loser would stay gone or bury himself somewhere.

How was I supposed to know that he looked better alive and was a whole lot less trouble?

Chapter 2

Steve Huntington learned about corrupt corporate behavior because his own company, the one he had babied from the ground up, was robbed blind. He now teamed with his just-younger brother, Mark. They were highly paid to investigate corporate shenanigans, and despite my best efforts, I'd ended up helping a time or two.

Huntington is smooth as glass and rich enough that you tend not to notice he is peeling back layers of a corporation, infiltrating himself right next to the other suits and extracting those who have decided on devious and illegal means to enrich their own pockets.

His brother Mark is, by my standards, even more attractive than Steve. Of course, I'm dating Mark, so I'm biased, but where Huntington—that is Steve—slides into the enemy camp like polish on an executive desk, Mark is more a mysterious shadow that darts in with deadly efficiency and, more often than not, leaves not a trace. He is a fascinating enigma with secrets, yet he is safety in a storm.

Me? I'm just an engineer. I honestly have no real love of intrigue. Huntington claims to this day that I excel at undercover work because everyone ignores me. There is a less-than-subtle intended insult in that assessment.

When he knocked on my door on this almost-spring April evening, I was immediately suspicious. Why was he visiting me?

He was Mark's brother, so I let him in.

"Huntington."

"Just call me Steve, would you? I brought you a sewing machine."

My eyes bugged out, but he kept talking. After the birth of my niece, Huntington had teased me about sewing. It had certainly seemed like a joke at the time, because I can barely sew a button on a blouse, but here he was babbling about infiltration and a matching baby bumpo or bumper something-or-other for Brenda, my sister-in-law.

"You want me to *what?*"

Huntington almost always looked smug, so the superior tilt to his head was nothing new. He flashed his baby blues in what he probably thought was innocence, but that was the one expression he could not possibly pull off, not even to a complete stranger, and we were far past that.

"How hard can it be? I need to obtain info about a guy who has been involved in some high-end burglaries, and his mother is in a sewing group. I promised Mark no more dangerous assignments for you so this time all you have to do is attend a few quilting parties and get in good with a bunch of old ladies." He held up a soft sided case, one that looked like it might hold bowling equipment. Even bowling, which I would have also turned down, would be better than sewing.

"I don't sew."

"So learn. How—"

My snarling lip stopped him short of professing how easy it would be. "Why don't *you* join the group if it's so all-fired easy?" I suggested. "This is the age of enlightenment. I bet the ladies would love to offer you a sewing lesson or two."

His pleased-with-himself attitude flew out the still open door. His eyes narrowed, hiding nearly all the blue. "I'm all for equality, but that would not work. I don't see them confiding in me."

He had that right. They might be more than willing to trade sewing for some manly chores, and a few would be thrilled to flirt with him, but Huntington did not inspire confidences. Not that you'd worry he would tell, but Huntington's personality ranged from impatient, competent businessman to shark. Sympathetic and helpful were not guises he could wear easily.

He shut the door with his foot and strode over to my small kitchen table. He set the bag on the table. "Top of the line for a beginner model. It's all computerized. You're good with computers."

"Radar's better. Why don't you hire him for this job?" Radar sewing had to be near the top of the most mind-boggling suggestions I'd ever proposed. He was a highly intelligent computer geek, and as such, his idea of fashion usually included items that were old and frayed at best. He'd even worn his t-shirt inside out to work without noticing because he simply did not care about clothing.

Huntington took a deep breath to answer and actually choked, the puff of air coming out in a cough. "Radar." He would have discarded the idea even faster had his brain not locked up at the idea. "Look, this is not a big deal. All you have to do is befriend one lady and get her talking about her son. Women love to talk about their kids. Once you're in, I'll provide a few pertinent questions. You don't even have to sew anything."

That's where he was wrong. My mother sewed. My grandmother had been an esteemed member of a crochet club. Hobbyists did not know the meaning of "I'm not interested in learning." They were zealous. They believed the world could and should be converted to their hobby. "Huntington—"

"Steve."

"Huntington—"

"How do you plan to address me if you marry my brother Mark? You'll then be Huntington. You won't be able to call me that."

The idea of marriage was not foreign to me, but I'd learn to sew before I'd discuss marriage with Huntington, especially before such an idea was even on the table with Mark. "My own name will work just fine in all situations," I snapped.

He frowned.

Before either of us could continue the argument, there was a rumble from the front drive, followed by a loud knock on the front door.

Huntington, who lacked the basic social graces to let me answer my own door, leaped to the doorknob.

A guy in jeans and a shirt smudged with dirt waited outside. "Delivery for O'Hala. You want this stuff on the front porch or out back?"

"Out back," Huntington instructed.

"No, you don't!" Okay, I had no idea what was in the delivery, but if Huntington was granting permission for someone to cart it to my backyard, it had to be a bad idea.

Huntington, once again feigning innocence, turned to me. "You want the plants on the front porch? I don't think the neighbors will like that."

"What are you up to?" I demanded, peering around his large shoulders. A white delivery van was in my driveway. The kid with the clipboard was already heading around the back of the truck.

"A long time ago, I promised you plants, remember?"

"That was for your condo, not my house!" Of all my requests at the time, it was the only one he had promised to fulfill. And the plants weren't for me personally, they were to make his condo, which I was using for a case at the time, look as though someone lived in it. "Have you lost your mind?" My father was an agricultural scientist who had made it a point of sharing his vast knowledge with all family members, thus the two plants being carted to my porch were easily identifiable as tomato starts. Dad taught at the university, and gardening was not just his profession, it was his passion. The only thing that superseded it was my mother, and there were times she had to take a sledgehammer approach to drag his attention away from a leafy frond.

"It's too cold out for tomatoes to be planted!" I protested.

"You want them inside?" the kid asked.

"I don't want them at all!" Instead of being nestled in small growing pots, someone had taken the trouble to plant them in large ceramic pots. The seedlings were only about six inches tall.

The kid shrugged. "We've been paid. I can take them away."

"No, we want them," Huntington intervened. "But I think I'll order a rack so they can be kept in at night for a while."

I flapped my arms. "Why not just install a greenhouse in the backyard? Why not buy the lot next to me and tear down the house so I'll have room for a half-acre plot? Maybe you should buy me a farm. Or a ranch."

While I was ranting, the kid didn't waste time. Four more plants arrived on my stoop, two of which were pepper plants. He didn't bother to have me sign for them. He simply continued to unload more.

I stared down at the delicate greenery. "These will not survive unless you plan on building a screened-in porch with plexiglass windows." I stomped inside and slammed the door, leaving Huntington to his delivery.

I pretended not to hear him call through the door. "The lady in question is in a gardening group too."

Chapter 3

Huntington didn't stick around. As soon as the guy was finished unloading the pots of potential vegetables, Huntington climbed into a sleek, black car. The midnight beauty pulled away from the curb without even a whisper of a sound. It was no wonder I hadn't heard him drive up. His current car was a gorgeous stealth model.

The plants on my porch waved back and forth in the gentle, but cold, breeze. Spring had not yet sprung in Denton, Colorado, especially at night.

I sighed. "Huntington, you are a pain in the ass."

It's possible there's a little too much of Dad in me. Even though they weren't my plants, there was no reason to let them die on the porch just because I hadn't bought them myself.

Maybe I could sell them. I rubbed my hands together. "Ha, I'll make a profit off of you yet, Huntington."

After I finished arranging the large assortment in my entryway, I turned around and spotted the sewing machine. My glee evaporated. "There isn't enough money in a few plants to cover your tab of annoyance, Huntington."

I had to wonder if Mark knew about this. I bet he didn't. And Huntington would expect me to explain it all.

I tapped my foot impatiently while considering my options. Eventually I decided that my day had been long enough. Tomorrow was Friday, and Mark was coming over. I could tell him all about Huntington's latest funny business then.

One good thing about the plants and sewing machine was that they didn't require babysitting while the owner slept or dragged herself off to work the next morning.

Friday was my favorite work day, and this one more so than most because, no matter what, I was not working this weekend. Since I had started at Borgot, the "suggested" hours had put a huge dent in my relationship with Mark. He had been trying to see me for two weeks in a row, but being new, I had been at the office all kinds of odd hours in order to make a good impression.

After slaving away for nearly a month at Borgot, I had started to wonder whether Mark's choice of a job was as bad as Huntington's assignments. Of course, that wasn't possible. But to avoid my boss's incessant nagging, I planned to steer clear of him until at least noon. Once I ran into him, I'd have to mention my plans to skip coming in during the weekend. The longer I put off notifying him, the better.

Luckily the restroom was on the way to the break room because my boss, Cary Waters, was on guard at the end of the hall pouring coffee from the dribbles of a nearly empty pot. His lack of a smile wasn't because the pot was dry, either. He spent a good portion of his paychecks on botox shots and face tucks. His skin was stretched so tight he *couldn't* smile, not without looking like a feral dog. He generally acted like one too, making it quite clear that I and all other employees were his ticket to the top.

I ducked into the ladies room and slowed the door so that it closed silently. If I continued on to the break room there would be hints that my failure to work overtime this weekend would make for late nights all next week. Never mind that you cannot bake the cake in less time. Turning up the oven just burns the cake, but he'd crank the heat until the project incinerated.

Listening to make sure he wasn't calling my name kept me from registering the smell of the bathroom for an extra nanosecond. "Good grief." Had the toilets backed up? Outright exploded? The stench wasn't exactly urine and excrement. It was more like someone had thrown up and left it to decay in a barnyard.

Our building was three stories; Borgot was only leasing the third floor. I'd have to use one of the bathrooms on the other floors and ask our admin, Kay, to call plumbing. Because boss-man was likely still lying in wait, I dithered over how to leave. It really stank in here, but it wouldn't be much better if I had to face Cary. I lifted my hand to cover my nose and mouth and glanced toward the stalls to make sure that the sewage wasn't anywhere close to reaching me.

A pant leg with a shoe attached stuck out from beneath one of the doors.

I gasped. The leg rested at a very disturbing angle. The person had to be…laying down, collapsed…hunched over the toilet?

There is a sound to being alone in a room. It is the absence of breathing, the absence of noise. Not only had the smell led me to believe the bathroom was empty, but the very lack of any presence had given me the impression of being completely alone.

I was still staring at the shoe when the door opened behind me. It was Doll Baby Monique.

"Oh, sorry," she exclaimed when the door hit me.

I concentrated on breathing and not panicking.

"Oh my gosh are you—" Her face changed as the smell hit her. She tried to cough politely over her shoulder in order to breathe in fresh air.

I swallowed hard, but it didn't help anything. My brain slowly processed the smell of blood and underlying puke. Without any intention of doing so, I kept parsing the facts.

Monique hadn't spotted the leg yet. She kept talking, inane stupidities about the cleaning crew.

I pointed and then darted past her out the door. Gagging, I leaned over, sucking in huge amounts of air. My legs wanted to run. Was there anyone else in there? Up on the toilets maybe? Waiting? What if…

Monique babbled. "Sedona? What on earth? Are you okay?"

"We need to call the police," I heaved out. "There's someone in there and…" I hadn't checked to see if the person was alive. All I had seen was the foot. What if they needed help? The stall door was closed. Maybe the person was just sick. Of course, the person's foot had been at a very awkward and uncomfortable angle.

My father is an agricultural scientist. I knew the sickly smell of blood meal and a lot of other disgusting, decaying smells. This smell was a taint worse than any and all of them.

"The police?" Monique whispered. Her eyes locked on mine.

"And an ambulance." I was going to have to go back in there to make sure the body was dead and not in need of medical attention. Oh, this Friday had just slapped me right across the face with a Monday. "Call 911." I straightened from my bent position.

Monique frowned, but she edged around me and headed in the general direction of cube city.

Where the hell was her cell phone now that it was needed? "Please hurry," I called after her. Maybe she would phone it in, thinking I was ill if nothing else.

I sucked in a huge gulp of oxygen. It wasn't enough, so I tried again.

Holding my breath, I ventured back into the bathroom. I edged forward as if walking along a cliff. You're supposed to check the artery in the neck, but the bathroom stall appeared to be locked, and if this guy was dead, breaking down the door wasn't going to win me any points with the police department.

I knew it was a guy. The pant leg was pulled up enough to reveal an extremely hairy leg. He wasn't wearing socks. Trying not to touch anything and gulping shallow breaths through my mouth, I forced myself to search for a pulse on his ankle. His face was clearly visible for half a second when I peeked under the door.

Monique must have decided I needed to be checked on. I didn't hear her until she started screaming behind me.

I nearly split my own eardrums with an answering screech.

I stood up so fast, dizziness enveloped me. The only thing that saved me was the single thought that I would *not* pass out in this disgusting, smelly pit where Joe Dork had died.

He had no pulse and his body was morbidly cold.

I flew out of that bathroom as if the devil himself were chasing me.

Monique was right in front of me all the way.

Chapter 4

My advice to the young and old: Do not find dead bodies. The police seem to think that if they ask enough questions, you will suddenly blurt out the killer's name or perhaps admit to the crime yourself just so that you can go home.

Because my brother Sean is a lawyer who works with abuse victims, I was well acquainted with a couple of cops on the force. Adrian, one of the guys I knew, was helping the lead detective, a Detective Saunders. Normally Adrian worked with Derrick, but for some reason, he was with the homicide division today.

When I entered the meeting room being used for the police interrogations, Adrian recognized me. He nodded his dark head of hair, and his tired brown eyes flickered with conflict. Being friends with Sean put him in a difficult position.

Detective Saunders handled the endless questioning. His muscular frame reminded me of a bear—a grizzly, to be specific. His hair was the right color too, a kind of dark brownish cinnamon mess that had probably started out military short, but was too long now. It stuck up all the way around his head.

At first he tried for kind and comforting. He didn't play the role very well because he was more war general than kindly uncle. His attempt to soften his voice made the demanding questions come across like a stalker whispering threats.

After we had gone over the questions three times, he finally switched personalities to pushy and insinuating. I relaxed. He fit this role and sadly, in the computer business, it was much more normal for men to act arrogant and demanding, especially around women.

I answered the questions as quickly as he shot them at me, searching my brain for details, but there was little to add. I hadn't seen Joe since Thursday morning when he'd been on the phone. "Other than mentioning he had moved back in with his mother and that she did his laundry, he only said he couldn't talk right then."

"About what?"

"No idea. He said something about being careful. Oh—and he spoke in Pig Latin." It couldn't possibly be pertinent, but since I had no other details, may as well give him that.

"The entire conversation?"

"No. Just a phrase here and there. I think the being careful part was in Pig Latin. Maybe a couple of other sentences."

Before Saunders could repeat himself again, Adrian stood, his chair scraping against the floor. The conference room was one of the few places in the building with actual doors, but it was a cramped space with a large table and too many chairs. "You know to call us if you think of anything else?"

Detective Saunders shot him a look of disgust.

Adrian shrugged. "If Sedona hasn't thought of anything by now, she isn't likely to." He turned back to me. "You aren't employed here because of the Huntington brothers, are you?"

Well, in a manner of speaking, I was, but not for the reasons he was worried about. "No. I took this job to avoid any investigations that the Huntington brothers might be involved in."

"Uh-hmm."

He'd ask Sean about it. My brother would then blow a gasket. Sean seemed to think that me working with Huntington was somehow endangering his wife Brenda. He equated the jobs with catching a cold—stand in the same room with me and suddenly you were infected. It was not my fault the last investigation had been at the hospital where Brenda worked as a nurse.

"I'll call if I think of anything, but I didn't know Joe other than seeing him in his cube or at meetings. We never spoke past a polite good morning." I wasn't dumb enough to mention the idiot annoyed me. No reason to even hint at a motive on my part.

It was past lunch time by the time I escaped the interview room. Not only was I starved, the entire floor was a no-go zone. Instead of being asked to work late, we were instructed to leave as soon as the police had finished questioning each of us.

Cary wasn't one to let us depart quietly. He stood at the exit on the first floor with a pile of phones. "They came in from the factory last night." He handed me a phone and an SD card. "In case you can't download the latest software over the internet from home, I've loaded it on the SD card. Just install the code from the card like we did with the early test units, and you'll be able to start testing the phones right away." His white button-down shirt was rumpled and had smudges of dirt smeared across the front. He might have actually carried the box of phones down here himself.

I accepted the phone and latest code because testing it was my job, plus he might chase me into the parking lot otherwise.

"The building should be cleared of police business by tomorrow morning. Too many startups fail. We cannot allow that to happen here. Remember you and every employee here are my early retirement plan." His chuckle was more of a cackle, held back because he couldn't stretch his lips properly.

The prototypes were cheap plastic, barely attached to the display. The thing was already powered on, probably running older code. The logo of the company splashed across the front display, mocking me. Cary may not have suspected my plans to play hooky this weekend, but he had not only managed to demand that I work, but that I do so from home.

Really, it's sad when you are employed at a company where the manager can't put aside his retirement plans for a day despite the death of an employee. The next rung on the ladder or the next botox shot was all that mattered to him.

I tossed the phone and SD card in my backpack. I'd have to at least load the latest software or risk being fired. Why couldn't the cops have kept Cary locked in a room somewhere?

On the drive home, I allowed my thoughts to drift to the upcoming weekend with Mark. That lasted right up until I pulled onto my street and saw a car parked at the curb in front of my house. It was not Mark's motorcycle or SUV. It was my parents' trusty white Accord.

My first thought was that Sean had called them to report the murder. That didn't make sense though because they lived hours away in New Mexico. Yet, here they were waiting on my porch.

Hoping nothing was wrong, I rolled the passenger window down while waiting for the garage door of my little patio home to open. "Is everything okay?"

Mom waved. "We had to come see the baby!"

They had visited Colorado right after Brenda gave birth just a couple of weeks ago. My brain scrolled backwards, trying to remember if they had informed me of a visit. "Let me pull in, and I'll open the front door." I pulled my Civic into the garage and hurried through the inside garage door. I dropped my backpack near the kitchen counter on my way to the living room to unlock the front door.

As the door swung in, Dad spotted the tomatoes and peppers in my entryway. His eyebrows rose in delight. "You're putting in a garden this year!" He rubbed his hands together. "Have you ordered the soil yet? You'll need a raised bed." He rushed past me without bothering with a hug. He didn't stop until he reached the window at the back door. Despite seeing no garden bed, he put his hand on the doorknob.

"Hi, Dad," I said, giving Mom her hug. We both gazed at him affectionately, me without the trace of annoyance my mother exhibited.

"Looks like you need some help," he said happily. "Have you found a place that sells composted turkey manure? You won't be able to buy elephant manure here. Hmm. I think I know a guy." He had his cell phone out before I had a chance to answer.

"Uh, Dad." I had no intention of putting in a garden.

Mom bustled over to him and grabbed the phone from his hand. She pressed some buttons and then gave it back. "Dear, I'm certain Sedona has it all worked out. You don't want to interfere with her plans." She turned to me. "We stopped by Sean's, but he is at work, and Brenda and the baby weren't home. So we came here to unload the luggage. We can't stay at Sean's since the guest room is now a baby room!" Mom beamed.

"Of course."

"You knew we were coming to see the baby!" Mom's green eyes positively glowed. Her strawberry blonde frizz was locked into a curly cap around her head. The fact that she had done such a masterful job of smoothing it down to impress the new baby made me grin.

"Wasn't that in two weeks?" I asked.

Dad grunted. "Your mother moved all my appointments around so we could come early."

"Oh, you wanted to come back and see Samantha, too," she said with a wave of her hand.

Dad mumbled, "We were coming week after next anyway."

"Well, no time like the present," my mom responded happily.

My brother, Sean, had his hands full between the new baby and doting grandparents. Served him right. He was always telling me how to live my life. He'd be too busy to worry about me now.

Dad gazed out into the backyard. "She has to have dirt. There's no dirt back there. It's too rocky." He faced me, hope etched across his face. His hand clutched his cell phone, but he refrained from dialing. For a broad-shouldered man standing nearly six feet, barely turning gray and muscles that came from working hard outdoors, he somehow managed to resemble a puppy about to burst with hope and excitement.

If Huntington had delivered dirt to my backyard, I'd have had no problem burying him in it. He had done more than enough pushing me around. Dad was a different story. I didn't have the heart to tell him that I was far too busy to take care of a garden. With a sigh, I said, "I haven't found any decent dirt yet."

Dad could have won a speed-dialing contest.

While Mom and I unloaded luggage and snacks from the car, Dad contacted every man, woman and child who might have the slightest hint of where to buy the best dirt. This wasn't his territory, but by nightfall, he'd know more about gardening in Denton, Colorado than the internet. Not even Radar, reformed hacker and computer expert that he was, could have found the places faster than Dad.

Since I hadn't eaten, I helped myself to a piece of the cake Mom had brought.

Mom finished in the guest room and bustled back into the kitchen. She came to a dead stop when she finally noticed the sewing machine sitting on the table in the little dining nook.

"Sedona!" She looked from the covered case to me. She knew that I didn't sew, had no interest in sewing, and possessed not a shred of talent in that area. "What is this? Can I see it?"

"Help yourself. It was a gift. I don't even want it. Not going to use it."

Dad interrupted with, "Do you want to plant blueberries?" He held the phone away from his mouth.

"Blueberries? I don't think I'll have room. The yard is very small, Dad."

"She doesn't have room for more than two," Dad said into the mouthpiece. "And make sure they are dormant. It's too cold to put'em out there if they aren't. Well, they might make it."

Mom gave my shoulder an absent-minded pat. "You shouldn't have invited us until the garden was in."

I nearly choked on the chocolate cake. I hadn't invited them. Not that they weren't welcome, but not only had I not invited them, I hadn't intended to put in a garden either. Mom took the cover off the sewing machine and gave a happy gasp.

I closed my eyes and stuffed more cake into my mouth.

Chapter 5

My parents were on the way out the door just as Mark showed up. He eased into the driveway on his motorcycle, set his helmet on the handlebars and pulled off one glove to shake Dad's hand.

"She's putting in a garden," Dad announced. "Chip off the old block."

Mark gave me a once-over that was rather more amused than usual and nodded his head. "She is something, that's for sure."

After basic pleasantries, Mark followed me to the open front door, unzipping his black leather jacket on the way. He shortened his stride to match mine. He was almost a foot taller, but for such a big guy, he moved silently. His chestnut hair was more than slightly tousled from his bike helmet, but I resisted the urge to comb through it with my fingers. Instead, I gave a last wave to my parents as they departed for their visit with the grandchild. Hopefully they would manage to drive my brother, Sean, nutty.

Before we stepped inside, Mark touched my cheek and looked me over again. "You okay?"

"You heard about the murder?"

"Did you really trip over the body?"

I wrinkled my nose. "I hope not. There was a dead guy, Joe Black, in one of the bathroom stalls. I tried to miss any and all puddles." The thought of the mess made the cake in my stomach suddenly heavy.

"What happened?" he asked.

Before I could recite any details, a disembodied voice from inside the house answered the question for me. "Babe, we are happening. Abebay, eway areyay appeninghay."

I let loose a half scream and pushed Mark sideways, away from the open doorway. "OHMYGOD!"

"Who the hell is that?" Mark demanded, pulling me closer as he tried to stuff me behind him.

"Pig Latin," I squeaked, peeking into the living room before yanking quickly back. My brain wrapped around the Pig Latin phrase, a repeat of the English one. "Babe, we are happening." I edged forward one step, my back to Mark, searching my living room for a ghost. Mark's arm was a band of steel preventing me from advancing any further.

There was nothing but empty air in the room. The dining nook contained the sewing machine, the table and little else. The bar counter separating the living room from the kitchen was low enough to allow me to inspect most of that empty room as well.

There wasn't any fog, no colored smoke, not a wisp of a creature.

Mark and I stood that way for at least a minute, me breathing hard with Mark keeping me tucked by his side so that I wasn't as exposed. The way he was holding me, I was half inside his leather jacket, but it was impossible to take cover when there was nothing to hide from.

Eventually, he eased away from me and stepped into the living room. I sidled close and kept pace.

"What—" I started to ask.

"Borgot at your service. Orgotbay atyay youryay ervicesay."

I jumped, ready to run, my eyes frantically roving around the empty space.

"Did that come from your backpack?" Mark swiveled sideways, honing in on my purple backpack sitting near the counter. I had tossed it there just like always when I got home from work.

I stared warily at my bag. "The phone. Borgot's phone."

"A phone?" Mark asked.

"Borgot at your service," it repeated.

I surged forward, dug through the backpack and extracted the cheap plastic phone. "Cary, my manager, insisted we take a phone home for testing since the police wouldn't allow us to work in the building until they were done with the investigation. He handed out phones on the way out."

"What's with the Pig Latin?"

I told him about Joe and his stupidity. While I talked, I switched the phone off. "Joe was hired as some ridiculous excuse of a language expert, but the only language he knew besides English was Pig Latin. He walked around spouting phrases and patting himself on the back as if he was a genius."

"He talked management into putting voice messages in Pig Latin on a phone?" Mark was incredulous.

"I doubt it. But he must have added it somehow. A lot of coders add a hidden personal signature to code even though they shouldn't." I frowned. "But he couldn't code his way out of a paper bag, so I don't know how he would have gotten any of his Pig Latin onto the system."

Mark shook his head. "He had the ego to add personal messages in *Pig Latin*? Was he an idiot or what?"

"Yeah, he was a dork. His last name was Black, but I always thought of him as Joe Dork because it fit better." I shuddered. "I don't know how he could have talked someone into uploading Pig Latin to the Borgot phones."

"Maybe he made one of the Borgot phones his personal phone, and he loaded his own phrases."

My first instinct was to drop the phone cold. If this was Joe's personal phone, I didn't want to touch it, and that would have been true even if he were still alive. "Eww. That's possible. But what was it doing in the box of phones being handed out for testing?"

"Hard to ask him now."

"I wonder where Cary kept the box. He did say they came in late last night."

"In which case, they would have been sitting around. All night, maybe?"

I nodded. "It's an open floor plan. Cary wouldn't bother to lock them up. He doesn't even track who gets which phone for testing. Although that doesn't tell us how or why Joe's phone landed in there. I should probably turn this in to the cops in case it really is his personal phone or the last one he used for testing."

His eyebrow lifted. "Only probably?"

Sheepishly, I grinned. "I was thinking it would be a good idea to have Radar duplicate whatever code and messages are sitting on it first."

"Don't trust the cops to do their job?" He held his hand out for the phone. He wasn't trying to confiscate it; he wasn't that controlling.

I handed it over. "The police might be able to glean something useful," I admitted. "But Radar's the best there is. He could copy everything on here and tell me when the code was loaded and whether those Pig Latin phrases were in the original load or something that was added."

"Good idea."

I was a little surprised at his quick acceptance since he had a tendency to warn me away from involvement in anything sinister, but if Mark was anything, he was logical. He wasn't one to pass up an opportunity just for the sake of stubbornness.

He used his own phone to call Radar, and then made a second call that I assumed was to Huntington.

Once he hung up I asked, "How did you hear about the murder?"

"Police scanner. I followed up with Derrick, and then headed over here hoping you were done and had come home."

"Derrick wasn't working the case. His partner was there, though. If Adrian hadn't been there, I might still be answering questions."

"Radar said he can meet us for Chinese and pick up the phone to examine it. You okay if I get the copy of anything on it to Steve?"

"Are you guys planning to investigate?" I hadn't thought past obtaining a copy of whatever was on the phone.

"It might be a good idea to check a few things, especially since you are working at a company where a guy turned up murdered."

I blinked. I hadn't seen enough to guess how Joe Dork had died, but it didn't take a genius to figure out that he probably hadn't ended up in the ladies room on his own. "Okay by me."

Chapter 6

By the time we finished eating and drove back to my place, my parents had also returned. From the front porch, the steady drone of the television could be heard. I stifled a sigh. Mark and I had barely had any time together lately. With my parents in town, the situation wasn't improving.

"Pick you up to hike tomorrow?" Mark asked.

I nodded. Had my parents not been around, I'd definitely have invited him in, but flaunting my personal life, even in front of them—*especially* in front of them, would be a huge mistake. I didn't need the complications, the lectures or snide remarks about good Catholic girls and "in my day." "Seven," I said. "I'll be up early even if it is Saturday, just for you."

He leaned in to steal a goodnight kiss just as the front door opened.

Mom was all smiles. "Hi, Mark! Sedona, did you know the sewing machine is a finishing machine? Sergers don't handle the regular stitching. You can't sew very much with it until you buy a regular machine."

My life was out of control. I pinched the bridge of my nose in the vague hope the gesture would keep my few remaining brains from leaking out. "Well, no, I don't know what kind of machine it is. It was a gift. I don't sew."

"A gift." Mark glanced at me and then leaned in close to look over my head. "Sewing machine." The gears in his brain were almost audible as they turned. "Steve? He gave you a gift? Why didn't you mention—" He bit off his question, either because he was angry or because my mother was dividing her bright-eyed curiosity between us.

Her mouth formed a little round "oh" before she remembered her manners. She stepped back and waved her hand at the living room. "Don't just stand there! You should come in. Oh, dear. We took the cake to Sean's house! I didn't think about Sedona having company."

"Thanks, Mrs. O'Hala, but I have to head home. Early morning date tomorrow." His smile was forced. "We do have a date, right?" He searched my face as if something had changed.

"Of course!" He wasn't thinking of canceling, was he?

"Well, there's no need to run off," my mother pattered. "Hmm. I'll make another cake. Or you can come for breakfast if you're making plans for early!" She beamed.

There was no answering happiness on my face. "Mom."

She sniffed. "Oh, all right. I'll mind my own business."

Before I had a chance to tell him about Steve stopping over, Mark gave a perfunctory wave and strode off the porch.

Great. Now I had another problem to solve and once again it was Huntington's fault. I turned around to find Mom watching me. From the thoughtful look on her face, my best guess was that a lecture full of not-so-helpful hints was coming my way, despite me trying to keep my private life private.

* * *

Dad hopped out of bed at five a.m. the next the morning, announced to the world at large that it was time to get started and took himself out back.

Mom was used to the morning flurry and ignored it. Since I had a seven o'clock date, one that I had originally thought would start *last* night and continue blissfully from there, I was less than pleased with this new arrangement.

I stumbled out of bed, showered, dressed for hiking and scrambled some eggs and bacon. Dad had somehow managed to have a load of limestone bricks delivered yesterday while Mark and I were delivering the phone to Radar.

Dad whistled while arranging the bricks alongside rolls of weed-blocking burlap. Maybe the neighbors would find the noise a cheerful awakening. His trilling was almost birdlike if you ignored the fact that it was interspersed with the clank of large rocks being plunked down. Yup, that was Dad, a springtime horde of melodic ostriches.

I packed sandwiches for later and then brewed tea and coffee.

Mom wandered in when the smell of coffee drifted through the house.

She peered into the backyard. "It looks like he's planning two beds? Did he okay that with you?"

I waved my hand. "If I installed a rocket launching pad back there it wouldn't stop him at this point. He'd just shift it aside."

She shook her head. "You should have hidden those plants, you know. He never could mind his own business when it came to gardens. Do you want me to help you pick out a sewing machine? To go with the serger?"

The doorbell rang, saving me from throwing myself into the washing machine and trying to drown myself. I grabbed the backpack with our packed lunch. With my free hand, I extracted Mark's foil-wrapped egg sandwich from the toaster oven. "Gotta go!" I yelled, giving Mom a quick peck on the cheek. "There's eggs and bacon in the oven in the covered dish."

I ran for the door, grateful that Mark had arrived fifteen minutes early. After his reaction last night, I was thrilled he had shown up at all. I opened the door and rushed out, bouncing sideways off of his broad chest when he was unable to move out of the way fast enough.

He caught hold of my arm to keep me from falling. "I take it you're ready to go?"

Mom ignored my antics and greeted Mark. "Sedona made eggs. Have you eaten?"

Mark smiled. "I think so."

He got the answer right without even checking with me first. Maybe it was the wild desperation lurking in my eyes or the fact that my feet were dancing in their hurry to depart.

"Well, I do hope you'll be able to stay for dinner." Mom winked at me as though I had any say in anything anymore.

I sighed. But honestly. I hadn't seen Mark in weeks. My parents had only been here one night, and they had already turned me into a lunatic.

"Sure," he said. "Good to see you."

He followed me to his SUV.

"I packed you an egg sandwich for breakfast."

"Thanks." He held the door open for me, accepted the sandwich and went around to his side. As he pulled out of the driveway, he asked, "Do you know how to sew?"

I slanted my eyes to him, but he was chewing and driving so he missed my suspicious gaze. "Nope. Unless you lost a button, you are out of luck. I can't sew. I've barely even threaded a machine before. I completed a pillow one time, but that was with Mom's help." This conversation was obviously a roundabout interrogation because of Steve gifting me a machine. Mark didn't care for his brother stepping too close to me. Sometime in the past, at least one woman had used Mark to get close to Steve, and Mark wasn't quite over it. "I did not ask him for a present, and I didn't accept it either. Or the plants."

"The plants? Those aren't from your dad?"

I groaned. "No, they weren't, but they might as well be. Dad saw them and started putting in a garden at five this morning."

A muscle in Mark's jaw ticked. "He didn't tell me about the plants. Neither did you, for that matter."

"When?" I threw up my hands. "I forgot all about them when we were telling Radar about Joe Dork's phone. I was actually enjoying myself for a few minutes there at dinner. And I haven't the foggiest idea why Steve—"

Mark held up his hand to stop my explanation. We were barely outside of town, but he pulled over, parking in a small dirt lot. "I wasn't too happy about him showering you with expensive presents so I went over to the condo last night after I left your place."

Instead of facing me, he crumbled the breakfast foil, and then gripped the steering wheel.

"Mark, Steve is not interested in me. Well, he's interested in me, because he still believes that I should work on his investigations and—"

"I told him to butt out." Mark's voice held a finality that sounded a bit like a threat.

"So did I!"

He finally faced me, but his face was not any less tense. "Steve talked my mother into joining a sewing group to gather information."

I was ready with a winning argument about how I planned to give the serger to my mother, but his sentence derailed me instantly. I snapped my mouth closed. I opened it again, but it took a moment for me to manage any sound. "What?"

Mark nodded. "His own mother. Then, after he involved her in his latest investigation, he decided it was too risky to send her in there on her own with no backup."

My brain turned. So did my stomach. "Wait a minute. It's too risky for your mother so he decided he'd hire me instead?"

Mark's teeth clenched. "His logic was missing past that point."

"Oh no," I disagreed. "His logic has been missing for a long time. And I'm going to tell him that I don't appreciate him deciding that it's okay for him to put me on risky jobs, but not his mother."

"He is putting you *both in a position of risk!*"

My ears popped. I sat back and waited for the windows to stop vibrating from his fury. "Well, I'm not in any danger yet because I haven't joined any sewing groups. Did your mom join?"

One perfunctory nod. "Mom isn't about to back out either. Steve has her convinced she is the only way he'll solve this case."

"Oh." I shook my head. "That's bad."

Mark slammed out of the vehicle and stomped down the trail. I followed, pretty certain this was not the original hike he had planned. As I marched along behind him, I tried to think of something clever to say to defuse the situation, but nothing helpful came to mind.

He strode ahead, and I half-ran to keep up.

This close to town, the trail was not as isolated as hikes we'd enjoyed in the past. We passed one other couple and two single hikers with dogs. At the pace Mark was setting, I didn't have time to smile and wasn't inclined to waste breath on a "good morning."

After forty minutes of pounding the trail, he finally stopped near a large boulder and a stand of scattered pines. He turned to face me, the shadows from the trees not nearly as dark as the clouds across his face. "Sedona, you know I don't want you in any danger."

I nodded, sucking in air. Before I had recovered enough to answer, a mountain biker approached from around the hillside, heading down fast.

We both scooted behind the trees.

Once the biker was clear, Mark said, "I don't want you to join the sewing group. And I have no idea what is up with the plants because my brother didn't bother to provide details on that, but I'll find out."

"I'll join the sewing group and the gardening group." I hurriedly shared the few details Huntington had let slip. "Apparently the mother of someone

Huntington is investigating, I don't even know whose mother, is in both groups. We can't leave your mom there all by herself."

Mark dropped his gaze and ran his hand across his face. "Sedona, I would never willingly put you in any kind of dangerous position."

"You wouldn't ask your own mother to be involved in risky business, either. And you didn't ask. Huntington did. But now it's done." I shook my head. "I wouldn't let my mom work all alone on one of Huntington's cases. We can't have yours shadowing some old lady by herself on his behalf."

Mark stepped to me and gripped my shoulders. "Sedona, it isn't just some random mother in the sewing group. It's Joe Black's mother."

I stared up into his eyes. They were the color of coffee and held enough stress and worry that the cup was overflowing. "Joe Dork?" I croaked out.

He nodded. "Yeah. That Joe. The dead one."

Well. This was an all new low where Huntington was concerned.

Chapter 7

When Steve asked his mother to infiltrate the sewing group, there hadn't yet been a murder. For that matter, he even attempted to add me to his employee roster before Joe Black was found dead, but I wasn't willing to forgive him everything because none of Steve's cases were ever simple.

Mark and I discussed what little we knew while we hiked back. There was plenty of time to talk because Mark had calmed down enough to stroll rather than run a marathon.

"Steve isn't certain Joe's mother is involved with whatever Joe was into, but Steve is pretty certain Joe was hanging out with a crowd that is pulling off some extensive burglaries. The group is very well organized and changes their pattern of operation frequently, which makes them hard to trace. We followed a money trail, and it appears Joe may have received cash from at least one of the heists. The bills were marked. Instead of laundering them through the system so that they weren't attached to him personally, he went on an obvious spending spree with the bills. Steve is hoping that by talking to Joe's mother you can find out the names of any friends, new ones in particular, or gather any other clues that might pop up."

"I can't believe there are two people in this world who would hire someone like Joe," I complained. "It's bad enough that Borgot hired him. You'd think criminals would be smarter and steer clear of such a lousy engineer."

"His lack of accomplishments is another reason Steve wants to watch Joe's mother. Joe isn't known for taking initiative or accomplishing anything on his own so it isn't clear how he might have become involved with these new associates. He has a criminal record, but he worked alone then."

"Borgot hired a known criminal?"

"The petty theft was buried in the records because he was using his father's surname at the time. After that arrest he changed his name to Black—his mother's surname. In addition to that incident, he had his car impounded due to unpaid traffic tickets, he missed court dates, and generally had a reputation for skipping responsibilities."

I shook my head. "Figures. Corporate America puts up with that sort of thing better than gangs or even two-bit criminal organizations. I wasn't paying a lot of attention to the phone call I overheard, but Joe said his mother would keep quiet even if she did see something. No idea what she might have seen or been at risk of seeing, but Joe was defending his move back into her place. Whoever was on the other end didn't want witnesses."

Mark sighed. "That implies she doesn't know about his involvement in anything shady."

"No, that implies Joe didn't think she knew. Those are two different things."

He smiled. "True."

"For all we know, Joe was involved in multiple shady deals, only one of which got him murdered," I grumbled.

"You're a suspicious sort, aren't you?" Mark draped his arm around my shoulders and squeezed me in a hug.

I poked his arm. "Whose fault is that? I hang out with sneaky types."

"Used to hang out with." He lost his grin.

I had been including him in that assessment, and he knew it. "Whatever you say. But the point is, Joe was the type to dive in well over his head. He was definitely sinking fast at Borgot. There's no reasonable way he landed the job by claiming Pig Latin as his second language. Someone had to want him there for another reason, or he lied on his resume or both."

"Probably both," Mark agreed.

"I'm not sure who hired him. To hear him talk, he was hired as a development engineer, but he showed up at the test meetings." I was suddenly suspicious that all of my co-workers were up to no good. Well, since Joe had met his final flushing at work, I'd already decided to be suspicious of them anyway.

On the drive home, much to my surprise, we stopped at Barbette's Bobbins. "We aren't attending the sewing circle right now, are we? Together?" I asked.

"You need a sewing machine, remember? Your mom said Huntington gave you a finishing machine. No one will believe that you are learning to sew if you don't have a machine."

His attention to detail was a million miles above Huntington's, but then Huntington had probably hoped I'd pay my own way when it was discovered he had only brought half the necessary equipment. "You're buying me a sewing machine?" Was this some odd competition between the two brothers?

He smiled and touched my chin before leaning in to brush a kiss across my lips. "My mom could lend you one, but I'm not sure how to break the news to her that you're on the case too. I think Steve should have to explain to her exactly why he needs to put every woman he knows at risk by assigning them undercover work."

Ah, family tensions. I was enough of an expert on that subject to keep my mouth shut and follow him into Bobbins without saying a word.

Barb of Bobbins was a nice lady, the owner and the sole creative mind behind the costumes that sold in the shop along with piles of fabric, patterns, ribbons and buttons. Barb also ran the local sewing circle in the back room of the shop.

No time like the present to start my undercover duties. I introduced myself as a beginner sewer needing the basics. As soon as I said "O'Hala" she beamed.

"Oh, yes, I remember you from when you came in here to help your sister-in-law shop! How is she? Brenda bought many a costume from me. Has she had her baby?"

"Yes, she did. It's a girl. Samantha."

"I'll surely miss her visits. She made a great Mrs. Santa Claus."

My memory of helping Brenda hide her pregnancy from her boss at work was not nearly as enthusiastic as Barb's, but then, as the proprietor of the shop, she usually wore one of her handmade costumes. Perhaps it didn't seem odd to her that Brenda had attended work dressed as an elf, a Mrs. Claus and possibly the Easter Bunny.

Today, Barb was decked out in happy homemaker attire, including a cute red-checked apron and a blouse with big puffy white sleeves. She also had a chef's hat, albeit a short one, perched atop her straight gray hair.

"I'm hoping to learn to sew a..." I stuttered to a halt. I couldn't think of a blessed item anyone would want to sew.

"Of course! You'll need to make baby outfits! And that baby will outgrow things as fast as you can sew them. Here, let me show you what I have in stock for beginners."

She was half right. The baby would outgrow things. She'd likely outgrow them before I could finish sewing the first item.

Barb made certain to sell us some "easy" fabric to sew, matching thread, needles, pin cushions, pins, scissors, a cutting board, a baby bib pattern and, of course, a sewing machine. Just before she rang it all up, I mentioned the serger. This led to scrap fabric and huge spools that contained enough thread to sew right across the state of Colorado. I hoped my mom could use some of this when the case was over.

Mark carried the various items to the SUV and loaded each parcel carefully. As he slammed the door shut, he said, "This case might be too much of a challenge for you. Every time she said the word 'sew' you looked ready to throw up."

"Nonsense." I sniffed. "This will be no more difficult than any of the others." They'd all been damned hard. In fact, previous cases had nearly gotten me killed. Surely, sewing couldn't kill anyone. Right???

Chapter 8

Mark and I skipped the packed sandwiches I had prepared and shared an early dinner at Italy's Canal before he dropped me off with all the new purchases.

I sighed with longing as he pulled away. My parents hadn't returned from grandparenting yet, but they would soon enough. Meanwhile, I had chores to do. Two of them, in the form of sewing machines.

Huntington, along with his other sins, had given Brenda the idea that I intended to make a bumpo or something or other for the new baby. What the hell was a bumpo? Or had he said bumper? Samantha couldn't even crawl yet so bumping into things wasn't a problem. Then again, by the time I learned to sew, she might be driving a car. Maybe Huntington had been getting in an early dig about my lack of sewing ability.

"Hmph. I know how to thread the regular machine at least." Well, not without double-checking the instructions and piercing my thumb with the sharp needle, but success was still success. "You probably couldn't have managed even that," I said to the not-present Huntington while sucking on my thumb.

Once the beginner machine was ready for actual sewing, I stared at the serger, the one Mom called a finishing machine. "Start small. One thread at a time," I muttered.

Machines don't scare me. I worked with them all day. I opened the panels and peered within the bowels of the great device that, according to the booklet, would make my creations "masterpieces" and "professionally finished."

There were more levers and notches than the inside of a computer. There were hooks and random color splotches and eyelets and sharp protrusions and tiny little numbers. "Unbelievable." The only thing missing was a keyboard. "How do you talk to this thing without a keyboard?"

The booklet was a sales tool, not instructions, so I turned to the internet.

Studying online manuals only made things worse. "Are you kidding me?" Threading the thing required all four spools of the thread Barb had sold me and quite possibly a PhD. "Why doesn't the thing thread itself? It has a computer chip installed, right?"

A little research revealed that Huntington had not purchased the *very* top-of-the-line equipment. No, this was a mid-range item that would not only not thread itself, it wouldn't sew articles without a lot of expertise either. "Oh, this is bad news."

The guy who designed the thing was obviously a very angry car mechanic. He wasn't an engineer, because no self-respecting engineer would have made such a mess out of four threads. The engineer would have simply designed a computer to control the thread tension. No, this guy had been repairing a Yugo the day his wife nagged him to finish the serger design. He had muttered, "You think working crammed in a tiny space with poor lighting all day is fun? You think I enjoy working by feel, hoping I get it right? See how you like it!" Presto, the serger was born, the most convoluted sewing nightmare ever to grace the earth.

Instead of four separate channels with tension levers that made sense, the threads had to be wound up and around, crisscrossing, looping under and over this lever and that thingamabob as if Silly String had exploded in one giant mess.

The end result was ugly. Very ugly.

"Maybe I don't need professional finishing." I turned to the baby bib pattern. It was a complex design with some kind of teddy bear sewn across the middle and a different colored fabric trimming the edge all the way around. The pattern mentioned something about "binding," but there was no definition. "Why do you have to trim the edge of the bib? Waste of time for something that is going to be spit on." I had made a pillow once. I could just sew the seams on the inside of the bib and turn it out like the pillow. "Who has time for trim? Samantha will love it because I made it." The real meaning of that mantra hit me for the first time.

I trolled the internet and found a simpler pattern, one that didn't involve a teddy bear on the front. The search for small sewing projects also yielded a pattern for a bra. That looked simple enough. I downloaded it as well.

"Gosh. Surely, this is enough for the day. I need a snack." There would be no sewing on an empty stomach in this house. And I hadn't even tested the serger yet. "Hmm." Progress was slow. "Good thing I decided against doing a bumper. Or bump-up. Whatever."

I made cookies. Priorities had to be adhered to in times of stress.

* * *

What with one thing and another, mainly the return of my parents, Dad's deliveries to my backyard and my ability to procrastinate as if my life depended upon it, sewing took a back seat for the rest of the evening.

Sleeping on the problem didn't help any either. When my alarm clock next struck me awake on Sunday morning, none of Cinderella's mice had shown up to produce a baby bib or any other useful pieces of clothing.

We all trooped off to church, something I would have skipped had my parents not been there with their high expectations. It was all for the best, however, because I needed to corner my brother, Sean.

It didn't take me long to find him and explain that the phone my boss had given me to test might belong to the murder victim. "You need to hand it off to the police."

Sean grabbed his hair and yanked on it. His brown locks were the same color as mine, but his eyes were a dark blueish gray to my greenish-gray ones. He used to keep his hair military short, but these days, he didn't have time to get it cut regularly. It was combed back and starting to grow out of even that style, drooping over his ears. "What makes you think I should turn over evidence for you?"

Because he was in danger of hyperventilating, I waved my hand in front of his face. "Hello? You're a lawyer?"

"You're hiring me to represent you? Do you know what I charge?"

I'd walked into that trap. "Sean."

"What do Mom and Dad think of this mess you're in? I thought you weren't accepting these bogus jobs from the Huntington brothers anymore? I knew you couldn't be trusted!"

"What about attorney-client privilege?" I hissed, eyeing our parents as they took seats in the windowed cry room at the back of the church. "No one needs to mention this to Mom or Dad. And who said this had anything to do with Huntington? I was at work. A dead body appeared. My boss was passing out phones for us to test, and somehow I ended up with a phone that may have belonged to or been programmed by Joe!"

Our heated whispers in the hallway caught Brenda's attention. Since Mom was caring for Baby Samantha, Brenda scooted through the still open door and headed our way. "You aren't discussing baby presents are you? Sedona, how is the bumper for Sammy coming along? Huntington said you were sewing one so I put off buying it, but now we need it!" She looked back at her daughter and blew her a kiss. Now that she had given birth, she was letting her pixie brunette hair grow out. Even though she almost had her figure back, she still sported the glowing complexion of a new mother. "Auntie Sedona is sewing you a present!" she cooed.

I didn't know who I wanted to smack more—my brother or Huntington. Mom caught my eye then, her eyebrows and head indicating we needed to get in there and sit down.

I handed the suspicious phone to my brother. "Derrick is here. I saw him drive up as we were on the way in. You can give this to him."

Sean might be a royal pain, but he was my brother. He frowned down at the cheap black plastic phone, his own temper at war with his lawyer instincts.

I hurried into the cry room, knowing that when push came to shove, he wouldn't desert me. He'd make me pay, but we both knew that me turning in that phone without a lawyer was not in my best interests.

He and Derrick missed most of the Mass. I made sure they both missed me on the way out, although I'm pretty sure Derrick had already left with the evidence, because otherwise he wouldn't have allowed me to leave without answering a bunch of stupid questions. Unfortunately, I didn't happen to have any answers.

Chapter 9

Some Mondays pretend they aren't really Monday, sneaking up on you before you're even fully awake enough to come to terms with it being that nasty first day of the week. The second Cary cornered me in the break room it was clear that this Monday had plans to flatten me like roadkill on the highway— over and over. If Cary hadn't been hiding behind the fridge door, I'd never have wandered into Monday unsuspecting like that.

His stare was as icy as his voice. "Sedona. You are the only employee who neglected to upload any test results this weekend."

Monique actually hung up her phone and blushed as though she feared what the person on the other end might think of the conversation. Kovid, one of the programmers, grabbed his coffee on his way to bolting. He was one of the really brilliant engineers, a young Indian guy with a great temperament.

Cary held up his hand to stop him. "No, by all means stay. Everyone on the team may as well know what was so critical that Sedona felt she could leave us high and dry. We all had our noses to the grindstone this weekend. You don't look dead or sick. Maybe you're not cut out to work at a startup. Or do you just want to reap the rewards of our hard work at the end?"

"Dead or sick?" He wanted me to be dead or sick? What kind of boss said things like that? My face flushed. He was deliberately dressing me down in front of co-workers. "Are you crazy? One dead body wasn't enough for you? You want the rest of us dead too?"

Monique gasped. Kovid's mouth fell open and stayed there.

His reaction helped me rein in my temper before it galloped away completely. I delivered my prepared excuse through almost unclenched teeth. "The police confiscated the phone you gave me. I had nothing to test. The police said there might be evidence on the phone that could help them solve the murder. They had a lot of questions." The last part was mostly a lie. They hadn't asked me any questions because Sean was fielding all related phone calls for me as my lawyer, but I was certain the police *had* questions. Close enough for this war.

My answer caught Cary off guard, but he was nothing if not persistent. "Why couldn't you find the time to come in and pick up another phone?"

I wasn't ready for that question, but I rallied quickly. "I didn't want to look like some crazed guilty person by returning to the scene of the crime." I nodded, liking this lie. "You know they say the killer always does that, and what if the police thought me coming in on a weekend was suspicious? Everyone else was testing from home." I shook my head. "No, I wouldn't dare mess with a crime scene."

"The project is already late! Companies that don't deliver on time get shut down. The police cannot be allowed to interfere with our schedule!" He jabbed his finger in the air to punctuate his point.

"Does this mean you won't be able to pull the schedule in three weeks like you promised?" Monique demanded. "You committed to that schedule! I've already told the marketing team you would do it."

"That's impossible," Kovid muttered. "We just requested an extra month."

Monique probably wasn't supposed to hear that comment. She sputtered and slammed her coffee cup on the counter.

I marched off down the hallway, my head held high. Okay. The seamstress job was now looking like a match made in heaven. A bloody, pin-pricked, crooked, unraveling seam type of match, but even Huntington wasn't this big of an ass when it came to managing. Had Cary deliberately tried to humiliate me in front of my co-workers, or had he planned on firing me right there in front of the others? Was there not a job on this earth I could keep???

The first message in my inbox was definitely a Monday message. I was "invited" to a mandatory code review at nine. I hadn't been at work ten minutes and the news was only slightly better than a dead body.

A code review wasn't entirely unusual except in this case it was the engineer calling his own code review. Engineers hated code reviews more than having their computer break down right as they are about to score the big Wizard level in the latest computer game. Code reviews were the equivalent of a colonoscopy, only slightly worse because you had to stay awake.

I sighed. Roscoe had scheduled his review for four straight hours. Was he crazy?

Apparently he was. I blasted through my emails and, determined to be able to say I had done some testing should Cary attack me again, I downloaded the latest code on no less than three test phones.

There wasn't much time before the meeting, but testing three phones at once had to count for something.

The phone assistant readily played various songs when I made my verbal request. The voice correctly reported stock prices and provided directions to a nearby store when I asked. I moved to my favorite list of oddball test questions.

"Borgot assistant, what is the meaning of life?"

There was a longer pause than normal, but the robotic phone voice finally came up with an answer. "The reading material on the subject appears to have no plot, but many pages."

"You know I didn't ask you for the meaning of *my* life, right?" I had a plot. I even had a burgeoning romance.

"Verily."

That was a new answer. "Verily? Who programmed this thing with that word?" I looked up "verily" just to be certain the phone wasn't equivocating or insulting me by using an obscure definition of the word.

Monique, with her lovely spandex pants, hurried by my cube. "Time's up," I muttered.

The phone answered me. "You may delay, but time will not."

"What?"

"Benjamin Franklin," the phone replied.

I shut the thing off.

Several of my colleagues had already arrived by the time I slid into my seat. Oddly, Lawrence, the executive attorney, was in attendance. Of course, he sat at the head of the table, his nose in his phone. Monique, who was supposedly dating him, sat next to him, staring down at her tablet.

Kovid was studying his computer screen, possibly trying to complete an important task even though we were obviously in the middle of hell and high water.

Roscoe stood at the door passing out photocopied sheets of his code "summary points."

It became clear in a hurry that he didn't care what we thought of his code. He was here to *tell* us what we thought of it, but four hours was way more time than even Roscoe could use to expound on his brilliance.

"What might have taken a normal engineer a thousand lines of code, I did it in a few hundred," he stressed. "Not only can this Borgot phone answer questions better than Apple's Siri assistant, Borgot's voice assistant will translate phrases into foreign languages. The translation feature is not only great code, it moves this phone from ordinary to groundbreaking. I spent the weekend filling out patent forms."

Ah, that explained Larry the lawyer. Patents meant patent lawyers to prove there was something to patent. Someone had to fill out reams of paperwork, understand every line of code and determine what ideas were unique enough to patent. I hadn't recognized the guy sitting next to Lawrence, but he was taking notes and paying attention. He had to be the lawyer assistant, and the guy who would do most of the patent work. His college-aged face and perfect haircut matched the lawyer he was striving to be. The disgruntled look of a guy who was putting in too many hours while his boss sent text messages to the babe sitting nearby made him look more like an engineer than a lawyer.

Of course, it was possible that Monique wasn't receiving suggestive text messages from Lawrence, but she was smiling at her tablet, and I'd seen her reach over to touch his leg under the table twice. Since they weren't talking aloud, it stood to reason they were conversing on their phones.

I shifted my eyes to focus on Cary. He was blathering about how two of the ideas for Borgot's invention were his. "That clearly makes the case for my name on the patent."

Roscoe didn't think so. "You didn't code a single line."

"The *idea* is worth more than the code. It's the unique idea that is patentable, not the actual code."

The lawyer assistant, introduced as Howard, muttered, "You can't just patent an idea. You must have enough proof of the concept that an ordinary person skilled in the area can make use of it. The idea must be novel and non-obvious. The more patents a company has, the better its chances of survival."

"I'm at this code review to make sure we're headed down the right path," Cary inserted. "I've read every line of code. I've got people testing it. I have the emails to show I submitted the improvements." He waved papers around. "I'll forward the emails around."

Roscoe rolled his eyes. "Kovid submitted those ideas before you did. We talked about them long before you sent those emails."

Kovid looked up. "The translation feature is one I've been working on for years. We just need time to finish coding each language. We're well past proof of concept."

"We're past proof of concept if you count Pig Latin code," Roscoe sneered. "My code will be far more important when it's completed. I'm working on actual *languages*."

I sat up straighter. "What?"

Kovid ignored the interruption. "No other phone assistant will have an active translation portal. Travelers can buy software separately for each language. The phone assistant will translate the phrases it hears or it can speak a selection of phrases as set up by the user."

"Can the phone really translate Pig Latin?" I asked. Joe's phone had spoken both English and Pig Latin in my living room. I wasn't certain how the phone was set up, but until this moment, I had just assumed that Joe had entered a few key phrases into his own phone. Could he possibly have obtained the code from the basics being worked at Borgot?

Kovid sighed. "Since Pig Latin is just a string of characters respelled, it was easy to program it to translate back and forth for one of our early test beds. It was a joke really." He shifted uncomfortably. "I think Joe Black did the testing on it, and it did make for a proof of concept, but only at the basic level. Real languages are much more robust."

"But it's actually part of the product?"

He frowned and shook his head. "That code was only in there for a short time. It's not in the current version of code or part of this code review. It was never intended for the end product."

He tapped on the keyboard, and then frowned. "Oh, wait. The Pig Latin code is still in there. That's odd. I know I removed it from the build."

I had no idea why it might have reappeared, but it did explain how Joe's phone had come to spout Pig Latin.

"Whose voice did you use?" I asked.

"Early days? Mine, Roscoe's, whoever was around. When we coded it, marketing hadn't yet hired the actor to do all the final voice impressions for the voice assistant."

The voice on the phone I'd taken home had clearly been Joe's nasal tenor. "Did Joe help with the voices?" Everyone in the room was staring at me, including the lawyers, Monique and Cary.

"You're not suggesting," Monique swallowed, "we include Joe on the patent, are you? I mean, I know he's dead and we all feel...sorry for him and all that, but just because he died..."

I blinked. She had mistaken my sleuthing for some kind of grand memorial intent. I wasn't that generous and Joe didn't deserve it in any case. "Well, no, not exactly," I said. "Using Pig Latin on a phone has zero practical use." I lied to cover up my curiosity. "I was just trying to understand the concept."

Howard, ever the eager assistant, sat up straight. "We could use Pig Latin to help explain the concept in the patent. Sometimes a simple diagram does wonders for getting expedited approval!"

Cary gave a hearty chuckle. "Excellent! I hired Joe. It was my idea to use his Pig Latin skills to lay the groundwork for the translation. I should definitely be on that patent." He slid a covert glance towards Lawrence, but Lawrence was staring at me. As soon as he noticed me notice him, he dropped his eyes to his phone again, ignoring Cary.

So now I knew who had hired Joe or at least the idiot willing to take the credit. Or blame. Or whatever the weasel was trying to do. "Did Joe have any other language skills?" I asked innocently. "Seems like Pig Latin could be coded without needing a specialist. It doesn't seem like such a simple exchange of letters would be patentable."

"Definitely not," Lawrence declared. "Pig Latin is completely obvious and trivial."

Howard nodded his agreement.

Cary spared a glare for me. My comment had not cost him a patent, but he probably didn't see it that way. I sighed. What kind of boss tried to use a dead guy to get on a patent, anyway?

The arguing continued. Being named on a patent did mean a bonus, but no one sunk quite as low as Cary to secure his spot of fame. From what I could tell, even Monique planned to be on the patent if possible. I wasn't sure how her boyfriend could pull that off even if he was the head lawyer at Borgot. To be on a patent, you had to be an inventor, not just the boss, the marketing specialist or some guy who happened to know Pig Latin. Roscoe and Kovid were easy names; they had both done coding.

The meeting might have ended then, but Cary, still desperate, took a new tack. "We finally have our official name for the phone assistant."

We did? The test phones still responded to "Borgot assistant," the phrase I'd always used. Of course, the executives had made a big deal out of the naming of the assistant for the phone. We had to make sure it was a better name than Apple's Siri so there was even prize money for the winning name. "The contest period hasn't ended yet, has it?" I asked, trying to remember the email from over a week ago.

Cary made a guttural snarling noise without his face ever changing from its surgical perfection. "Whoever comes up with the name for the assistant *must* be on the patent. Any of us can do better than Apple's 'Siri' or Amazon's 'Alexa'." He snorted and rolled his eyes. "The name I submitted is quite obviously the winner. It will become a household name! We can't afford to leave it—or me—off the patent."

Monique piped up with, "Oh, I'm *quite* certain marketing will win the naming contest. And, I do agree that it's a great idea that whoever comes up with the winning name be on the patent." She beamed a thousand-watt smile at Lawrence.

His eyes widened slightly, perhaps in panic.

"Marketing should be disqualified from entering since you've been assigned to select the winner!" Cary sputtered. "That's corrupt!"

"Why not make the naming of the phone assistant user configurable?" I suggested. I certainly wouldn't vote for whatever name Cary had submitted. And it was possible that Monique's pick would be worse. The woman wore pants that said "Doll Baby" across her butt. "There at least needs to be the ability to select from one of two names, maybe one a female name and the other a male name. But honestly, when you consider what some people name their pets, it's probably best we leave the naming up to the user." Everyone was staring at me again. The room had gone silent.

"What?" I asked, spreading my hands.

"That's actually a very good idea," Kovid said.

Howard opened his mouth, sputtered out a half squawk and then fell silent.

Cary waved one hand as if batting at a mosquito. "Let the user choose? That's hardly enough of an idea to get on a patent. We'd do better with a unique name, one we can trademark. We need it to represent the company!" His face had gone blotchy red. Interestingly enough, the area around his mouth didn't change color, but it was kind of puffed out as if it might fall off or explode at any minute. Wow. Just how much silicone was in there anyway?

The meeting dissolved into a shouting match between Howard and Monique, with Cary throwing in wild ideas and more than a few new patent demands.

When we finally disbanded, I checked company policy to see just how much of a bonus we were talking about for being named on a patent. "Ah. Five thousand dollars—and the possibility of an executive position." I scanned through the executive officers. Lawrence already had a patent, apparently. The CFO, CEO and COO all had patents. Most of the board members had patents. It must be some kind of badge of honor with these people.

Well, if they had obtained their patents the way Cary was going about it, the intellectual property award was probably not what the U.S. Patent Office had in mind.

An email from Cary popped into my inbox before I could leave for lunch. Of course it was marked "urgent." All of his emails arrived with flames, threats and exclamation marks.

"All feature changes, enhancements and product ideas must be submitted through me from now on," the email read. It went on to stress the necessity of being a team player and discussing any possible enhancement to code, to products, and to company policy with him before so much as sharing it with yourself. He included a long list of examples such as color, phone skin designs, handicap improvements and so on.

"Yeah, little late, buddy. This thing is halfway done." He probably didn't even care about the cash, but a chance at an executive position? He'd sell his boat and house for that.

I grabbed a sandwich from the break room and went outside to call Mark and fill him in on how the Pig Latin had possibly gotten on Joe's phone.

"The code existed in a past build. The only weird thing is that Kovid seemed to think the code had been deleted."

"Can Joe have added it again?"

I hesitated. "He had access. Even I have access to the build server. But I don't think he knew how to change code in and out. I doubt he did it, which makes things even more strange."

"Okay," Mark acknowledged. "Are you going to pass this along to your brother for the police?"

"Shouldn't I wait for them to ask? I'm still not sure whether or not it was Joe's personal phone, although the voice assistant was in his voice."

Mark didn't argue the point. "I'll let Radar in on what you told me. It would be a good idea if he were hired on there. He might be able to track who added code and when just in case it's important."

"That's a good idea, but I don't think it will work. I've heard rumors we're under a hiring freeze until we get the first product out."

"Oh really? Money must be tight or running out. When the money leaves, some people get desperate."

"Desperate enough to kill Joe, anyway. But I'm not sure how him being dead helps anyone." I sighed. "I'll check some basic things. I already know how to access the code if I want to, and Joe could have done the same. It would still take someone with brains to add that code back in. I don't think he could do it."

"Okay. Should I stop by tonight? And bring Chinese?"

"Definitely."

"Enough for your parents too?"

"They're having dinner at Sean's. Mom is cooking over there so we're good."

I ate my sandwich on the way back upstairs. Gosh, working for a startup sure was fun.

Chapter 10

The only reason I was able to sneak out of work at six was because Cary was busy writing up his memoirs in the form of a lengthy thesis on why he should be listed on the patent as the number one inventor. He'd already sent around two drafts.

There hadn't been nearly enough quiet moments in my life lately, but at least Mark met me in my driveway after work. He had Chinese food in hand.

"Radar had a date so he couldn't make it, but he said to ask whether the old version of code containing the Pig Latin was still readily available if someone went looking."

I nodded. "I checked the server. All the old builds are still available, including the Pig Latin modules." I led the way inside, turning on lights and setting my backpack down before grabbing dishes from the cupboard.

"In that case anyone could have changed a few lines to call the Pig Latin code back into the latest build?"

I nodded again. "Anyone who knew what they were doing. I just don't know why anyone would bother, and if Joe did it, that's not really enough of a reason to kill him." I finished setting plates out. The serger was in the way, but Mark moved it off the table.

"It does seem like it would be easier to take the code back out than kill him."

"He was pretty annoying. Maybe the Pig Latin code was the last straw for someone." I shrugged. "I forgot to tell you that Cary took credit for hiring Joe today." I gave him more details about the patent meeting.

"Was Cary smart enough to put the Pig Latin back in there? Perhaps he thought he'd get a patent?"

"The Pig Latin angle on a patent probably didn't occur to him before today because it *isn't* patentable. He's grasping at straws and trying to make a house out of them."

"Was Joe dumb enough to think he'd make it on a patent?"

"I doubt he even knew anything about patents. He's more the type to have thought he could use Pig Latin as a secret code to impress people. Huntington seemed to think Joe was involved in moving or selling stolen contraband. Maybe Joe thought it was worth talking someone into putting the code back in so that he could use it to set up the deliveries of the stolen goods."

"Considering these burglaries have been impossible to trace, I suspect the culprits are not counting on something as obvious as Pig Latin," Mark said.

"Probably not, but Joe was very proud of using it. And none of this really gives us a clue as to why someone murdered Joe."

"I'd feel better about your safety if it has something to do with the burglaries and nothing to do with Borgot."

"Maybe. But if that is the case, it's very odd that he was killed at Borgot."

"True."

When we were finished eating, Mark lifted the serger back onto the table. "Looks like you already have this machine ready for your first project," he noted.

"I threaded them both if that's what you mean. I'm not sure the serger will actually run, but it has enough threads in there to make a pair of pants by itself."

Mark grinned. "You sound like you'd like that."

"Better it than me." I showed him the inside. "Can you believe this mess? Every time a thread breaks the instructions say to unthread every single one of these and start completely over. It's like a bad joke." I sat down at the controls, which in this case meant sitting in front of the machine with my foot over the pedal. I turned it on. "It's set to do a rolled hem, but I haven't tried it yet."

I pulled a small piece of blue cloth from the bag of odds and ends Barb had sold me. She had called it broadcloth, but this was only a "remnant" about the size of a large scarf. "Okay." I stared at the blue cloth. I looked at Mark.

"Are you going to try it now?" His bemused challenge was just short of a laugh.

"Why not?"

He didn't answer. Neither did the machine. It sat silently, not telling me whether to first roll and press the hem and then stick it under there or just put material in and see what happened. I'm big on the "try and see" method of learning. "Rolled hem plate. Yup. Got that. Threads. Check. Light, check. Machine set to thin material. If I did it right, anyway." The machine was as ready as it was going to get.

"Looks good to me," Mark said.

"What do I have to lose? Other than fingers. Maybe my whole arm if the thing sucks me under there. My hair could get caught. If this thing hurts me, I'm going to set all of your brother's clothes on fire," I muttered.

Mark laughed, filling the room with a warmth only he could ignite.

I placed the end under the guide, feeling more confident with Mark there to save me should the machine decide to attack.

Gently, I pressed the foot switch. The serger was loud. Very loud. It sounded like a plane was taking off. If Mark was still laughing, I could no longer hear him above the roar of the engine in this thing.

Determined to show no fear, I pressed harder on the foot pedal.

The machine grabbed the material and yanked it from my fingers. Needles pounded, and snapping noises filled in around the plane engine. The spools of thread jerked hard. Vibrations shivered across the table like thunder booming after a lightning strike.

"Aaaagh." As I scooted back in self-defense, my foot slammed down on the pedal, sealing the fate of the scrap of blue material. The needle slashed into the cloth like a knife, cutting it to certain death with threads.

As soon as I remembered to take my foot off the pedal, the roaring beast stopped. There was no smoke, but the thread running through the needle had snapped under the pressure.

Mark peered over my shoulder. "It isn't a very straight hem."

"No, but it's definitely rolled." I tugged on the cloth tentatively. "You might even say it's bunched." The machine had not fed the material under and then out the back end. It had added a lot of thread to it though. "I think this piece may be bound to the machine permanently."

"Yeah. Sewn tight. Open and sewn case." Mark grinned down at me. "Mom sews. She can help you with this."

"What?" I blinked. "The one who made the flowers for me?"

"I only have one mom, so yes."

He must have sensed my fear. "You have to meet her anyway because Steve hired her to infiltrate. Before you go undercover on this one, it might be a good idea if she tells you all the right things to ask and gives you a few sewing pointers. I've been wanting you to meet her anyway."

My heart stuttered. "You have?"

"She's been asking to meet you for even longer." His eyes softened with affection, a rare expression for him.

I fingered the ruined material. It wasn't budging from the machine. "Maybe it's best if we not mention the sewing right away. I'd rather make a good first impression." And a second and third. And anything to do with sewing would make me look like an incompetent idiot.

He laughed and pulled me to my feet for a mind-numbing kiss, the kind that drove my brain from "meet his mother" to "Who cares?"

It was going to be a long time before my head cleared. Maybe never. Mark was firmly under my skin and lodging more securely in my heart every day. Meet his mother, indeed.

Chapter 11

Tuesday I delved deeper into the server where the code was stored. Each engineer checked in his own segment. Once compiled and built, we loaded the newest code onto the phones for testing. I'd been a "build master" in the past. There was a lot of recordkeeping involved with the job, and there was always at least one engineer who managed to either load the wrong code, not be ready, or not have his piece working.

Being the build master was a lot like herding cats; the cats don't care and no matter how many times you put a cat where you want it, it's going to go elsewhere. The code, nevertheless, had to be assembled eventually. Like a giant puzzle, all the pieces had to be in the right place.

I had access to all the directories. The modules had archaic names, but there was no indication that Joe had ever written any of the code. Most of it had been written by Roscoe or Kovid. There were a few earlier modules written by Kevin, but he quit after a few months to become a snake charmer. Some of the basic phone functionality had been purchased from another company. That code covered phone calls, camera and non-unique functions.

Joe had probably had access to the modules, but would he have bothered to put the Pig Latin back in? And could it have been just for his ego?

Kovid worked in a line of cubes on the other side of mine, two down from Doll Baby. She was on the phone when I walked past. She had been talking to the same person for at least an hour.

"Hey, Kovid," I said.

He looked up.

"Did you take the Pig Latin out yet? I need to request another phone or two for testing, but I want the latest stuff before I bother to load the code."

The thunderous frown on his face stopped me from inventing more random excuses that were merely a ploy to obtain information from him. "What's wrong?" I asked.

"He wants it left in."

"Joe?"

The frown vanished, replaced by astonishment. "Joe? He's dead." Kovid waved his hand in dismissal of our expired co-worker.

"Then who are you talking about? I thought Joe must have put the Pig Latin back in after you took it out."

Kovid sighed. "Cary demanded I leave it in."

"You've got to be kidding me." I lowered my voice, but only because Cary's cube wasn't very far away. I was starting to wish it were in Siberia.

Kovid nodded. "I did the Pig Latin thing as a joke after Cary hired Joe. It was easy, quick. The translation worked with almost no failures because Pig Latin is merely a matter of rearranging letters. It was stupid, but something management could play with while we started the real language translations."

"And Cary really thinks that Pig Latin is enough to earn him a spot on the patent?"

Kovid shrugged. "I don't know if the Pig Latin was really his idea or not, but he's not letting us eliminate anything that might give him a chance."

"But it's not even original! And there's nothing inventive about it!"

"Agreed. But if we take the code out, he can't even claim an idea. He's now swearing he hired Joe for his language expertise to prove the concept." His forehead wrinkled. "Or something like that. But I'm pretty sure I did the Pig Latin after hearing Joe interrupt a bunch of us engineers with his stupid phrases. No one suggested it as a real language for the phone. Honestly, I was making fun of him, which might not have been nice, but instead of shutting him up, he thought it made him important!"

I groaned. "And now all the phones are going to ship with a Pig Latin option? I thought being hired at a startup company was supposed to mean working on cutting edge technology!"

Kovid rubbed his forehead as though trying to erase a headache. "Right now, it's a hidden option."

"He at least let you hide it?"

Kovid shook his head. "That's the weird part. I took that code out, I know I did. But whoever put it back in added a special key sequence to select it. Once it's turned on, the phone will translate and answer questions in both Pig Latin and English.

"All the other languages are selected by typing in the first four to six letters of the language after a verbal request. For Spanish, you say 'Spanish,' and then you type 'S p a n.' But when the modules were dropped back in, the Pig Latin was coded behind the words Joe Black. And the entire name had to be typed in, no spaces."

Goosebumps ran across my arms. "Joe must have put that Pig Latin stuff back in after you took it out."

He looked away, staring blankly at his screen. "Who else would bother?"

My mind scrolled to Cary, but that didn't make sense. Cary couldn't have been planning the Pig Latin thing from day one because no one in their right mind would think it was patentable. "You can tell that the Pig Latin stuff was put back in before Joe died, right?"

"Of course he had to have done it while still alive!!" He swallowed hard. "When I saw that in there...It was like a bhoot, the ghost of Joe, was standing right next to me." His glance shifted behind me as though he might be able to see the bhoot right now. I rubbed at the goosebumps and had to force myself not to look.

"I can tell from the date that the code was reinserted almost immediately after I took it out, but there have been two updates to the Pig Latin modules and one of them was yesterday."

From the look on his face, it was obvious he hadn't done the updates. And Joe had already been dead for a couple of days by yesterday. I gulped. "Oh."

He nodded. "Yeah. The file had been accessed. Something changed because the date changed, but whoever made the changes didn't update the change log." He raised one hand helplessly and then shook himself. "Look, none of that matters. It's just weird, is all. I'm almost finished with the code to allow the user to select the voice assistant name. If you don't tell anyone, I'll do a build with that code and you can start testing it. It will be in the official drop at the end of the week."

I straightened and backed out of the cube opening. "Thanks. Shoot me an email when you have the latest ready. Meanwhile I'll brush up on my Pig Latin because if Cary gets his way, it will be our number one language."

Mind boggling. Just mind boggling.

Chapter 12

There were only so many nights I could continue to escape at a reasonable time, but tonight had to be one of them. My parents were leaving tomorrow, and I'd promised Mom I'd invite Mark over "for at least cake" before they left. Was it my fault they had been busy at Sean's until the last night they were in town?

I waited until Cary made his rounds just after five and then started a random test loop on one of the phones to run overnight. The battery would likely die long before the test finished, but running any test still counted.

I also dutifully packed a phone to take home. Maybe I'd find a second or two to run a trial on it while I was brushing my teeth before bed. There weren't likely to be any other available seconds because I had a cake to bake and people to entertain the rest of the evening.

Just as I stood to head out, Cary's voice drifted from somewhere down cube. I ducked, but clearly heard him say my name and something about, "Of course, we discussed the idea of letting the customer choose a name for their phone assistant! Sedona was already testing the idea at my request."

"Oh, for the love of patents, you liar." Of course, now he'd come to my cube with some made-up test document. I didn't have time for him. He probably wouldn't let me leave until I agreed to sign an affidavit swearing the customer naming the phone assistant was his idea.

I crouched lower, adjusted my backpack and duck-waddled over to Joe's old cubicle. Monique was talking into her cell and walking out of her cube. If she glanced over the tops of the walls, she'd see me scurrying along like a mutant marine.

I quickly grabbed my earlobe, but who had time to put earrings on in the morning? I was lucky to get my clothes on straight! The "lost my earring" excuse wouldn't fly.

Joe's cube was as sterile and empty as every other cube in the building. No one had bothered to clean it after he died, although the police had taken his laptop. There was nothing but standard issue desk, chair and cabinet.

I wasn't desperate enough to climb in the cabinet to hide, was I?

Cary's voice closed in.

With a grunt, I pulled Joe's chair aside and scooted under the desk, my back to the hallway side. I yanked the chair back in with me. If Cary found me, he might be dumb enough to believe I was testing the cell phone reception under a desk. And if he didn't believe me, who cared?

I shifted my backpack around in order to scrunch further into the corner. My butt landed on one of the support bars, sending a shooting pain into my rear. As if Cary wasn't enough of a pain in the ass without the extra jab.

I kept quiet. Cary's khaki pants were just visible as he walked past into my cube. I leaned my head away from the opening and held the phone to my ear just in case he caught me.

There was the sound of papers being shuffled. He was either leaving me a note or wadding up his latest "plan for a patent" draft. I held my breath. There was nothing saving me but a thin cube wall.

His cell phone buzzed. He must have had it set to vibrate mode, but this close, the sound was quite audible.

After a silent moment, he said, "As soon as I find it. He wasn't wearing it." After another pause he said, "It's hardly going to be discovered randomly, and even if it is, no one will know where it belongs."

I peeked around the side again just enough to glimpse one of his legs. Who was he talking to? Who cared? If he had to do some chore or other, he'd forget about me.

His voice faded, accompanied by the sound of footsteps and slacks swishing.

I pushed the chair the tiniest bit. No sound of anyone. I scooted and had to clamp down on a squeal. The support post was either following me out or I'd sat on something that had moved with me, bruising more of my butt.

I felt along the floor until I located the offensive object. It wasn't too dark to recognize Joe's watch because it lit up when my hand hit one of the buttons. "Eww."

I had never noticed much about the watch other than suspecting Joe used it to help him translate Pig Latin faster. The thing obviously did more than tell the time, but the leather watchband was stretched oddly as though forced to fit the watch. The holes for the buckling prong were very distorted.

A closer inspection revealed that the space between two of the holes was cut, forming one larger hole. The watch must have fallen off his arm because it wasn't possible to securely buckle the broken band anymore.

I gulped. Had he raised his arm in defense and the leather been sliced with a knife meant for his head? I stuffed it in my backpack. I didn't want to think too hard about it. My hand froze as the conversation I'd just overheard played in my head. "He wasn't wearing it." Who wasn't wearing what?

I fingered the watch. Obviously, Joe wasn't wearing it when he died. Ick. I dropped it in the pack. Cary couldn't have been talking about Joe's watch. Why would he care about a watch? Like it or not, I was obligated to return this to Joe's heirs. I guess that meant his mother. Oh wait. His mother could be involved in illegal dealings just like her son. Yeah. I did not want to involve myself with her any more than I had to. Well, Huntington could give it to her, maybe after he arrested her.

I peeked around the chair. A pair of jeans went by without stopping. From that attire, it could have been any of the engineers, including me, except I was huddled under a desk like a fool. Why hadn't I just run for the exit? It was well after five. I had a right to leave!

With a sigh, I pushed my way out. Would it be overkill if I crouched down on my way out of the rat maze?

Probably.

Roscoe and Kovid were chatting just outside cube city. I gave them a weak smile and dodged around them on my way to the stairs. My walk was not a run, but it might have won a few races.

Someone called my name from behind me, but it was impossible to tell who with as hard as I was breathing. Besides, I could take the stairs way faster than Cary could ring the elevator up to the third floor. I'd be out of the building and in my car before he arrived down on the first floor.

If you never look back, you can claim you never saw them.

Of course, just sneaking out of work to bake a tiramisu wasn't enough of a challenge. At six o'clock when Mark was due to show up, I was outside helping Dad install the last of the blueberry plants in my new raised bed. Darkness was already creeping into the yard.

I didn't remember gardening being this dim. "We could wait until morning," I grumbled.

Dad ignored me, of course.

We dug about in the soil, unwrapped the roots and set them in the ground. The blueberry bushes were nothing but twigs, with no sign of spring budding whatsoever.

Mom was busy puttering about inside, having generously offered to unbind the material from the serger and rethread it.

We hadn't finished installing the last bush when she bustled out the back door and leaned over to whisper. "Mark's brother is here. It was very nice of you to invite him too."

Of course I hadn't done any such thing. Huntington always invited himself places. "Steve?"

"He looks just like Mark, but his eyes are blue. I think he's taller too."

"What's he doing here?" I slapped my hands mostly clean and then brushed them on my sweatpants.

Mom said, "Well, of course I invited him in for cake. It was obvious he is family since he looks just like Mark."

"Yes, I know. Dad, are you coming?"

"There's still time to mulch these in. I'll finish that. You don't want them to dry out or for the roots to get too cold."

Mom rolled her eyes at me and tugged me to the back door.

By the time we hurried back inside, Mark had also shown up. Steve, being Steve, had had no problem letting Mark in while we were out back.

Mark had made more of an effort with his hair than normal. Instead of it just being combed, it had been gelled into place. I gave him my best smile before turning to his brother.

"Steve," I said coolly. "You've met my mother?"

He smiled, ever assured. "The elegant and lovely lady who answered the door, yes. You look nothing like her. I'd never have guessed."

He was right, but it was rude to say so. Mom's strawberry blonde curls were completely untamed, but gave her a soft, feminine glow. My brown hair was almost always pulled into a messy ponytail that bespoke my laziness. Mom had bright green eyes and a smattering of friendly freckles. My eyes were darker, nearly gray, and I had a tendency to frown a lot, especially lately.

That changed when Mark moved to my side. Either because his brother had also shown up or just because, Mark put his arm around me and leaned in to give me a kiss. He left his arm around my shoulders.

I grinned up at him. "I hope everyone likes tiramisu. I need to wash up."

Mom started pattering and asking mom-type social questions.

I hurried to change clothes and was just out of the bathroom when Dad came in.

Mom, ever the smooth social hostess, handled introducing Dad to Steve. Dad hadn't washed up yet, but he shook Steve's hand anyway. That was Dad; absent-minded and not too worried about a bit of dirt. As soon as he spotted me, Dad said, "Don't over water, now." I helped him finish with, "Just keep the root ball damp."

Steve peered around Dad's shoulder at the backyard. "You already put in the garden bed? Great!"

Dad gave a proud nod as he headed to the kitchen sink to wash his hands. He continued with his instructions. "You don't need to fertilize for a few weeks. I made sure to mix molasses in there. I didn't put in any corn meal because I knew you'd want to plant onions from seeds. Don't put the tomato plants out until the nights are above forty. You can probably get away with slightly cooler, but you know those cold nights will drift in there anyway."

"Uh-huh."

Mom busied herself cutting slices of tiramisu.

She handed me a plate. Her eyes widened. "You better move the sewing machines. I'll finish serving."

Dad grabbed two plates from Mom and handed one to Steve, leaving Mark to relocate the machines.

"Did you boil the eggs?" Dad asked.

I nodded dutifully. "Yes—"

He interrupted around a mouthful of tiramisu. "For a minute at full boil."

I had probably cheated, but nodded anyway. I only bothered to boil them when Dad was likely to ask. Usually I took my chances with raw eggs, but with Dad, the only way to avoid a lecture was to follow his rules. This time, even my precautions failed to avert the lecture. He turned to Mark.

"Food poisoning. Could die of the shits if you get it bad enough and can't obtain medical help in time. Hell of a way to go. Of course," he interrupted himself and faced me, "if you used eggs from a free-range farm, you probably wouldn't have to boil them. Did you?"

Mom blushed a bright red. Dad was spoiling another of her dinner parties, and at the rate he was spouting, his tab was going to run so high he'd never be able to make it up to her. If I didn't intervene soon, Mom might make up an excuse to lure him back to the garden and then lock him outside.

"Uh, no, they weren't from a local farm. They were from the grocery so I—"

Back to Mark, Dad's original target. "If a chicken is allowed to peck along the ground and eat bugs and pebbles for digestion, and even some chicken poop from other chickens, it has a healthy digestive tract. They lay eggs with a protective barrier," he said. "You don't want to wash eggs unless there's obvious shit on them and then just spot clean them. The chickens take care of the rest."

I smiled weakly at Mark. Steve inspected the tiramisu with sudden suspicion. I hurriedly reassured him. "Don't worry, Huntington. Your egg came from the grocery. That chicken only ate grain right from the feed trough."

He glanced up at me before Dad took back over. "It's a lot healthier to eat the eggs from chickens that roam. More protein, better natural antibiotics in the system, the whole nine yards. 'Course it's best to nab the eggs right after they are laid or you could end up cracking one and the bacteria—"

Mom twisted her napkin in her fingers and pushed her chair back to stand.

"Dad, they are from the grocery!" I yelled. "No issues with freshness. Plucked right out of the hen house. Fresh and boiled!"

Mark grinned at me and spooned in another bite of tiramisu. Huntington frowned down at his plate, his doubt obvious. "All of this cake was made from the same batch?" he asked. "You didn't make a special piece or two for anyone?"

I hadn't thought of that, but it made me smile. "Yes, Huntington, your cake is from the exact same batch as everyone else's. Plus, I didn't know you were coming."

He didn't look as though he believed me, but the tiramisu was excellent so he didn't refuse to eat it.

Mom muttered something about making Dad's with special eggs. "No, Dad is safe, too."

Mark laughed, but changed it to a cough when my mother glanced his way.

The tiramisu and coffee disappeared despite Dad changing his lecture to how chicken poop was excellent fertilizer for the garden.

When it was time for Mark and Steve to depart, and gosh, they wasted no time after eating, Steve handed me a piece of paper. "Garden club meeting time and place. Sewing ones too." He smiled innocently, knowing I wouldn't discuss a case in front of my parents since it was better if they remained completely in the dark about *any* case, past or present.

"Thanks."

Mark shot him a cold glare and opened the door, urging Steve along in front of him. I followed them both out. My parents probably would have opted to allow me some privacy, but Dad spotted Steve's new stealth car sitting in the driveway.

"Is that a Porsche?" he asked, his head tilting as he stepped outside. It was already past dusk, but because of my involvement with Huntington and his investigations, my porch light was more of a lighthouse beacon than a normal bulb. Good lighting might keep any escaped convicts or friends of Huntington who were roaming the neighborhood from wandering onto my property. If the glare of discovery didn't stop them, I'd at least be able to see them clearly if I had to shoot.

Steve failed to hide a note of pride in his voice when he answered Dad. "It's the Panamera electric hybrid."

I looked back to find my mother leaning against the door jamb with her hand over her eyes. "Mark, you might want to come back inside and have another piece of cake. This could take a while," she said.

Mark glanced at me. "Car buff?"

I shook my head. "Not really. But you know how I work at technology companies and like cool gadgets?" He raised an eyebrow in lieu of answering, but I continued. "I get that from Dad. I noticed Huntington's new car the other day, but didn't know it was an electric hybrid."

If it had been anyone other than Steve, I'd have gone and admired the car too, but there was no point in feeding his ego. To be fair, Dad also asked about Mark's Lexus hybrid. Mark didn't even have a chance to leave the porch, never mind answer the questions. Huntington knew every feature on Mark's SUV as if he owned it himself.

Mom retrieved her sweater, and we loitered while Steve extolled the virtues of his new hybrid, including the all-important zero to sixty in "just under five seconds."

Mark put his arm around me, and we leaned on each other.

Just another night with my oddball family and eclectic friends.

Chapter 13

I fully expected Cary to read me the riot act for disappearing "early" two days in a row. Never mind that five-thirty was a perfectly normal quitting time, and never mind that I started work at seven. He would choose to recall that I hadn't worked the previous weekend, so by his standards, I hadn't shown up for a solid week.

Huddled in my cube, I downloaded the latest code and started testing. My spreadsheet already listed several hours of completed tests.

Now that I knew the secret, I activated the Pig Latin on one of my three test phones. "Yup. Still there." Thankfully on these phones, the robotic assistant's voice pronounced the words, rather than Joe's voice. His nasal translations from the grave had been far too creepy. But it did beg the question of just why the phone that I had been given had contained Joe's voice recordings. It had to have been his personal phone.

I shuddered.

All of my test phones readily went in and out of Pig Latin translation mode. If there were any coded messages on Joe's phone, maybe Radar would find them, because as far as the Pig Latin went, it seemed to work the same— and perfectly on every phone in the bunch.

The test for sending text messages worked fine as well. The phone assistant was supposed to be creative enough to handle a variety of tasks, including answering questions that relied on artificial intelligence to come up with an appropriate answer to miscellaneous questions. The AI was my favorite part of testing. "Recommend a good book to read," I instructed.

"Anything by Frank Tuttle."

"Tuttle? Who is Frank Tuttle?"

"An author. Or Big Foot."

"*Big Foot*???"

The phone repeated itself. I felt like shaking it, but stared at my test sheet instead. "I don't know if this is a legit bug to report or if Borgot's phone has solved the mystery of Big Foot. Big Foot? Who programmed this thing?"

I tested Kovid's new code for naming the phone assistant. It was a bit of a hassle at the moment because it required both typing in the name and speaking it into the phone. Without both steps, the robotic voice mangled the pronunciation. Despite my careful pronunciation, "Unicorn" still came out Un-

I-Corn. Worse, the phone stuttered, making it sound like listening to rap music while popping popcorn.

"You can't say 'unicorn' but you can pronounce 'Tuttle'?" Maybe Tuttle was some famous monster hunter or something.

I tested the phones all day, completing all my usual tests and creating several new ones. Despite expecting Cary to stop by, he was a no-show. Without him around to nag me, I scooted out of work at five. It was almost like being on vacation. And my parents had left that morning. I called Mark before reaching the car. "Want to get together for dinner?"

"What did you have in mind?"

"Who cares? We can get Chinese or I can cook. Mom left the pantry stocked."

"I could grab some steaks."

"Works for me. There's tiramisu for dessert."

"That wasn't the dessert I had in mind."

It hadn't been the dessert I'd had in mind either, but I there was no way I would say that out loud.

For once, traffic didn't attempt to kill me on my way home even though I was in a hurry. This time, I left my backpack in the car because this was a "no phones" kind of date.

Before changing out of my jeans, I stepped out back to ready the grill. I stopped cold in the doorway. "Oh, my God. Who? Why?"

My beautiful garden and its neatly arranged rows was a mess. The blueberry plants were no longer in the ground. One lay on its side by the cute brick edge Dad had installed. Another was halfway across the yard. "Who?" The entire backyard had been sprayed with the garden hose. In fact, the water was still on.

I hurried to shut it off, my shoes squishing in the mud. "Crap." I was still in my work sneakers and jeans. No point in ruining them. I raced inside and changed into my oldest sweatpants and a shirt that should probably have been thrown out two decades ago. I never wore it anymore, but it had a picture of a cow skull and desert sun with the words, "But it's a dry heat" across the front. I loved that saying.

My oldest sneakers weren't that old, so I grabbed up the beach water shoes meant for a trip to Hawaii. I'd never gone to Hawaii, but I had big plans for someday. My feet would be cold in the shoes, but at least I could hose the mud and dirt off.

Back outside, I slogged over to the first blueberry plant. I grabbed the trowel that was practically still warm from Dad's hands from planting the day before. "Huntington if you..." But that made no sense. He wanted me to garden. Why would he, or anyone for that matter, tear my garden to shreds?

"Hmph." With an energy that was mostly fury, I used the hand trowel to dig a hole in the corner where the blueberry bush had been. Whoever had gone through here had used a shovel and water to smooth everything inside the raised bed back to an even, muddy mess.

I moved to the next blueberry bush, but that was a mistake. The dirt in the garden was soft. My water shoes were meant for traction on sand, not sinking into soil and swimming against loose dirt. Halfway across, I was buried nearly to my knees.

I opted to step backwards onto the dirt already traversed, but my foot slid against an unsteady surface. My butt took the brunt of the fall.

Thankfully the ground wasn't wet enough to splash. Not so thankfully, as I scrambled to my knees, I realized the ground beneath me was wearing clothes.

"Wha—?" I sucked in a worried breath. Maybe Dad had lost part of his sleeve? Tentatively, praying, I scooped dirt away from what had once been a gray or white shirt. Using the spade sparingly, I verified that the shirt was still on the body that had worn it. For the second time in a week, I felt for a pulse, knocking more dirt aside. Even mostly buried, I knew who was wearing the clothes. No one else had lips frozen into that botox expression, and his had been preserved like that long before rigor mortis set in.

Like an angel with wings, I airlifted myself out of that garden plot, the ghost on my tail. One water shoe remained suctioned in the dirt. The other stayed with me as I flew to the back door, reached in for the phone and dialed 911.

Chapter 14

The 911 operator demanded that I stay on the line until the police arrived. That prevented me from calling Mark and annoyed my last nerve. I didn't have a lot of remaining nerves to begin with, not after finding Cary in my backyard.

When Detective Saunders finally arrived, I hung up without saying good-bye. Having already soiled the crime scene with my presence, I stomped closer to the raised bed to answer his questions.

He ignored me for several minutes.

When he finally stopped bellowing at his team about "taping off" and "watch your step," he turned to me in disgust. "Could you have possibly contaminated this scene worse? You're a mess."

I crossed my arms and glared. By a small margin I resisted tapping my foot. "Sorry. I didn't stop to bathe before calling the police." I blew my bangs up with a puff of air. My hair must have been well past "fashionably windblown" and more "matted down with mud" because it barely moved.

The detective snorted, giving me another disapproving quick up and down. He turned around and grabbed a very large plastic bag from one of the technicians. He held it out with a smirk. "I'll need to take those clothes as evidence. I need every speck of dirt that may have been in contact with the victim."

Was he implying that I should just get naked in front of everyone? My eyes narrowed and the foot tapped. Before I could verbalize my opinion of him, a stealthy male voice from behind me said, "I'll make sure she gets these out to you with all the dirt intact." Mark's arm snaked around my waist.

Then, to my embarrassment, Mark reached up and removed a clump of soil from my hair. He took the plastic bag from the detective and dropped the clump inside, shifting so that he was planted firmly between me and Detective Saunders.

I sighed. "I was much cleaner *before* I found this mess." I waved my hand at the taped off area. "Those prize blueberries cannot be replaced. My dad looked high and low before he found the varieties he wanted." I refused to acknowledge that my voice was shaking. "I don't imagine Cary is feeling all that fixable either."

Truth to tell, I was probably sorrier about the work lost. The gardening had been something Dad had helped me with, and after the police were done sifting through each molecule of dirt, I'd be left with nothing but sifted mud.

"No, looks like his next job will be manning the compost bin," Detective Saunders said with a smirk.

Both Mark and I glared at him. His comment might be a good gardening joke, but it was in extremely poor taste.

Saunders wasn't the least bit perturbed. "No sign that anyone was inside your house?" he asked.

"No. Nothing inside was disturbed. The place was still locked up."

"We found drag marks from the front," he said. "Looks like they came in from the side gate."

At least they hadn't broken out a window and swished him through the living room.

"You know of any reason someone would want to leave a dead body in your yard? Revenge? A warning of some kind?"

I shook my head, searching my yard for a reason, but not finding one. "No," I said softly.

"Well, someone doesn't like you very much," Saunders drawled. "You'll want to watch your back."

If the body was meant to warn me away from something...Borgot? Did someone want me to quit? The person who had disliked me most was probably Cary, and I doubted he'd buried himself in my yard to prove it.

Mark tightened his arm around me, and we withdrew inside. A detective was just finishing up an inspection.

Before I could change clothes, the doorbell rang.

Turbo waited on the porch, his hair uncombed and his shirt looking like he might have grabbed it off a hobo. For him, programmer extraordinaire, this fashionable attire was entirely normal. My old boss from Strandfrost was silent for a moment as his brain assessed all the data in front of him. Finally, he let out a huge sigh of relief. "I heard about the body on the police scanner." He gulped. "They didn't say if it was the owner of the house or not."

"Come on in, Turbo. I'm fine. Thanks for worrying. I didn't know you had a police scanner."

He blinked at me a few times and adjusted his glasses. "How else do you get accurate news?"

He was such a geek. I didn't bother to explain to him that I didn't have *time* for news, not from any source, really. There was another knock on the front door just then, saving me from what was sure to be a lecture on the best scanners from Turbo.

It was Radar. He was staring down at his watch, one that reminded me of Joe's watch because the display was flashing information so fast, it looked like blue Christmas lights. As soon as Radar saw me in one piece, he nodded happily.

"Let me guess," I said. "Police scanner."

"Nah. Well, sort of. My smartwatch hooks to Twitter via my phone to pick up certain feeds, like police scans pertaining to certain addresses or keywords. I need something more sophisticated to sort the tweets though so I'm working on the code."

"What program do you use for voice recognition to create the tweets from the scanner?" Turbo asked. "Even with the best scanners it must come across garbled. The police communication equipment is shit at the front end."

"It is," Radar agreed. "I run it through a transcribing program and a signal processing program to remove some of the noise. An alert then goes to my smartwatch with the text," he held up his fancy watch. "If the tweet looks interesting enough, I can check my phone for more detailed info. Heard there was a dead body here."

Mark eyed the two of them warily, but Turbo didn't notice. Turbo was more interested in peppering Radar with questions about the setup for getting text messages of police scans. "Is that a Pebble Smartwatch? Is it advanced enough for what you're doing?"

Radar babbled the specs of his watch, along with more of his plans. "It will function okay for me until the Netflix Smartwatch comes out. That one has a bigger screen and a more powerful processor. But for now, not only does this one handle text messages without me having to pull my phone out, I can see who is calling and text back one of six standard replies. The watch handles maps, the weather and can even control a camera or video recorder remotely."

"Those two are kind of scary, aren't they?" Mark said to me.

I worried my friends would be insulted by his question, but neither engineer noticed. They were too busy scribbling notes on a stray piece of sewing cloth they had grabbed from the kitchen table.

"I need to change clothes," I said with a sigh.

"Do you have any cookies?" Turbo asked.

"There's some cookie dough in the freezer." They hadn't even asked who the body was after discovering it wasn't me. Should I be flattered or dismayed?

I changed into clean pants and a shirt, bagged the dirty ones, and handed them out the back door to be labeled and taken away.

Only then did I locate some cookie dough. It didn't take long to chop the brick into individual pieces. Someone had turned on the oven.

Even though no one had asked, I told them about the garden and the body I'd stumbled across.

When I was finished, Turbo and Radar both stood up from the kitchen table and stared out the back door. "There's a fence. How'd they haul the body over the fence?"

"Blood is actually good for growing plants. But the cops probably hauled it all away as evidence," was Radar's contribution.

Mark shook his head. I checked the cookies.

"Did whoever it was who murdered your boss really think you wouldn't find the body when you started planting?" Turbo asked. "Sure, you had fresh dirt back there, but you were bound to notice."

"Maybe they didn't know it was Sedona living here," Radar said. "If it was a little old lady, maybe she wouldn't pay as much attention as Sedona does to weird things."

Abruptly, Turbo opened the door. Radar followed him out.

Detective Saunders demanded they retreat. The two of them stopped at the edge of the porch, ignoring him. The investigative team was keeping to the raised bed and the side of the house, having decided that only I had gone from the back door to the raised bed. The whole area had already been photographed, including the spot where my final water shoe had been abandoned. It was gone now, probably bagged.

"Those cookies ready yet?" Mark asked.

I checked, took them out and scooped a cookie off the pan, but it squished and collapsed. "Too hot yet." I handed Mark the squashed mess on a small plate.

He blew on it and ate it as it cooled. In the backyard, my two friends walked around the police tape and discussed...scarecrows?

"She'll need to rebuild this part and there should be fencing. Without a scarecrow or a cat or something the birds will eat all the blueberries."

"Hey," Radar's face lit up, "I have this cool robot! It doesn't do much yet, but all the arm and leg movements have been completed. I've been looking for a project! This is perfect." He rubbed his hands together.

He and Turbo kept talking, planning and waving their arms like two mad scientists on speed. Turbo asked something about "protection in case of invaders" and "karate chops or just spinning."

"They're definitely scary." Mark put his arm around my shoulders.

"Nah, they're just being engineers. They're good guys."

"Whatever you say." He nudged me inside with him and then scraped another cookie from the pan. "I'm not sure, but I think they are talking about booby trapping your backyard."

My brow wrinkled in concern. Not that they wouldn't do a good job. But how did they plan to keep *me* from setting off their traps?

Chapter 15

What with one thing and another, we never did eat dinner. And there certainly wasn't any dessert.

Because I had to provide another statement at the police station with my lawyer present on Thursday morning, I called in at eight to tell Kovid that I'd be working from home as time allowed. "I don't know who else to notify that I'm not coming in," I explained. "It could take a while before they decide who will replace Cary."

Kovid disagreed. "Got an email first thing from John, the CEO. Monique got the job."

"Marketing Monique? Doll Baby on the back of her pants, Monique?"

"We don't have any other people working here with that name, so yeah, her."

Monique was mid-thirties; maybe a tad younger if she had aged badly. She wasn't old, but her outfits painted an unflattering image of a woman desperate to attract a man before it was too late. In the corporate world, dressing like she did was an invitation for innuendos and attention of the wrong kind from guys who assumed the attire was an attempt at a promotion. Despite all that and talking on the phone all the time, she did get her job done. That didn't mean she deserved a management position over the engineering department. Then again, Cary hadn't really deserved the job either.

"Huh. How did she get the job in charge of engineering and test? She's in marketing!"

Kovid grunted. "We have a hiring freeze so they couldn't go outside the company. They aren't even going to replace Joe. No hiring."

It was very polite of him to mention that as an excuse, but I knew what he was thinking, because unkind though it was, I was thinking the same thing. She was sleeping with the executive attorney. Lawrence had to have pulled some strings, because there was no logic that would put her in charge of engineering.

After Kovid hung up, I asked my Borgot voice assistant for her number. The test phone didn't know so I had to call Kovid back. I pointed out that my test phone was flawed because it didn't know Monique's number. My job was to test these things, after all.

"She's not in your contacts list, right?" he asked.

"Shouldn't all the company numbers be in there?"

"No. Not unless you specifically add them. We aren't Facebook here, grabbing every phone number we can get our greedy hands on."

"Okay, okay."

I called her number, but the line was busy and went to voice mail. Huge surprise, just huge. I left a message and tossed the phone in my backpack on my way out the door.

* * *

Sean was an experienced lawyer, and he'd assisted the police department often enough that many of the guys knew him. He had me in and out of there in an hour. Since he had been sitting beside me while I told the story twice, I didn't bother to defend or explain myself as we left.

"I'm sewing a baby bib for Samantha," I said instead, to break the chilly silence.

"Hard to believe you have the time."

I didn't, not really. "Sean, I was at Borgot all day Wednesday. I did not have anything to do with either of those bodies."

"Are you working for Huntington again?"

I shrugged. "Not exactly. After the first guy showed up dead, Mark decided to investigate. He doesn't like the idea of me working in a dangerous environment."

Sean stared at me and sputtered. "Stay away from Brenda and the baby until they arrest the guy who did this!" He stalked off to his beat-up Accord.

While it would have been possible to make it into work, I drove home. Out of sheer guilt, I dug through my backpack for the Borgot phone to run some tests. To my dismay, I found Joe's forgotten watch instead.

"Ugly thing." Unlike Radar's timepiece, this watch resembled a prototype with cheap plastic and a big outer rubber piece holding it together. I stared at it for a while before I dared try it.

"Borgot? Joe?" For the phones to activate Pig Latin, his entire name had to be typed in. But this thing had a relatively small screen, making it difficult to use. "Joe Black?" I guessed.

Nothing.

My mind ran through what Radar had said about speech recognition. That sort of thing was exactly what Borgot hoped to be very good at, in addition to providing translations for foreign languages. Radar had also said his smartwatch was essentially just a watch without his mobile phone. The cell phone was the brains; the watch was just spitting out text messages or supplying basic information that his phone had already obtained.

Joe had a phone that talked Pig Latin. If this watch worked with that phone, it probably had some of the same basic functionality loaded. "Oh-Jay?"

"Owhay, ayay oingday?" the watch asked in Joe's voice.

Chills ran up my arm, freezing my teeth shut. I set the watch down rather than fling it across the room. As often as I'd been forced to hear Joe's voice after he was dead, it felt like his ghost was stalking me. "How ya doing," I translated in a whisper. Louder, I said, "Better than you."

I swallowed, studying the watch. "Burglaries. Was he stealing high-end watches?" Huntington hadn't exactly specified why he wanted Joe's mother questioned. This watch didn't look high-end anything, either.

"What is the current temperature in Denton, Colorado?"

"Sixty-two degrees."

The watch responded to the same question asked in Pig Latin. This thing was definitely set up to work with Borgot code.

I played with questions and features. The watch appeared to try to synch to a phone or other smart device more than once. Without the right phone in close proximity the functions were very limited.

I needed Radar and the code from Joe's phone. Maybe there were calendar events or other meaningful appointments we could access once the watch connected to the phone.

I called Radar and told him what I'd found.

"If there were appointments on the smartwatch, they'd be on the phone too," he said. "And that phone didn't contain anything very useful. From what I can tell, it may have been his personal phone, but the only real difference between it and any other Borgot test phone is that his voice was used for a lot of the commands."

"That's the same with the watch," I said.

"What kind is it? There aren't that many smartwatches out there. They are very expensive and the more capabilities, the more the watch will cost you."

I checked, but there was nothing on the watch casing, no name, no insignia.

"I'll come by in a couple of hours," Radar promised.

While I waited for Radar to stop by, I called Mark and left him a message about the smartwatch.

Since neither he nor Radar was available right away, rather than chew my fingernails asking a watch stupid questions, I started on the baby bibs and the bra. It had to be easier to cut the patterns all at once.

Then too, maybe I was procrastinating using the sewing machines because once those patterns were cut, I downloaded and cut out a t-shirt pattern. I messed up the sleeves, so decided it was going to be a tank top. "Everyone needs a tank top."

I checked the time on Joe's watch. It had only been an hour.

"Fine." I sat down and shoved the first bib under the regular machine. Sewing a back to the front meant I didn't have to put a binding along the edges. Binding looked hard and time consuming.

The bib turned out more rounded than square. That is to say, the corners were funky diagonal edges. And one diagonal was way larger than the other. "I'll make a round bib instead."

I cut some off the edges and sewed it again.

It was now rounder, but extremely lopsided with one side higher than the other. "Well, Auntie Sedona made it, right? The next one will be better." I added straps to tie around the neck, but boy did they make the edges bulge where they fit against the bib.

Since I was practicing and learning, I tried to use the finishing machine for the top. According to the pattern, that part should have the mystery binding sewn across it and then made into the ties, but I'd already affixed ties.

The serger was every bit as noisy as before. It was possibly faster. It cut straight through one of the ties I had just sewn on.

I checked the pattern and instructions again. Apparently the top was supposed to be done *before* adding the ties. And the instructions didn't say anything about correcting for ties that might have gotten cut off.

The thing now had one tie, was crooked, uneven and ugly. "Maybe I better start over. Then again, Samantha is too young to know the difference between a washcloth with a string and a bib. Hey, maybe this is one of those things you tie to the high chair and use to wipe her mouth. Yeah. I'm an inventor. No ordinary bibs for this family." Not at the rate I was sewing anyway.

The doorbell rang, providing a reprieve, at least until I discovered it was Huntington and not Mark or Radar.

"What?" I asked.

His eyes narrowed. "Mark said I owed you some replacement plants because you lost some kind of heirloom blueberries working on the case. I don't see how that is possible since you haven't even attended a single garden club meeting yet."

"Mark is correct. But more important than blueberries, I need surveillance equipment. You have access to the good stuff that works at night, right?"

"At night? What are you up to, and what makes you think I can provide that kind of thing?"

I rolled my eyes. Not only had I caught Mark installing cameras during one of our cases, both brothers did investigative work at the highest levels. "You run a company that involves high-tech companies. Are you telling me you don't have the latest and greatest espionage equipment?"

"Are you crazy?" he asked. "Of course you are." Another thought occurred to him. "Who do you want watched?"

"I want it installed in my backyard."

His eyes flicked to the back door before he strode over. "You think someone is planning to bury another dead body there? I did order you more dirt from the same place your dad ordered from." He stepped outside. "I don't think you have to worry about this happening again."

I just glared at him. He sighed. "You're in more danger of a squirrel digging up your plants than another dead body finding its way here. There is no way you need state of the art equipment to catch a squirrel digging up a tomato plant."

"A squirrel did not put Cary in that garden bed." I pointed out.

"I am not wasting my time or equipment on—can't you just set an alarm every hour, run outside and check on the garden until you get over your unreasonable fear that people intend to make this a cemetery?"

Leave it to Huntington to decide my sleep was unimportant. "No. This gardening thing was your idea, you know."

He snorted. "Fine. I'll install some equipment. But we are not even."

I agreed heartily. "Damn straight. You owe me way more than this."

His eyes narrowed, but I didn't drop my gaze. He finally asked, "Do you know the names of the blueberry plants?"

"I'll text them to you. The detectives took all four plants. Two of them were Sunshine Blue, but I don't know the other two. I'll ask Dad."

Huntington snagged two cookies when he stepped back into the kitchen.

"Were smartwatches part of the contraband you think Joe was stealing?" I asked.

"What makes you ask that?"

I was just about to tell him about the watch when the doorbell rang. It was Radar and Mark. Their timely appearance meant I only had to tell my story once.

"This is an odd looking watch," Radar declared after a quick inspection. "Yet it runs high-end code. It has Pig Latin on it?"

"Just like the Borgot phones, but Borgot isn't producing a smartwatch to run with its phones."

"Joe couldn't have loaded all the Borgot code on here, but if the Pig Latin is on here, that means at least part of the phone code runs on this without the phone being nearby. And I don't recognize this watch model." He held up his own very snazzy unit.

"By 'not recognize,' I assume that means you have considered purchasing every smartwatch available, memorized the list of specifications, and know the price of all of them?"

He grinned. "The price is the least useful because they are all expensive. The good ones start at around three-fifty and run to well over a thousand dollars. I got in on the first Kickstarter for my Pebble so I actually only paid a hundred and fifty, but it is barely a prototype compared to what the newer models can do."

"Joe's watch doesn't look high-end," I said slowly.

"No. And it will be very interesting to see what this watch can actually do when it's running with his phone nearby. Was he smart enough to integrate the Borgot phone with a smartwatch?"

"He didn't code. Ever." I shrugged, nodded and then shook my head. "I suppose it's possible he kept his talent hidden. I avoided him for the most part."

"I'll check it out and get back to you. Meanwhile, can you get me the raw code you're testing now and a Borgot phone?"

"Why?"

"If Joe's phone worked with this watch, I can check the raw code to see if it has any kind of support for a watch. If it doesn't, that means someone added it to whatever was running on his phone."

"Okay, sure." I grabbed my backpack and took out one of the Borgot test phones and the SD chip Cary had given me. "This isn't the absolute latest code drop, but it's close."

Radar blinked. He looked from the card to me. "You transfer test code on an SD card?"

"We can download code easily at work over wifi just like any kind of phone update, but the early phones locked up sometimes. We often transferred the code the old fashioned way using the SD card to transfer it. Cary handed out the SD cards when he gave us phones to test on the weekend, but I never loaded this drop because Joe's phone started talking, and we realized it was probably his personal phone. But the code on this card is pretty current for all our other test units."

Radar took the phone and stared at the slot on the side where the SD card would fit. "You transfer valuable code on a card." He nodded. "That would make it very easy to hand off the latest version of Borgot code by slipping someone this little card. Give them the phone as well, and they have everything they need to code another device, including a competitor phone or a smartwatch."

"But he didn't code!"

"He could have given it to someone who knew how to code a smartwatch, all without any kind of email or download that could be traced." He smiled. "No trace. They have the code if they want to make it work with a watch and sell the watch without Borgot ever being the wiser."

"But who would he give it to?"

Radar wasn't listening. He was already halfway to the door.

Mark and Steve followed him. "I need to make some calls," Huntington said, already frowning over his phone.

"Don't forget you promised to add cameras to my yard!" I yelled after him.

He ignored me, of course. Mark gave me a quick kiss. "I need to follow up with Steve on a couple of things and make sure I stay in the loop. The heists he was working on don't look like the real problem here."

I sighed and watched him go.

Chapter 16

Having taken most of the previous day off, I was behind on my testing. So, of course, there was a mandatory meeting taking up the entire morning. Monique came by to remind me and to hand me a copy of the new product launch schedule.

"This schedule is also attached to the email with the meeting plan. I want to make sure when we leave that room everyone has agreed to this more aggressive product ship date."

I didn't even need to look at the schedule to know it was a disaster. "Uh, Monique, did you run this by Roscoe and Kovid?"

"What for?"

"They are the ones who have to code the phone features. They know how long it takes. I can't test until they are done coding. The schedule Cary was touting was overly optimistic. We haven't hit a single date on it yet."

She blinked and stared down at the paper in her hand. "That's one reason I did it over. I want to make sure we meet my schedule."

"But if you didn't ask Kovid or Roscoe how long it would take them to add the features, how do you expect us to stay on schedule?"

"Wait." She put one hand on her hip. "Are you saying I should come to you and ask how long these tasks take and *then* come up with a schedule?"

I nodded. "Well, yeah."

"Don't be ridiculous. We'll never get stuff done if we just let you decide on the schedule!"

She flounced off.

At least her management style wasn't any different than Cary's. There would be no adjustment curve.

The meeting did not start off with donuts or other goodies. Monique dug right into the schedule without even mentioning that she had taken over Cary's position. Of course, several emails had informed us of the change so there really wasn't a need to dwell on it. We could move straight to the arguing.

"There is no way we can code all this by next month." Kovid didn't even glance at the display at the front of the room. "To meet the first ship date, we already had to take out all the foreign language support except Spanish."

"What?!?" Monique shook her head so emphatically, her hairspray was in danger of flinging off onto the walls. "The languages are what sets our product apart! We can't not have them. We need every single one."

"Nothing patentable without at least one foreign language," Howard, the lawyer assistant, intoned. "A patent would give us a stronger case with the venture capitalists for more funding, and if we have a patent, the company would always have that asset to sell, whether the company survives or not."

Roscoe pounded his fist on the table. "Last meeting Cary insisted we put Pig Latin back in. That was doable. Some of the Spanish is functioning, but that was assuming the old date." He pointed at the PowerPoint slides on the display. "If you move those dates in where you want them, you won't even get the Spanish finished."

"Do not ask me to consider writing a patent for the Pig Latin," Howard said. "I already told Cary no dice, and it's still a no go, I don't care who asks me to do it."

"None of the Spanish language has even been loaded on the phones for testing," I added.

The good news was that since neither of the programmers would agree to the ship dates, Monique didn't care about the test dates. I sat through most of the meeting wondering who had killed Cary. Had he died because the programmers were sick of his bad schedules? Kovid never showed anger, but he wasn't backing down from Monique's demands. Roscoe's face turned beet red, and he had no problem shouting Monique down, yelling about his expertise not being properly appreciated. Had either of them hated Joe because Joe never did a lick of work? In fact, with his Pig Latin claims, he only added to the workload.

Monique tried pulling rank. She even offered bonuses. That did quiet the room, at least temporarily. Since Lawrence had sent his assistant and not shown up himself, I had to wonder if anyone in this room even had the authority to offer a bonus.

"What kind of bonus are you offering?" Roscoe demanded. "Cary once suggested he'd throw in a thousand dollars per language, like we were dogs that would snap at stale and rotting bones."

"If you take out all language support other than English, we can get a phone out close to that date," Kovid said. "We can add in languages one at a time after that."

"That would be a nice marketing move," I inserted. "Just think. More announcements, more press releases about our fabulous phone."

"No language, no patent," Howard snapped. "Why not just shut the company doors now and save the venture capitalists the trouble?"

"We must have at least Spanish!" Monique wailed.

Roscoe's neck was still a dangerous purple, but the rest of his face had toned down. "It's not ready. Testing hasn't even started on it."

Oh sure, throw the ball at me. "I haven't seen any code with language support other than Pig Latin. Cary hadn't even finished the test plan for the other languages." I lobbed the ball back at Monique.

She was in marketing. She didn't even duck. "You'll need to create the test plan now that he's gone. Hopefully he left you some notes."

How had his job become mine? I hadn't been promoted, she had! Rather than point out her manipulation I merely said, "If the code isn't in the phones, I can't test."

The meeting went on for another hour, but the code didn't exist. Monique lost her cool babe look long before we adjourned.

She stomped off to report to upper management that we were refusing to do our jobs. She was new at this though. Upper management would just blame her for not being able to get our "buy-in." No matter how beautiful or how she dressed, no way would upper management take the blame for a late product. That left her as the responsible party now that Cary was dead.

I frowned. Had upper management killed him because we weren't making the schedule? Nah. That implied they knew and had lifted a finger. Killing him hadn't improved Borgot's chances of producing the product on time. Of course, him being dead probably didn't hurt our chances either.

I worked late to make it look as though the meeting had given me some incentive, but I was actually pleased that we might ship the phone without all the language support. Of course, I now had to come up with a test plan, but if we shipped English first, there was time to figure out the other languages later. No doubt Roscoe and Kovid felt the same way.

Monique, unlike Cary, didn't stay late to make sure the rest of us did. At seven, I headed for the stairs.

I've never been a big fan of hearing about endless executive perks while the worker bees toil and hope for raises. That said, I'm also not into employees who believe a company is a benevolent parent. Obviously, there were others who did not share my view. I stood and stared into the break room where Roscoe stuffed pizzas, quiche, frozen ice cream bars and a pack of Starbucks cold coffee into a cooler. I seriously doubted he was taking all this food back to his desk to thaw and eat while he worked.

Management bought these things to keep us here longer, not as take-home for our kids and the kids in the entire neighborhood.

Roscoe finally noticed me staring. He froze for a second and then recovered. "Big work weekend at home."

"Uh-huh." I folded my arms and my foot started tapping.

He shrugged and closed the cooler. "I'll have the work done to prove it. What can they say? Besides, who will notice?"

"Gosh, you're right," I agreed, slapping my forehead. "No one will notice that the freezer has been emptied out overnight." A corner of the break room was suspiciously empty. "They'll probably think that those few people who stayed all night managed to suck down two or three cases of soda, too."

He snickered as he edged me out of the way with his cooler. "The delivery to replace this stuff is early every Monday morning. And this month there's a big meeting with the venture capitalists who fund Borgot. They always restock heavily before those meetings so the next delivery will be huge."

I waited until he was a good ways down the hallway before yelling, "Should be a fantastic weekend coming up with all that food, Roscoe! Have fun at the lake!"

Some detective I was. I hadn't even known when the food and sodas were restocked.

Chapter 17

I had promised to attend sewing meetings and gardening meetings, and here it was, Saturday, the regularly scheduled day for the garden meeting at Dave's Garden. The internet said we'd be talking about spring planting. I was on my way out the door when Turbo and Radar showed up, followed by the truckful of dirt that Huntington had ordered.

"We brought a few things for your garden," Turbo said.

"The replacement dirt is here too." I gestured at the guys in the truck to go ahead and take the dirt around back. "I'm on my way out to a meeting."

Radar's head tilted with curiosity.

"It's at Dave's Garden. I have to replace the plants that the police confiscated for no good reason, and there's a meeting there to discuss what to plant and when." That was a reasonable enough explanation that it didn't require mentioning Huntington had asked me to spy on someone.

His head leveled again. "I bet they don't have any advice for when to plant dead bodies."

"Anytime the ground isn't frozen," Turbo said. "Be too hard to bury them then."

I pinched the bridge of my nose. "Why did you stop by again?"

Radar said, "To tell you that Joe's watch locks onto the phone code and the two work together. But the latest code drop you gave me from Borgot on the SD card doesn't have any watch support. Not even a hint of any watch support."

I thought about that. "Can you tell if the code that ran on Joe's phone is Borgot code?"

"Whenever you turned the phone on, a Borgot screen appeared, so there was definitely Borgot code on his phone in addition to smartwatch support."

"There's no mention of Borgot doing a smartwatch in our schedule or product description. And yet he has a version that supports his watch."

"You sure the guy wasn't a genius programmer? Maybe he added the code to work with the watch."

"He wasn't playing idiot, he was an idiot," I said.

Turbo held up a phone and another smartwatch, one I hadn't seen before. "We're also here to beef up security. This is one of Radar's old watches. The phone app will control the security we're adding to your garden. You can then monitor the garden from this phone or the watch!"

I tilted my head. "The phone will run my security?"

He nodded. "But you can keep the watch in your bedroom and from there, you'll get alerts."

"Couldn't I just keep the phone in my bedroom?"

Radar nodded. "Sure, but it's cooler to check the smartwatch. The phone app is your control unit for the system. We'll let the dirt guys do their thing, and then we'll install a couple of things to monitor the garden for you. You won't have to worry about anyone burying dead bodies back there without you knowing about it." He started babbling about alerts and scans and a passcode for on and off.

It was nothing short of a miracle that Huntington had responded to my request for security this speedily. He usually pontificated, argued and waited until he was tired of me nagging. Maybe Mark had lit a fire under him. I held up a hand. "Tell me about it later. Do not break anything while I am gone."

Turbo pouted, which is not a good look for a geek with hair that hangs low over the tops of his eyebrows and a shirt ratty enough to have come out of the rag bin. "Have I ever broken anything?"

I used logic against him. "Statistically, it would be impossible for you to have reached this age and not broken a single thing." I headed for the garage, keys in hand.

"We'll leave the phone and smartwatch on the kitchen table," Turbo called after me. "You can wear the smartwatch and use our phone instead of that simple Borgot phone. It doesn't have a smartwatch."

"Uh-huh. Unless you're Joe and you found a watch that works with Borgot phones." I went back and took a spare key from the kitchen drawer. "Here. Lock up when you leave." I glanced at Radar. "And don't give Radar the key. He'll make a copy because he can't help himself."

"Heh-heh," was Radar's response.

Turbo frowned. "He wouldn't steal anything."

"Of course not." I don't know why I bothered. Radar probably already had a key. As a hacker he prided himself on getting in anywhere, anytime. His skills might very well have spilled over into houses, libraries, and Fort Knox for all I knew.

* * *

Technically, I'd met Dave of Dave's Garden a few weeks ago. Huntington had sent me on a quick mission to obtain a guest list from one of the garden meetings. The assignment had turned into a bit of a fiasco, but I'd gotten the list and assumed my job was done. Apparently that hadn't been enough because here I was, headed to Dave's establishment, this time with instructions to spy on Joe's mother. She wasn't likely to admit to any funny business Joe might have been involved in, and now that he was dead, striking up a conversation about her son was impossible.

Dave's Garden was on the outskirts of Denton, a flat, somewhat barren tract that had been zoned for businesses. Dave's Garden took up a good four or five acres on one side of Old Ranch Road, but the land across the rural route was built out with a brand new office building complex. The front of the office complex had a beautiful blue granite clock with the time, the temperature and a list of the buildings' occupants below it. There was also a concrete garage that was not very cleverly hidden by a few large pines and a tiny strip of land for flowers. I felt lucky to be headed to Dave's Garden rather than the office-type garden.

Even though spring wasn't blossoming yet, Dave had a good head start. Snap peas, tomatoes, lettuce and a whole host of flowers were growing in the outdoor greenhouse. The place smelled of water and dirt and good things growing.

I asked first thing about the blueberry plants. Dave didn't have the right variety, but could order them for me.

"If you spot any computer scammers this time, could you quietly alert me?" Dave spared a desperate glance around the two of us. "Or, if I'm already lecturing, tell my new assistant, Rohit." He pointed to a young guy working at the information stand. Even though it was still quite cool out, the guy was wearing sandals and shorts. Perhaps as a concession to the weather, his shorts did extend past his knees.

Rohit saw Dave pointing and raised a hand to wave in our direction.

"Rohit has a good head on his shoulders," Dave said. "I was lucky to hire him this winter after he was laid off from his old job. We don't need any incidents in my shop like happened the last time you helped out, so alert him or me if anything seems amiss."

I had been hoping Dave wouldn't remember the past incident. "I doubt any scammers would come here." For a six-foot guy in coveralls and hefty work boots, Dave sure was turning out to be the nervous type. He had a few gray hairs, but he was younger than my dad and in good shape. You'd think a guy his size would exhibit more confidence.

"Just don't go setting a mob on anyone. I'm trying to expand my business and some of these gardening types get carried away."

They had done more of a tackle than a carry away when I pointed out there was a scammer in their midst. "Okay, I'll be sure and tell you or security on the sly if I notice anything."

He leaned in close. "I don't have official security. That's why I said to tell me or the new guy. He's been fantastic. Most people a year or two out of college don't have much gardening experience, but he's got real know-how. He's even convinced me to grow hops this spring." He stepped over to a box near the greenhouse. "Lookee here. I've got some rhizomes if you're interested. Easy to grow, and I'll be packaging the hops right here and selling them with other organic grains for beer brewing."

I grinned and put my hands behind my back so that he couldn't hand me the gnarly brown root he was waving around with enthusiasm. "Thanks, but I think the blueberries will keep me plenty busy."

"You never know when you'll want to try something new." He smiled and gazed around proudly at his kingdom.

"And I'll come straight here if I need more supplies." I nodded. "I'll be sure to tell you first if I see anything suspicious." I did a quick check to see if there were any geek-wannabes with tattoos trying to sell unnecessary computer services. There were a few hippies, but I think they worked for Dave. During my scan, to my surprise, I spotted Monique in the crowd that was gathering for today's lecture.

Dave noticed my eyes widen. "Who? What?"

"Just someone I know from work. Nothing to fret about." My voice trailed off at the end. She worked at Borgot. There were two dead bodies to account for. Maybe she was a scammer in cahoots with Joe. Now that he was dead, was she his replacement at the garden meetings? Or had she been his partner?

I glanced around at the plants, pots, chair, benches, hoses and rows of supplies along the outside of the main building. What nefarious deeds could possibly take place in a garden store???

I gave Dave a good-bye nod and casually sauntered over to Monique.

Dave headed for his assistant, no doubt with dire warnings.

I ignored him. I wasn't here to cause anyone any trouble. Monique turned as I approached. "Monique! I didn't know you were a gardener!" She wore clothes that for me were work clothes—jeans, a nice sweater and sneakers.

She grinned and flicked perfectly manicured fingernails at me in a finger wave. "Hi Sedona! I didn't know I was into gardening either. Not until Lawrence suggested," she stopped and put a hand to her heart, "that maybe I could help him with landscaping this spring!" Her voice was a hushed squeal. "I think he's finally planning to ask me to move in with him. He owns a great house over in Alpine Hills." She waved one hand. "Oh, you probably don't know the area. But it's gorgeous."

She was right about Alpine Hills being way outside my normal social circle, but I'd helped with a case there. From behind me, I could hear Dave start the meeting. "I'm here for the free class. Are you attending it as well?"

She shook her head. "No, I don't need a class. What do you think of this piece?"

I hadn't noticed we were standing near the garden sculpture area. She ran her hand down the side of a copper can.

"What is it?" I asked. The thing was just taller than me, a mass of metal with bits of wire decorations.

"Isn't it gorgeous?"

The base was some kind of twine stuff that would probably grow moss or grass once permanently installed. There was a long tin can opposite the copper one, and some sort of ceramic blue octopus with holes all along each appendage. Maybe you could plant strawberries in that part. An ugly metal flower sprang from the middle of it. What might have been a snake looped in and around various pieces. Then again, maybe the snake was just random metal. "Uh..."

"I know, it's kind of expensive. But Lawrence can afford it and really, a thousand dollars for something this unique? He'll be the talk of the neighborhood!"

I blinked and stared harder, but with focus. Maybe I should abandon sewing and gardening and become a sculptor. I'd only have to sell one piece a month. "It's unique," I agreed.

"He'll love it."

"You know, if he does love it, I think you should marry the guy because you two were made for each other." I found it hard to believe there was one person who could love this thing, never mind two.

Monique giggled with delight. "I already know we are perfect together, but you're so sweet to say so. That reminds me—this week I'm going to announce a team building project. I was telling Lawrence about how this phone will be super late unless we pull out all the stops. We've got to do something even if it means spending our entire training budget. Luckily, Lawrence knows a guy. After this guy did a team building exercise at Lawrence's old company, everyone was totally on board and completely motivated. I know it will work for us!"

My dismay must have shown on my face because she frowned back at me. "I am counting on you."

"Uh-hmm. I hope Lawrence likes his gift."

Thankfully, Dave's assistant walked over to see if we needed help. Sure, his appearance was probably because Dave had told him to keep an eye on me, but in this case it worked out in my favor.

"Can I help you ladies with anything?" From the rich tones to his skin and his accent, he was probably originally from India. His dark, nicely trimmed goatee and polite smile rounded out to make him a handsome fellow. He pushed dark sunglasses on top of his head, making his hair stick up all around the frames, but a good salesman always made eye contact.

I stepped back, grateful for the interruption. "My friend here is interested in this sculpture. I need to get to the gardening meeting myself."

Monique pressed her hands together with excitement and turned back to the looming object of art. "Do you deliver?" she asked. "Lawrence is never going to expect this. What a great surprise!"

"Yeah, it'll surprise him. For sure. See you." Maybe the new assistant would get a nice commission on the piece. Lucky him.

I scurried to the back row of seats. Not only was this location far from Dave's suspicious gaze, it allowed me to search the crowd for Joe's mother. Given the death of her son, I couldn't count on her being here. I also didn't know what she looked like, but I spent the entire lecture eliminating possibilities.

Sitting in the back, I received the sign-in sheet last. I scanned it for her name, Wanda Black, but as suspected, her name was not on the list. Thankfully I had a few extra minutes to study the old sign-up sheets behind the current one. Pretending to pay attention, I flipped the top page over the clipboard, and when Dave was looking elsewhere, I skimmed across the names.

An older lady asked Dave what plants would attract young people to gardening. Someone shouted, "Pot!"

Another voice in the crowd yelled, "Hell, we don't need pot. We need Viagra plants!"

The mind boggled.

I used the distraction to flip more pages. The meetings had only been held monthly over the winter. There were less names than on today's showing, too. On page three, I hit paydirt. Very carefully, I extracted the page and then found two more containing the name Black. The real surprise was that the first name attached to Black wasn't Wanda. It was Joe.

Chapter 18

I hadn't been home an hour when the doorbell rang.

The second I opened the door, I recognized Mark's mother even though we had never met. Her eyes were the same confident brown as Mark's, but hers were larger and touched up with mascara. She carried a giant cloth bag, much as Mary Poppins might if she were part of our modern world.

"Hi, I'm LeAnn—"

"Mark's mother," I chimed in with a huge smile. "Come on in." I held the door wide.

She matched my smile, only hers had dimples. Light brown hair nearly touched her shoulders, a tucked under look with a few rogue curls that didn't stay in place. "I know it's rude to invite myself over, but truth to tell, I wanted to meet the woman who had Mark so interested and Steve so annoyed."

"Huntington is annoyed with me?" I sniffed. "His annoyance is nothing compared to mine. It was his idea that I learn to sew. He could have asked if I had any inclination, but—" I stopped myself before the full rant mode could spin out of control. She didn't need to know right off what I thought of her eldest child.

She laughed. "Mark mentioned Steve hired you for the case without checking on whether you could sew or not." She held up a large blue and yellow canvas bag decorated with ribbons and a handle that could withstand the lugging of a sewing machine if necessary. "Steve isn't just irritated about the sewing. He's stewing because you never gave him a second look after meeting Mark. I do believe he thought it should be his choice."

My face clouded, and my eyebrows gave me an instant headache when they smashed into each other with the force of my scowl. It's possible horns popped out the top of my skull. I pressed my lips tight to keep from making any more unkind remarks about Huntington.

"Hmm. You are suddenly very quiet. I do hope you aren't thinking you can date them both. It's been tried and failed before."

I stared at her, quite unable to keep the gurgle of surprised sputtering from exploding. There was no taking it back, but stuffing it down was almost manageable. On a gasp I said, "No, you don't have to worry about that. I don't even *like* Huntington—Steve—most of the time." I immediately apologized when her eyebrow raised, a female imitation of Huntington's sneer. "Sorry. I know he's your son, and I'm sure he's quite beloved. But the man is overbearing, obstinate, and has more dumb ideas than anyone I've ever met."

"For example?"

I sighed. "For example, the sewing thing. Some nonsense about every woman being able to infiltrate a sewing circle simply because of the proper chromosome. I'm an engineer. I test computers. The last case he hired me for? To infiltrate a hospital. More nonsense thinking that all women wish to aid ill people." Well, there went first impressions. My shoulders drooped. "Sorry. I'm sure he has better qualities."

"Such as?" Her voice had dropped a degree or two.

I blinked. "Uhm. He, uhm." My brain raced frantically. He was good looking, but that wasn't really an asset at the moment. Even if he was ugly, his mother wouldn't think so. "He hired Marilyn!"

"His maid?"

I nodded. "She needed a job and self-confidence. And he's been very kind to her. Although he adopted that cat, the one from a previous case, which probably made her job harder, but I suppose that shouldn't be held against him. Well, not very much."

She held up her hand to stop my flow of words. "Wouldn't adopting a homeless cat be a positive?"

My eyebrows locked again. I hadn't really liked that cat much, not after it left me bleeding from several scratches. "Not if you're the maid," I muttered.

She laughed.

I desperately tried to think of something else. "He seems to be able to obtain information on people. Although that isn't really a great thing depending which end you're on."

"Enough. You don't seem to be the least bit enamored of him."

My retort came out a half swallowed, "Hmph."

I led the way into the living room and invited her to sit down.

She headed instead for the kitchen table and the sewing machines. She checked the threads, giving me an approving glance when she found them properly threaded.

I shook my head and confessed before she could be too impressed. "I could take the whole machine apart and put it back together. I can probably even improve the design. The one thing I can't do with it is sew." I held up the "baby bib" which, upon closer inspection, looked a lot like a rag that had been used as a chew toy by a rabid dog.

"Ah, but I can teach you," she declared. She pulled two chairs together and beckoned me over. "Come on. It won't be so bad."

I lacked her easy confidence by a large margin, but I accepted the chair.

She was very well organized and knew her subject. After a couple of demonstrations, she scooted over and let me take the wheel.

There was more than one false start on my part, but with her careful instructions, I soon managed a seam that only partially looked like I was trying to design a Jewish skullcap for Frankenstein.

"See?" she said. "And once you have the material sewn together so that it doesn't shift, you sew that exact same line on the serger. The seam on the regular sewing machine is like drawing the line in pencil. You then ink it permanently on the serger."

I gave it a try and was ridiculously proud of my first perfect seam off the finishing machine. It was so neat and had *so many stitches.* "It almost looks like I know what I'm doing!"

"Let the machine do its job. Everyone is happy."

I eyed the enemy. "Until it does a seam too small and my pants suddenly fit a four-year-old."

"Then you have gifts! You won't be the first person to instantly decide to make things for people smaller than you, bigger than you, or when that fails, you'll make enough pot holders to open a store."

"Your faith in me is amazing."

She laughed. "Hey, you should see the pot holders I have! I wasn't putting your skills down. We all do it."

"That wasn't what I meant. I meant I wasn't certain I could manage to make the potholders."

She laughed again. "The sewing group we've joined is making pillowcases for a charity. As long as you know how to do that, no one will guess you are working undercover to obtain information." She pointed at the seam. "Pillowcases are an easy place to start."

"Yeah. This is easier than what I was working on."

"What was that you had started on?" she asked.

"It's a baby bib." I left it buried under our practice fabric. "Maybe you can help me make a proper bib. That is, if you'll come by again. Let me finish a couple of these pillowcases. All I have to do is repeat this seam you just taught me, right?"

She nodded. "Two sides and a bottom. Nothing fancy."

"I hope it's enough to keep my cover. If I have to sew in front of anyone, it will be touch and go."

She patted my shoulders. "Don't worry. We can make this work."

I wasn't so certain, but at least I wouldn't fail the undercover sewing job right out of the gate.

Chapter 19

Mark showed up shortly after his mother left. I was still sewing, gaining confidence with my third pillowcase.

I ushered him in and said, "Let me finish this, and we can have dinner." I sat back down at the machine, certain that it would betray me now that I had an important audience. "This had better turn out or else," I muttered.

"Or else, what?" Mark asked.

I raised my eyebrows and then frowned. "You don't want to know. Never mess with a woman who is sewing who says 'or else'."

He nodded sagely. "Something tells me that I don't want to mess with you when it's 'or else' on any subject." He was not interested in letting me finish my project. He pulled me up for a kiss, taking his time and being thorough.

Well. That kind of kiss could put a lot of 'or elsing' to rest.

He stepped back. "I'm hungry. You can sew later."

"Okay," I agreed, a bit breathless. "Let me get my jacket."

After a very nice dinner, I wasn't about to return to the sewing, but as I went in the kitchen to make coffee for Mark, the pile of material reminded me of his mother's protectiveness and third-degree concerning my intentions with Mark. Mark wasn't really in Steve's shadow, not so far as I was concerned, but her questions did leave me wondering a few things. "Why does Steve get to be CEO of your investigation company?" I asked.

Mark shrugged. "Because he was a CEO before, and in the world in which he travels it's all about rubbing shoulders with people at the same level. It's okay for companies to hire him because he is one of them. A board of directors is too busy to talk to a private investigator—but a CEO of an investigation company puts him at their level."

"I meant why him and not you?"

"Because he's good at it. He has the credentials from his previous company. His name doesn't look like some guy on the street hung a shingle and named himself CEO. It gives it a legitimacy that not everyone can bring. Plus, I don't care one way or the other."

"No?" I teased. "You two seem competitive."

His eyes caught and held mine. "I care what some people think. How they feel about titles. How they feel about loyalty."

I didn't drop my gaze. "Do you really think a lot of women would go for him strictly because of the title?"

He didn't answer, but anger flashed across his face, the kind of heat that tenses facial muscles, but is gone so fast you're not sure it was there. "Why the fifty questions?" he asked.

I handed him his coffee. "Your mom warned me off trying to date both of you, as if she was worried about my honest intentions." I put my hand over my heart and smiled.

Mark sighed, his exasperation obvious. "Steve and I competed over a girl a time or two in high school. It was stupid, and for a while we were more interested in the number of girls we could date than the who or why. Mom was less than pleased with us, especially when Steve lorded it over me when he asked a couple of girls out that I had just dated and they both said yes."

My eyebrows raised. "I could see where that would be a problem, especially if you actually liked one of them."

His expression was guarded, but he didn't drop his gaze. "It was high school."

I nodded and waited because his frown was still fierce. "What else did she say?" he finally asked.

"Nothing. She asked what I liked about Steve."

"And?"

"It was one of those socially awkward moments."

"Why?"

"I couldn't think of anything to say."

He studied me before asking, "Why didn't you tell her you like working for him?"

It was my turn to frown. "Strictly speaking, I don't. He keeps hiring me, and I keep losing my regular employment. I can't decide if that is because of him or if every company I work for is corrupt."

"You're not bringing this up to try and tell me anything in particular, are you?"

"Just that your mom seemed concerned and I wondered why. You and Steve get along okay from what I can tell, so it seemed odd that she mentioned it first thing."

Mark let out a big breath of air and took a sip of coffee before setting it aside. "I bought a ring once for a girl named Charlene. I never actually asked her because...I don't know why. Mom was more upset than I was by the end of it. Steve had just finished investigating who had been skimming at his old company and left him holding the bag. He decided to use his investigation skills to prove one way or the other if my potential fiancee was really offering what he thought she was offering him."

I groaned. "He didn't."

"Far enough to make sure it could have gone further. Mom was furious. She walked in on them." Mark grinned.

My mind stumbled over the possible scene and didn't find anything to grin about. "I would imagine your mother was way less pleased with him about that than the high school shenanigans."

"Hysterical is probably a better word. For a while there, we thought she might beat Steve to death with her purse."

"You saved him?"

Mark laughed. "No way. Even if he had a good excuse, he was on his own. As far as Charlene, I'd already realized that it wouldn't ever work, and that had nothing to do with my brother. Charlene didn't even realize he'd been fighting for his reputation. All she saw was the glamor of his CEO title, the cars, the swagger. She missed the important things, obvious things about me, about him, about...everything."

I nodded and put down my tea. "To be perfectly clear, I'm not after him."

"I am not my mother. I do not need reassurances."

Since my body was now skimming his, I wiggled and put my arms around his neck. "But I'm sooo convincing when I really try."

That got his attention.

"I suppose it wouldn't hurt if you spent some time convincing me," he allowed.

His eyes had a tendency to drown me, stealing my breath and my concentration. I was drawn to him as if he held the key to the universe, at least my part of the universe.

"It's a shame you don't actually have a sword tattoo on your arm," I murmured against his lips. When I'd first met him, he had been impersonating a thug. He not only had a motorcycle with a gorgeous sword along the side, he had a fake tattoo on his arm, fake contacts and the same attitude he had now.

He laughed, nuzzling my neck. "What? You want me to get a tattoo?"

"No, I don't like tattoos, but it went well with your bad boy image," I whispered in his ear as I nibbled.

He lifted his head to look at me. "My what?"

"Your image." I ran my hands down his arm and soaked in the scent of him. His eyes dropped to my chest and that made me take another big breath, although for a different reason.

His hand on my lower back tightened, pressing me closer. "And just why is a tattoo important to my image?"

"Well, you know. It made you...dangerous."

"A tattoo made me dangerous?" He didn't sound convinced.

"A guy with a tattoo was likely to be..." He lowered his head, hovering above my lips impatiently. With my breasts pressed tight against his body, I could feel his hard muscles against my heart. "Be demanding."

"Don't worry," he threatened softly. "It wasn't the tattoo."

Chapter 20

We spent significant time reassuring each other of our loyalties before falling asleep. I was wrapped tightly in his arms when a long but faint beep woke me. I reached for the alarm clock out of habit, but quickly realized the buzzing was coming from the kitchen. A fourth beep was my final warning.

A siren blasted across my backyard. An unholy cacophony of bells and lights joined in. Mark sat up and rolled off one side of the bed. In the next two seconds, I was on my feet ready to run for my life. Cary's ghost must have risen from the dead because haunted wails penetrated the closed window.

"What the hell?" Mark didn't waste time getting dressed. He went for his gun and headed for the back door in his boxers.

I had on a t-shirt, but wished for a pair of shorts. Since he had the gun and was already halfway to the back door, I grabbed a pair of light sweatpants from the floor and stuffed myself into them on the run. "Why is it so bright?" It wasn't the sun because a quick glance at the clock showed it was three in the morning.

Mark was outside already and couldn't have heard my question over the noise.

The lawn was fully lit by floodlights. "I don't own this many lights," I muttered.

The odd ghost wail continued to shriek banshee threats. A jet spray of water shot sideways from four different sprinkler heads that I didn't own. That is to say, I hadn't installed any sprinklers in the back and instead of watering the lawn, these things formed a square around the garden, forcing anyone who had gotten inside to run through the nearly lethal blasts of water on their way out.

"I guess we're looking for a soaking wet burglar?" I blinked against the bright glare, staring at the grotesque ghost bobbing about my garden. It was beyond frightening.

"Is that scarecrow having a seizure?" Mark kept his gun pointed at it.

"That's a scarecrow? I think it's channeling Miley Cyrus."

Mark actually backed up a step. "Your friends made a scarecrow that *twerks?*"

It was hard to know for certain what the thing was doing. It flopped over at the waist, jerked its butt back and forth and convulsed, much like Miley Cyrus did when she tried to dance. "If it sticks its tongue out, shoot it," I advised.

Mark's eyes widened in fear. He obviously didn't know whether he should grab me and run or just start shooting. It warmed my heart. Mark was becoming more and more like family.

With one final butt jerk, the head flew off of Radar's robot. My ears rang from the sudden silence, but I was fairly certain none of the noise had been Mark shooting. Yet. "You're right. My friends are scary."

"Damn straight. Not only will birds not go near your garden, you're going to have to start carrying liability insurance for shock therapy if your neighbors see that."

"I can't believe Turbo and Radar thought this was a good idea. Did you see what set it off? Or hear anything?" I asked.

Mark just stared at me, his mouth opening and then slamming shut. "I'm going to get dressed. You might want to figure out where the off switch is in case that thing starts up again."

Good point. What had Turbo said about the security features? Hmm. Something about looking for the app on the phone or smartwatch. I hadn't picked up either, never mind attempted to run any apps.

As I turned to follow Mark inside, my gruff older neighbor's face popped up over the fence planks separating our yards. Thankfully, he was too short to peer over without a stepladder. Retrieving one must have delayed him long enough that he had missed the worst of the show. An orange Broncos cap was smashed down against his tightly curled, nearly white head of hair. His black-rimmed glasses blended well with his skin, but the frames were somewhat lopsided as if shoved on in a hurry.

I shivered from the cold air and apologized. "Sorry," I called out. "False alarm."

Mr. Jackson was a nice neighbor. He used to plow my driveway now and then. Since I'd been involved with the Huntington brothers I hadn't seen him much. I owed him cookies to make up for this little incident—the whole pan. "I'll stop by tomorrow and explain?"

He gave me a very truncated nod before disappearing back into his own yard. Luckily the house on the other side of mine was further away and was occupied by an old lady who was renting the place. She was almost completely deaf without her hearing aid in.

I hurried inside to hunt for the phone and hoped Turbo had left written instructions for controlling the lights, robot and watering system.

The phone was right on the counter where he said he'd leave it, lit up and loaded. I stared down at the app. The watch had a message scrolling across it that said, "Security Breach! Security Breach!"

I already knew that.

Since I didn't have any idea which buttons to push or what to swipe on the smartwatch, I tried the phone. It warned me of a security breach too and there were rows of icons. I pressed the one that looked like a light. When that turned the floodlights off, I hunted for the robot controls and hoped for the best.

* * *

Mark and I spent the next hour showering, getting dressed and inspecting the yard. There were paw prints coming into and leaving the yard from over the privacy fence. A fairly large hole had been dug in one corner of the garden, but no bodies had been left behind.

"They came in under the alarms." Mark shone his flashlight across the yard. We kept the floodlights off since at least one neighbor had already been woken up. "Maybe it was a skunk," he mused.

I shook my head. "We'd be able to smell it. Shoot, after that thing went off, a skunk would have sprayed every inch of this yard."

"Good point." His flashlight found a pile of scat. He studied the nearby prints. "Whatever it was, it shit its pants when Miley started her dance."

"Probably not the first creature to do that," I said.

"I can look up these paw prints in the morning." He continued to shine the light around, hunting for clues.

I stomped over to the kitchen window and peered in. "It's five. Not much point in going back to bed."

He agreed. "Let's go eat breakfast."

"At this hour?"

"I know a place."

"Okay."

The tiny restaurant he chose was perched next to a truck stop on highway twenty-four. Mark held the door open for me. "They serve a great breakfast."

Since my stomach was growling, who was I to argue?

The diner contained two rows of worn tables and a waitress pouring coffee behind a long counter with stools. An order window was behind her. I never saw a cook, but a hairy arm slid a plate onto the pickup ledge. The counter was half full of sleepy truckers and a biker couple.

We were the first to take a table even though it was nearing six o'clock. The place smelled of fresh coffee and syrup with a hint of french fries from the night before.

The waitress had Mark's coffee poured and a teabag for me within the first minute. It was warm in the restaurant, so I slid out of my coat.

We had just put in our order when the gal with the bike leathers stood up and grabbed her bright red and black leather jacket off the back of her chair. In her struggle to wrap herself in the snug coat, she managed to expose an alarming amount of flesh at both the bottom and top of her shirt. Her short top showed off an impressive muffin top tummy roll, and even though the leather pants weren't super tight, they weren't flattering because they squished even more of her out the top of the pants.

When she was finally settled into her tight jacket, she pulled out a phone to check her text messages while she waited for the guy with her to collect his change and leave a tip.

The basic black phone looked just like a Borgot phone. I sighed with guilt over the testing I had not gotten done.

After they left, Mark shook his head. "Why do women wear that kind of stuff?"

"Because when we get dressed and look in the mirror, we suck in our guts and pull the shirt down nice and neat," I explained, automatically sitting up straighter, but trying not to be too obvious about it. "We don't stare in the mirror when we're hunched over our phones and our fat is hanging out." My back was ramrod straight now, but there was no easy way to suck in my stomach without being completely obvious.

"Uh-hmm."

"And we *never* look at our butts because no matter how long we study the problem or what we wear, our butts are big. Trust me. There's no truth to that whole 'black is slimming' thing." Black leather pants hadn't helped the biker gal's cause.

Mark took a sip of coffee and gave me a full grin. "You have a cute butt. And for the record, I was asking why anyone would wear a top that was glaring purple with bright yellow flowers."

I blinked. "Oh." I shook my head. "I don't have an answer for you on that."

Mark laughed. "That's okay. Your answer was better anyway. I'm not dumb enough to bring up some biker chick and ask why she was wearing something to show off her fat. It's not something you ask your girlfriend."

I grinned a goofy grin, but it was more because I loved hearing him refer to me as his girlfriend than my dumb answer.

The pancakes were as good as Mark promised, but the cafe attracted an odd collection of customers. Four more bikers came in and sat alongside a couple of local ranchers. By the time we left, the place was filling up with truckers making a stop to eat and fill the trucks.

Mark dropped me off at my place with a promise to come by for dinner.

I spent Sunday morning practicing my sewing. Not only did I finish a few pillowcases, I got brave and started on the tank top. When that didn't work out, I switched to the bra pattern.

Mark's mom showed up just before lunch.

"Are you ready for the meeting this afternoon?"

I nodded and showed her the pillowcases. One had turned out really short for a pillowcase. "I added straps to this one, so it's a grocery bag."

"You're really getting the hang of this! All of these pillowcases will fold and fit in the bag. You'll look like a pro!"

I beamed until her eyes caught the mess that was currently in the machine.

"This doesn't look like a baby bib."

The soft pinned material was little more than a tangle of thread and elastic. It would make a better bird's nest than a bra. A used dust rag would provide more support.

That gave me my answer. "A dust rag?"

"Working with elastic is one of the hardest things to learn." She lifted the part of the bra not actually under the needles. "And a waistband might have been a better place to start than a bra. Goodness. You are ambitious, aren't you?" She smiled. "No wonder Mark likes you."

I was pretty sure my ambitions—in jobs and in sewing—were not an ongoing attraction for Mark. "Uhm..."

She sat down at the machine and managed to extract the bra in under my usual hour. "Have you tried it on?"

I nodded. "One side fits. The other, not so much." My face could not possibly flush any redder. Was there anything more embarrassing than getting caught making underwear??? If she asked me to try it on, I would just die on the spot and save us both the trouble.

Something on my face must have signaled, "Not in this lifetime. You could be my mother-in-law someday, but at this point you are my boyfriend's mother. I do not know you well enough to get half-naked and work on intimates even if those intimates don't involve lace."

Her mouth twitched. She turned to the machine, picked up the scissors and then the seam ripper.

"Can I make you some coffee? Or tea?" I asked.

"Iced tea would be great."

Tea I could do. Sewing, not so much.

She fiddled with the bra and the elastic while I baked cookies and made tea. By the time I was done, so was she.

"You'll have to size it and sew the clasp on to create a good fit. But I straightened out the other part and finished the elastic."

"Thanks." I was so relieved she didn't ask me to try it on, I helped myself to another chocolate chip cookie. If I kept eating cookies at this rate, I'd need to make myself bigger pants.

After our snack, we gathered up our pillowcases and headed off to the meeting.

Barb had more snacks for us and a cute little cookbook for sale that contained the recipe for the coffee cake and jelly roll that she served. Frankly, I was more interested in the cookbooks than discussing "pinmoors" for quilting. The pins were supposed to be better than safety pins and keep me from pricking myself when sewing the quilt that I had no intention of ever starting.

All the attendees sewed pillowcases while Barb talked. Every now and then one of the other ladies chimed in with advice. No one expected me to say anything, so I didn't. Gossip and machine noise filled in around the sewing talk.

I perked up when someone mentioned "basting" but they weren't talking turkey so I lost interest in a hurry.

After the sewing discussion and demonstrations, Barb reminded everyone to leave their pillowcases for the charity.

As we filed past the counter to drop off our pillowcases, she sighed. "Joe used to deliver the pillowcases to the charity." Three of the ladies ahead of us hurriedly dropped their parcels and scurried for the door.

"You mean Joe Black?" I asked. The lady behind me gave a bit of a gasp and put her pillowcases down on the counter. She made a beeline for the exit, but her friend dithered behind us, not sure about the proper protocol for cutting in line just because the topic at hand had gotten morbid.

"Yes, Wanda's son," Barb answered. "This is just terrible. We need to get these delivered before Wanda comes back to the meetings."

There was a dead silence, the kind you have right after the priest asks for volunteers for the latest project. No one knows what to say and no one wants to be noticed.

"I can't deliver them this week because of the store hours," Barb added.

Mark's mom took a deep breath. I knew what was coming, and I couldn't allow her to deliver anything that had involved Joe. He was a suspect in a case, and he'd been murdered. "I can probably fit it in," I rushed out. "When do they have to be there?"

"Nonsense. I'm retired. I can do it," Mark's mother piped up, shooting me a warning glare.

"No worries," I looked her right in the eye. She wasn't doing this alone.

"Oh, that would be wonderful!" Barb chirped. "I will have all of them by Tuesday. Can you two deliver them after that? That would be such a relief."

Yeah, peachy. Just peachy.

There was no telling what Joe might have delivered with the pillowcases. From what Barb told us, the pillowcases would be boxed and ready for us to pick them up. She expected two or three large boxes to be filled for the delivery.

As soon as LeAnn and I settled in the Mercedes, I turned to her. "Mark and Steve said that Joe was a suspect in some kind of thefts. Do you think maybe Joe's mother puts something in the boxes while she's sewing or helping pack the boxes? Then Joe takes the next leg, either delivering them to the charity that might also be involved, or stopping to deliver contraband on the way to the charity?"

"I bet she sews messages or some important code into some of the pillowcases," LeAnn declared.

"Sews how?" My skills were so lacking, I couldn't even imagine adding a secret message.

"A code could be sewn into a seam or just the colors of certain pillowcases could mean something to someone. From what I've gathered, the women make most of the pillowcases at home and bring them in. Not every meeting is for the pillowcase charity and besides, if it's anything like the other groups I've belonged to, most meetings are about gossip and maybe learning a new sewing tip or two."

"But how would anyone know Wanda's pillowcases from the others?"

"Maybe she writes on the pillowcases or adds her initials. I noticed a few of the ladies stitched their initials on the top corners. One of the ladies I used to know who does similar charity work sews a label with her name and a number."

"Really? She puts her phone number on the pillowcases? Isn't that kind of desperate? Or risky?"

Mark's mom laughed. "Not her *phone* number. She keeps track of how many pillowcases she has sewn for the project. So each one has her name— which isn't her real name, it's CloudSoft, a name she made up for her donations, and the number for that pillowcase. She's made over five thousand of the things for various charities. She does other sewing too, sometimes children's dresses, sometimes book bags."

"Oh. So a label or even a coded number wouldn't stand out."

"Exactly. The ladies could sign them or put doodles on them, and I doubt anyone would notice or care unless a person knew to look for a certain word or symbol."

"If the messages are in code, we might not be able to figure out which ones have special meanings."

"We can stop and sort through them when we do the delivery."

I nodded. "And if there is anything else in the boxes that he was delivering, we'll find it."

"Exactly. Unless we insert ourselves in the process, how else are we going to find out what Joe and his mother were up to with the pillowcases?"

How indeed.

Chapter 21

The sewing circle left me desperate enough or inspired enough to finish sewing the bra clasp on when I returned home. I was pretty sure the task wasn't supposed to be difficult, but sewing it on there got complicated in a hurry. Maybe ripping hooks out of an old bra and triple sewing each eye and each hook to make sure the bra didn't fall off wasn't the best idea.

My technique resulted in two broken needles, one very bent hook and a lot of used thread. But hey, huge amounts of thread were required because this thing was not going to pop off if I happened to sneeze at the wrong time.

Oh, who was I kidding. I wasn't about to wear the thing in public even if I used half a spindle of thread on each hook. No sense in taking a chance.

It was rather ugly when I finished, but I tried it on anyway. I kept my expectations low. Very low.

It was a nice pink color. Very soft cotton. I hadn't ruined that part. And, hey! Mark's mom had fixed the one side so it no longer pulled halfway around my back. I could get my arm through the arm hole and everything.

The first hook was a bit snug. I wrestled with it some. Using so much thread made the openings smaller. And the hook caught on bits of extra thread twice. But with a little forcing, I was able to fasten all of the hooks. I peeked in the mirror.

Okay, no one would award any prizes for the thing, but it held everything in! There were a couple—or a hundred—threads hanging from it, but it actually resembled a bra. Maybe not one you'd *pay* for, but it was a bra, and I had made it myself. Well, almost.

I tried on a t-shirt. Nothing bulged where it wasn't supposed to. No bits of material floated under or over the shirt. I smoothed a hand down over the front. "Not bad."

I flounced into the living room. Nothing fell out. "I'm not fooled by you," I addressed the sewing machine. "I know you will betray me."

The bra was comfortable. Maybe I would wear it in public. After all, no one could see it, right?

Chapter 22

LeAnn and I decided to hold a pow wow Monday after work to discuss the delivery of the pillowcases. I dithered about whether or not to mention the discussion to Sean because, while he had been dutifully acting as my lawyer, he was also a pain in the ass. My instincts were to leave him out of the process entirely, but there was a chance he could be useful—and that he wouldn't dump me as a client if I included him.

Unfortunately, Sean showed up first, and began pacing like a trapped lion. One such caged route took him past the mess of sewing on the kitchen table. He zeroed in on the baby bibs I had never finished.

He stared at the misshapen bits of cloth. He fingered the edge of the tan material gingerly, his mouth set in a firm line.

Well, good. After a few years of marriage, he might have learned the value of keeping his mouth shut on occasion. "I am pretty sure the baby won't notice if the bib isn't perfect," I said. "I made that one so you can tie it to the highchair and grab it when you need to wipe her mouth."

He shifted his lawyer gaze to me and then back to the bib. He muttered something about Brenda that sounded remarkably like, "I can't show this to Brenda."

I sniffed. His wife could set off the smoke alarm just by getting a pan out of the kitchen cupboard. I doubted she'd be any handier around a sewing machine. So much for hoping they'd like my creations just because "Aunt Sedona made them." I'd fallen short of even that save.

Sean muttered again, this time something about calling Mom.

I don't know what good he thought that would do. Not even Mom could save that baby bib.

Huntington showed up with Radar, saving us from a family argument. LeAnn and Mark weren't far behind.

LeAnn gave everyone the rundown on what had happened at the sewing circle. The cookies were already baked, so all I had to do was serve them with tea and coffee.

The Huntington brothers were not sanguine about inserting LeAnn and me into the pillowcase delivery process.

"If there's contraband from a burglary in those boxes and you turn it in to the police, you mark yourselves as informants. It won't prove Joe's mother is guilty, but she'll know you were responsible as soon as she asks Barb who delivered the pillowcases," Mark pointed out. "You do not need a target on your back."

Sean was against the entire idea too and demanded we turn all evidence over to the police immediately. The problem with his argument was that we had no evidence yet.

"We don't even have a pillowcase at this point," I said. "All we know is that Joe sometimes delivered them. He probably had a dual reason for being involved, but we don't know that for a fact."

"Tell Detective Saunders and let him confiscate the pillowcases," Sean said.

"That would mean we couldn't ever attend another sewing meeting." The idea actually had merit on that basis alone, but I plowed onward. "If Saunders shows up, it would blow our cover and any chance of our gaining any additional information if the pillowcases are guilty!"

LeAnn chimed in. "We have to do this right and make sure that no one suspects we are undercover."

I nodded quick agreement. "What if we managed to meet the cops on the way to the charity? How about a routine traffic stop...Hey, I know. What if I used Huntington's new car? The cops could pull me over because they see a cool, hot looking car and then find the contraband if it's in the pillowcase boxes!"

"You are *not* using the Porsche," Huntington sputtered. "It's a brand new car!"

"They can't pull you over without a reason," Sean said, lawyer mode at the fore.

"No, but the Porsche is perfect for a speeding ticket! How many seconds from zero to sixty?"

"You are not using the Porsche!"

"Maybe I can just take off quick from a traffic light when there is a cop at the intersection." Huntington changed cars every month or two, but the Porsche hybrid he currently drove was a step above his normal cars. "I need something that screams 'I'm up to something' without doing anything illegal."

"Anyone who knows you at all has plenty of reason to suspect you of illicit activity," Huntington groused.

Sean nodded in complete agreement, but he was in lawyer mode, never losing focus on the legal aspects. "A speeding ticket will work. That would be the easiest for me to deal with after the fact."

"With the Porsche, the cops will know right away that it's me. How many other people are cruising around Denton in one of those things?" I asked.

"You do not need the Porsche for this. You can speed in the Mercedes."

"The SUV?" I snorted. "It's a family car. No, I need something that looks illegal standing still. That way the cops instinctively know the driver is up to something."

"A speeding ticket is a speeding ticket!" Huntington yelled. His blue eyes flashed with annoyance.

"She doesn't have any speeding tickets in the SUV, even though it's a pretty fancy Mercedes," Radar said. "No infractions at all. Might look suspicious that she suddenly gets one when she's on a charity mission."

Huntington and I both glared at him, albeit for different reasons. "Stay out of my driving record," I ordered.

Radar took too much pride in his skills to bother acting innocent. "Heh-heh." Hacking the DMV was not something he'd consider the least bit challenging.

"Your mom will be with me," I said to Huntington. "She'll make sure I take good care of the car."

His mother grinned. "Of course I will."

"Mom." Huntington had lost any trace of humor. "Do you know how much that car is worth?"

"We want our cover to be perfect," LeAnn said. "Sedona borrowed the car from her boyfriend, who borrowed it from you. Got a little carried away with the foot pedal and gets caught speeding." LeAnn spread her hands. "It fits."

He snarled, an actual guttural growl. "Not one mark on it. And don't drive more than five miles over the speed limit. I can track every single inch of that car from my phone."

"Ten miles over," I said, glancing at Sean for verification. "They don't normally pull people over unless it's eight to ten, and we have to make this realistic. I don't want anyone thinking I'm a narc."

"We don't want any lasting trouble, that is for certain," Sean agreed. "And ten over won't require any special favors to have it removed from her record."

Huntington glared at Mark next. Mark didn't smile. "You hired her."

They stared at each other wordlessly, letting the seconds tick by. Huntington didn't lose an ounce of his glare when he said, "I'll bring the Porsche by in the afternoon. You drive it straight to Bobbins, get the stuff, get pulled over and then return it right to me."

"I still have to deliver the pillowcases."

Sean shook his head. "The police will confiscate them all as evidence if there's anything in those boxes. Just make sure that if there is contraband, it spills out. Give them every reason they need to demand a search and take everything off your hands."

"Well, if they take the pillowcases, I hope no one expects me to sew enough replacements for the charity," I huffed.

Mark broke the staring match to grin at me.

Chapter 23

With Cary dead, no one nagged me to stay after five. I went in at seven and bolted at four o'clock to allow me enough time to meet LeAnn and Huntington at my house. Huntington had insisted on providing lessons on driving the Porsche.

Predictably, he had to lecture about every detail, when really, no matter how fancy the dash, whether it takes a key or a push button to start, the concept is the same: Push one pedal to go and the other one to stop.

When I finally backed out of my driveway with LeAnn in the passenger seat, I grinned. "Ready?"

She nodded. "Yup. I hope this solves Steve's case for him."

"Uh-huh."

"What? Do you think we'll fail?"

I shook my head as I cautiously steered the Porsche around the corner at the stop sign. The car drove like a magic carpet ride without the sound of wind to distract from the smooth ride. "No, we won't fail. It's just that his cases are never easy. At least they haven't been."

"Well, he never had my help!"

I had to smile. "True."

Driving Huntington's expensive car made me more than a little nervous, but we made it to Barb's Bobbins without incident.

Barb was ready for us.

We loaded three boxes in the backseat where LeAnn could easily dump them out once we were well away from Barb and her bobbins. When the cops pulled us over, they'd be able to see anything and everything in those boxes.

Our hands were dusted off, and we were ready to leave when a Harley blew into the lot at full throttle. Well, it was a Harley so it probably wasn't at full throttle, it just sounded like it was about to run us all down.

"OhmyGod, what is Wanda doing here?" Barb gasped.

I hadn't met Wanda yet, but who else could she mean other than Joe's mother?

Wanda sputtered to a stop and yanked off her rainbow-colored helmet while dismounting. She wore jeans and leather boots with a fringed pink leather jacket.

"I've got pillowcases," she said. Her eyes were nearly obscured behind heavy black designer eyeglasses. Instead of complimenting her, they overwhelmed her brown-turning-gray hair, making the glasses more memorable than her face, except for her nose. She had shared her nose with her son; it was just as large, and neither the glasses nor the nose stud distracted from its size.

She untangled a long skinny box that was strapped down on the Harley and hurried over to join us, a tornado spinning and then stopping in front of the car.

"I made some extras. Came to help. This was my...my son's route." She swallowed hard. Her arms shook.

"You didn't need to come," I said. "We have this covered."

Her chin, a foot under mine, lifted. "It was his route. Now it's mine."

I waved at the already crowded backseat. "If you want to add yours, we'll get them all delivered."

"Nonsense. I'm small. I'll fit just fine in there. I gotta live up to the boy's memory." She yanked the door open and wedged herself in without ever taking her hands off the cardboard box. The thing resembled a tall, unwieldy shoebox, one that would easily fit a size thirty shoe.

With the other boxes already packed in the backseat, she couldn't set her box down. She propped it upright on her lap, extending it almost a foot above her head, blocking a good half of the rear window.

"I'm not sure it's legal to have a package blocking the right side like that," I said hesitantly, just as my brain realized the benefit.

LeAnn and I shared a glance. This wasn't according to plan, but with her sitting there blocking the back window, we might not even have to speed to get pulled over. Maybe this was a boon rather than a bother. And maybe she had brought her coded pillowcases, all neatly packaged in a separate box. So far, she was the only one who had touched that box, too. Maybe there was enough proof of wrongdoing in the box for the cops to arrest her.

Wanda's presence bumped my nerves up another two notches. I was even more thankful that we had decided the cops would pull us over with a reason rather than us just turn in the contraband. We'd look all the more innocent this way.

Of course, I wasn't counting on the gun.

Chapter 24

Conversation was nil. Wanda didn't offer even a lame attempt at polite social niceties, and I was too tense to bother. The route we had mapped out was as short as possible from Barb's to the charity, but the charity was on the outskirts of town because rental space was cheaper there.

Mark's mother turned around and began rearranging the boxes in the backseat, almost as planned. She shoved one box off the seat onto the floor, opening it in the process.

"We can make room for your box," she said as she grunted and toiled away. Barb had done a nice job of packing the pillowcases, forcing LeAnn to take some out of the box on the seat and put them on top of the box on the floor. It wasn't actually creating any additional space, but maybe Wanda wouldn't notice the shuffling was somewhat pointless other than to expose the contents of the boxes.

"There, I think you can set your box inside this other box, kind of on top," LeAnn offered. The words squeezed out of her lungs rather painfully because her seatbelt had locked tight across her chest.

Wanda mumbled something I couldn't hear.

"Well, you could slide it across the top," LeAnn suggested.

There was no response from the backseat. LeAnn finally faced forward with a heavy sigh.

A couple of teenagers in a Silverado pulled up next to us at the red light. We had at least another two miles before the cops were supposed to ticket us for speeding.

The young gal in the Silverado slid her window down. She wore a black and red biker jacket, and her wide bulging eyes made her look remarkably like a cockroach with a bandana. She pointed a 9mm at me through the window. I hadn't seen much of her face at the truck stop restaurant, but I recognized the leather coat. She was a biker. Wanda drove a Harley. It was possible the two of them knew each other.

"Nice car," the biker chick shouted at me. Her window was open; mine was not. She hollered, "We're takin' it for a ride." She kept the gun steady while opening her truck door.

For all I knew she and her boyfriend were really interested in stealing Huntington's Porsche. It was a super cool car. The light was still red.

"You're clear on both sides, go!" LeAnn yelled.

I hit the pedal without bothering to take my eyes off the gun pointing at me, testing the zero to sixty. The car was rated at somewhere around 5 seconds, but I believe I set a new record at three. Maybe they could tell from the tire marks. There was definitely some extra black left on the road.

The dash and front panel of the car was state-of-the art with more whistles and bells than my phone. Somewhere amongst the display that included camera monitors, a GPS system, and the latest in anti-theft protections, there was a dial that told me how fast we were moving, whether we were using gasoline or electric, and whether or not the oil was low. All I noticed was that the assholes behind us started shooting. "All these cool features and this thing can't emit a lethal plume of gas that might kill them?" I complained.

LeAnn shook her head. "The idea behind these hybrid electrics is that they don't emit enough fumes to kill a grasshopper."

"Damn shame."

"Yes, yes, it is."

"You can't just take off!" Wanda screeched from the backseat. "OhLordHeavenHelpUs, they'll kill us for sure. You have to stop!"

There went the very slight possibility that the occupants in the Silverado were randomly after the car. Well, they'd probably take the car too, along with the pillowcases, but Wanda was obviously expecting them and afraid of them.

I hit highway twenty-four doing ninety.

"Hey! This isn't the way to the donation center!" Wanda protested.

"I'm not driving this thing to the donation center with someone shooting up the town behind us," I snapped. "Don't worry. We'll outrun them." I caught her eye in the mirror. Hers were dark pinpoints behind her glasses. It was not hot inside or outside the car, but beads of sweat dotted her forehead.

"You can't outrun them!"

It didn't matter what she thought. If I had any say, the Silverado wouldn't catch us, and I'd never see the guy or his girlfriend again. Of course, if the cops didn't get their ass in gear, they might not catch us either. And we were now nowhere near where we'd planned on being pulled over.

Apparently, Wanda wasn't about to give up either, because as I pressed down on the accelerator, she smacked me with her purse.

"Hey!"

"Stop! They'll kill us. You always give them what they want. They mean business!" She undid her seatbelt, the better to reach me. The Porsche started beeping a warning.

"Ow! Hey!" I used my right arm to grab at the purse while steering with the left, but I had to let up on the accelerator or risk running off the road. Another audible warning from the front panel began complaining, but I was too busy trying to keep the car in my own lane to investigate.

LeAnn was no lightweight; Mark and Steve would have been proud. She twisted in her seat, grabbed the purse, Wanda's arm and Wanda's hair. She stuffed everything backwards.

The Porsche emitted another shrill warning, but there was no time to figure it out. The Chevy's grill was bearing down on us like giant grizzly teeth. The driver was about to rear-end Huntington's hundred-thousand-dollar stealth car.

The road was clear for at least five hundred yards. I floored that gas pedal hard enough to channel shades of Fred Flintstone when he was late for work.

Hundred-thousand-dollar cars have good stability. We shot away like a rocket booster was strapped to the trunk. I had no problem holding her steady until we caught up to the chicken farmer in front of us.

"What did Huntington say about that noise?" I yelled over the numerous shrill beeps.

"I think it's her seatbelt," LeAnn shouted, still fighting off Wanda's slaps.

The car shrieked again, a different, longer wail.

"Shit." I had to switch lanes to dodge around the pokey farm truck. Now that we were closer, the crates in the back of his truck didn't seem all that well tied down. There were three large mesh boxes stacked across a broad bed. Each crate held six or so shelves of chickens. The truck took up more than one lane, but with the Silverado determined to mash us into the chicken truck, I had no choice.

I swerved into the left lane and punched the accelerator again. Huntington's car complained the entire time. This car was made for that man. All he ever did was complain at me.

"I think it warns you when you drift across lanes or drive too close to another car," was LeAnn's opinion.

"Hang on! That chicken truck is too wide." The truck itself wasn't oversized, but the crates were a foot or two over the sides, hanging into my lane. One wrong move on my part or that of the chicken driver and we were all going to be tenderloins. The chickens knew it too. They flapped and squawked, sending a steady snowfall of feathers across the window. Even with the windows closed, there was a distinct smell of chicken poop.

"Where the hell are the wipers?" My eyes weren't leaving the view of the road to search for the switch. With a death grip on the steering wheel there was no leeway to start pushing buttons hoping to discover where the genius design engineers had hidden the wipers. At this speed most of the feathers and stray bird shit didn't stick anyway.

My cell phone, nestled in my jacket pocket, rang. "As if."

The cameras on the Porsche flashed a picture of chicken wings as we sped by. With the windows closed and warning beeps at full orchestra, the squawking was akin to one elongated peacock hoot trying to make itself heard above the din.

The Chevy didn't wait for me to clear the front of the chickens. With a swerve worthy of a monster truck show, it slammed off the road on the right, churning dust.

The chicken crates swayed dangerously, caught between two vehicles, feathers, dust and a driver who had just panicked enough to slam on the brakes.

"They aren't stopping!" Wanda split her attention between us and the back window.

"Neither are we," I muttered. The wheels barely held the edge of the road when we returned to our lane because I oversteered.

Wanda shrieked, deliberately careening forward, grabbing at me, at buttons and LeAnn. The radio stared blaring.

Mark's mom slapped her. Hard.

I finally found the windshield wipers, but not before somehow accidentally turning on the GPS. It started talking too. Did it give directions to hell in a handbasket? Because I'm pretty sure that is where we were headed.

I overcorrected again. We wobbled back into the right lane, the swinging finally slamming Wanda into the side of the car.

"Put your seatbelt on," I yelled at her.

The problem with highway twenty-four was that it didn't have much for side roads. There wasn't a lot of traffic, which was fine for speeding, but we were on a one-way ticket with no way to lose the guys behind us.

The Silverado was no slouch in the speeding department, but the Porsche, electric or not, wasn't having any problems keeping distance between us, not until a motorcycle passed the Silverado. "Uh-oh." Mark had a motorcycle.

A black car, one that looked suspiciously like the Viper Huntington had driven during the first case at Strandfrost, tried to pass the Silverado next. The Chevy nearly sideswiped him.

Wanda grabbed me around the throat, but LeAnn smacked her with her own purse. I slowed down. No way did I want Mark driving a hundred...I looked down and took my foot completely off the accelerator.

Mark gained on us. Huntington kept the Silverado busy, dancing close, pretending to pass, causing the Silverado to lurch from side to side in an effort to keep him from passing.

Where were the cops? If the Huntington brothers were smart enough to follow us, why couldn't Sean's friends be that smart?

The box of pillowcases in the backseat, the one that Wanda had insisted on keeping with her, slammed into the side of the car. Wanda tried to grab the box, but it started ringing. It was one phone at first, but then the voice assistant kicked in on at least two other phones. "Borgot at your service."

"What?!?" No one heard my shout. The seatbelt audible never stopped screaming at us, the GPS was still giving directions and LeAnn had managed to turn the fan speed to full rather than turn the radio off.

Finally, ahead of us, flashing red and blue lights decorated the highway. Luckily they didn't have their sirens on or maybe they did, but we couldn't hear them.

Wanda punched the box as if that would stop the phones from talking.

I didn't care how the cops managed to get the jump on us as long as they kept Silverado and pals from shooting Mark. Or us. "Should I go faster?" I asked LeAnn.

She couldn't hear me with the continuous din inside the car.

Eight-five was still well above the limit. I took my foot off the gas again. I let the car slow at its own pace before pulling over. As soon as the wheels drifted over the white line, the audible for the lane warning started in.

"Huntington can keep this car," I griped.

Wanda let out a screech from the back. "What are you doing?"

"Stopping. Cops ahead."

"You can't stop now!"

This was the same lady who had insisted we stop just moments ago.

As soon as the Porsche rolled to a stop, two of the audibles went silent. Now I could hear the sirens even with the phones still babbling like a bar full of drunk idiots. "Would you shut those pillowcases off?" I yelled at Wanda. "They're making a hell of a lot of noise."

Mark glided next to us. He wasn't driving his bike with the lightning streak. This was a sleek yellow model with panels that shone in the sun. The side said Ducati 1199.

I rolled the window down.

"Everyone okay?" he asked.

I nodded. "In one piece, no blood."

"Stay in the car."

He took cover behind the front of the car and hopped off the bike.

Good idea. A state cop car screeched to a stop nearby. Two policemen bounced out, their hands on their holsters, but none of us were threatening.

All eyes turned to track the Silverado. Without hesitation, it spun off the road and turned around, disappearing momentarily behind a billowing dust cloud. Two cop cars closed in from our direction and at least one other was coming at it from Denton.

The chicken truck driver ambled to a slow stop not fifty yards behind us. None of the crates had fallen, but at least one cage door had burst open. Chickens were running and half flying at full squawk. There were white ones and brown ones and at least two roosters. The roosters might have been trying to herd the chickens, but they stopped to yodel every time the farmer flapped his hat at them.

The phones were still babbling in the back seat of the Panamera.

An unmarked car pulled up next. To my intense dismay, Detective Saunders stepped out. Of course he'd show up. He was in charge of the case.

I opened the door and climbed out.

He eyed me up and down a little too gleefully.

Chickens were still pouring off the back of the flatbed truck. One of the crates was tilted, having slid partway off. Two others must have opened as well because there were chickens all over the road.

Wanda climbed out and pointed at me. "I'm just delivering pillowcases! To a charity! She's the driver, and she was the one speeding!"

Mark sidled next to me, but not in time to distract me from the chicken that hopped on the roof of the Porsche.

"Oh, crap." And that is exactly what that chicken and two more proceeded to do on the top of Huntington's dusty, but expensive vehicle. I grabbed the white chicken, gently tucking its wings. I handed her to LeAnn.

"Got her," she said, holding the chicken a bit tighter than necessary and keeping her carefully away from her clothing.

"Just hang on, she'll settle down."

I closed the driver side door of the Porsche, but a brown chicken burbled a hearty cry and defied my attempt to capture it. The other white one flew off and landed on Mark's Ducati.

"Hold still, bird!" The chicken ignored my orders. The passenger side of the car was still open wide. Two more birds approached, one landing on the top of the car, the other flapping at Detective Saunders.

"Sedona..." Mark rolled his eyes, but he went around the front of the car.

"If any of these birds poop in the front seat, Huntington will kill me!" I flew faster than the chicken. My little brown friend hopped from the roof of the car to the top of the car door, balancing easily.

Mark shooed it away before it could enter the Porsche, but with me coming at it from the other side, it flew in my face. "Hey!" One claw caught my arm. It beat me half to death with its wings as I attempted to subdue the beast. Good thing Dad used to have chickens or I'd never have caught it.

"Okay," Detective Saunders bellowed. "That's enough. Hands up on the car and spread'em."

"What?" I was still fighting feathers. None of us were the least bit threatening if you didn't count Wanda, who was still busy shouting about her innocence and convicting herself all at the same time.

"I'd never have been involved if not for Joe," she sobbed. "It was all him. I had to deliver the phones or they would have killed me. And I can't get any more untraceable phones because Joe is dead. I've told them he's dead, but they won't listen."

I stared at her and then at the box that still rang and talked, but not as often. Her back door was still wide open. "Untraceable phones..."

"Hands up and turn around," Detective Saunders demanded again, coming around the car at me. He was worse than the chickens. I didn't like the gleam in his eyes. This guy was not patting me down.

I stared at him over the top of the squawking chicken I held.

"You heard me." He would have been in my face, but kept his distance because of the flapping wings of my feathered friend.

"What do I do with the chicken?" I asked.

"What?"

"The chicken. I can't release it. It might get run over. Or escape." I had her feet secured, but her wings flapped and then randomly tucked or stayed out. "Here, you better hold her." I offered the bird up.

He took a step back.

Mark was suddenly next to me again, his arms at his sides. He was wearing his black leather jacket. On the best of days, he could look threatening. Today, he'd had more than enough playing around. His eyes were flat and cold.

"You'll probably want to start with me," he growled. "No telling what I might be hiding under my coat." He lifted the edges, clearly showing nothing but a t-shirt. He made sure the two state guys could see that he wasn't carrying.

"Do you want the chicken?" I asked Saunders. More birds approached, two more flying onto Huntington's car, competing with the ones already there.

"Put that damn thing down," he bellowed.

The chickens on the roof took umbrage with his tone. Two of them launched off the side of Huntington's car and headed for the road. The other one came at me, but I stepped away, using the chicken I already had to push the new one into Saunders. "Grab it before it gets away," I yelled at the detective.

Saunders gave a good imitation of a chicken squawk as he batted at the flapping bird. Feathers flew. Poop dropped. "Get that thing away from me!" The more he danced, the worse it went for him. The first chicken landed, but went right up again, catching his arm. Several others flapped, landed, pecked and ran rampant.

Mark coughed away what might have been a stifled laugh. The chickens now had us surrounded. It was the farmer's fault really. He was chasing them our way, grabbing them one at a time and stuffing them in a cage. When the cage was full, he went back for another cage, but in the meantime, our bunch of cars and humans looked like the nearest roost.

A bawking beast rushed us. Saunders dodged, causing those that had settled to fly again. He took a direct hit in the chest, a lone feather sticking solidly on his jacket. It looked to be smeared with a smelly offering from the chicken.

LeAnn handed her bird to one of the troopers. "I'll get it."

She was off, chasing chickens. She clapped, a mistake if you wanted to catch a bird, but it worked well for making several more take flight, including at least three landing on the front seat of Saunders' car. She seemed determined to bury the detective's car in chickens.

I grinned.

The next vehicle to pull up was the one I wanted to see. Huntington could barely inch the Viper forward, forcing Sean to pop out several yards away.

My dear lawyer brother didn't appear much calmer than Mark. His face was an unhealthy red. "Sedona!" He shot me a glare dark enough to kill the chicken I was holding, but if there is one thing we O'Halas understand, it's loyalty and family.

"I'm fine," I told him.

"Were you speeding?"

I shook my head. "Um, there was a Silverado chasing us and they shot at us!"

Sean was already in lawyer mode. Saunders didn't have a chance, and he knew it. Within a minute, Sean had the troopers admitting they had nothing conclusive on radar. How could they? All of us had been speeding, including the Ducati. But by the time they aimed radar at us, I was probably traveling the slowest of the lot.

"I'm impounding this car," Saunders announced.

Sean switched gears. "We'll allow you to inspect the contents, but the car is legally registered and up-to-date. No reason to impound it."

Huntington added his two cents, but he was fighting off a chicken as he tried to extract the talking phones from the back. "This isn't my stuff. You can have it." The phones hadn't gone silent either. As Huntington yanked the box from the back, the voice of the phone assistant clearly read out a location and time.

Wanda froze and so did I. I knew that voice. I'd recognized it right away. It was the Borgot assistant voice, which meant these were not phones that had ever been sold. They had to be test phones that should have remained at the company. Untraceable, unowned, unregistered phones would be very valuable to a criminal.

"That's supposed to be a box of pillowcases," I said.

"Your fingerprints anywhere on those talking pillowcases?" Sean demanded.

I shook my head and pointed at Wanda. "She brought them. She's the only one who touched that box. LeAnn, Barb, and I put the other pillowcases in the back."

"I had to do it. They killed Joe! If I didn't deliver the phones Joe stole, they woulda come after me." She pointed back down the road. "You saw them! They had a gun! I promised I'd bring them, but they didn't wait at the charity where Joe usually delivered them. I thought maybe they'd leave me alone if I came with you and delivered the last batch of phones he had taken from his work!"

Saunders started reading her her rights. She'd already confessed to having the phones, but she hadn't been the one to steal them. Joe had. He'd taken the phones from Borgot and sold them to the bikers—or whoever wanted to buy them.

Even though the phones had been stolen and probably used to commit crimes, Joe's mom couldn't have been the one who had murdered Joe. Although, having known how annoying Joe could be, anything was possible.

LeAnn handed her chicken over to the farmer. I gave mine up too, and since I had already been pooped on, decided to help catch the rest.

Sean and Detective Saunders argued over who would keep the car. Huntington tried to get in a word edgewise while still holding the box of talking phones.

I was almost relieved when Radar and Turbo drove up in a white van. "Need a ride?"

Neither of them owned a van. This one looked as though they had borrowed it from an airport shuttle service. The old lettering had peeled away, but it was still possible to read the "Ride'n Fly" logo.

"How'd you guess we needed wheels?" I stuffed a last chicken into one of the cages and inspected my pants. There was only one or two poop smears, but no way would Huntington let me drive any of his cars back. I wasn't even fit to ride on the back of a nice Ducati motorcycle, not that I had a helmet.

Turbo turned to Radar. "Good call on the vehicle."

LeAnn strolled up behind me. "Is this our ride? Oh, how low we've fallen already."

"Heard on the radio there were phones in the box," Radar said.

"They announced that?"

He shrugged. "Not exactly."

I nodded. "Yes, phones. From Borgot. Free minutes because they are test phones, I'd bet."

"Did you snatch one for me to examine?"

I shook my head. "I was never near the box, but Huntington pulled it from the back seat. Maybe he'll be smart enough to confiscate one."

"And we thought maybe information was sewn into the pillowcases." LeAnn shook her head.

"Those phones are unmarked, unowned, and Borgot is paying for the air time." Turbo waggled his eyebrows. "Untraceable and if used in a crime and dumped later, it's a test phone assigned to nobody."

Radar nodded. "Even if conversations are recorded or locations tracked, that wouldn't prove who was using the phones unless they were caught in the act because no one ever bought them. Perfect for heists, kidnappings, bank robberies, whatever."

"Probably drug drops," Turbo declared.

"If Huntington can get us even one of the phones, we'll know more," Radar said.

I shook my head. "I don't know if he can pull it off. There are enough cops over there to open six donut shops. They're planning to impound the car."

"Yup." Radar held up his smartwatch even though I couldn't possibly read any of the text from so far away. "Someone called in for a wrecker so we figured you might need us to bring transportation."

Most of the chickens had been captured. The ones that hadn't were probably going to run wild and free until a coyote or hawk spotted them. I slid the back door of the van open and let Mark's mom in ahead of me.

I waved at Mark and climbed in. The van smelled of stale smoke and failing air fresheners. LeAnn was right. We'd been driving in the seat of luxury only moments ago, but things had taken a downhill turn, fast.

Chapter 25

Radar dropped LeAnn off at her house so she could get cleaned up. At my own house, I rushed my shower because Radar and Turbo went out back to reset and "improve" the garden security. The danger was in their definition of "improve."

"Leave precise and detailed instructions for shutting things off," I yelled as I raced into the bedroom. "Precise and detailed!"

"Arming it is easy," Radar said.

"For shutting it off!" I slammed the bedroom door.

Even showering at warp speed, Mark and Steve had arrived by the time I finished. I grabbed clothes and dressed fast, not wanting to miss any details. My newly sewn bra was half on before I realized it was the one I'd made.

I nearly tossed it back in the drawer, but it would hold well enough. In fact, the hooks were so snug I could barely force them through with all the sewing I had done around the area. Well, no one was going to see it anyway.

By the time I staggered into the living room, Radar was hard at work examining a phone. Huntington had, indeed, pilfered one of the Borgot phones from Wanda's box. "The investigative team is working on extracting every possible clue from these things, but Joe's mother spilled her guts," Huntington said. "Joe was selling the phones to a gang who used them for heists, at least one blackmail and one kidnapping for ransom."

"Was this gang a bunch of her biker friends?" I asked.

He shook his head. "She claims they were Joe's friends that he met through a single biker her group used to know. The criminals not only used the phones to coordinate crimes, they had branched out and were selling the untraceable phones to other entities for criminal use. That's why the pattern of crimes wasn't always the same. Several of the crimes were happening in other states. We knew some of the perps belonged to a local bike gang here that included the two in the Silverado."

"Good thing you managed to snag one of the phones," I said.

"The gang hadn't taken control of these phones yet, so there probably isn't any incriminating evidence on any of them. This particular one spouts Spanish phrases, and I didn't know how to switch it to English."

That got my attention. "What?"

"It's doubtful any of the foreign phrases are a special code for the gang, because they hadn't taken possession of the phones."

"Are you sure it was Spanish? It wasn't Pig Latin?"

He scowled at me. "Spanish."

I turned to Radar. "Joe's phone—or his watch, did it have foreign languages on there?"

"Yes and no. There were apps for Pig Latin, Spanish and Italian on the watch. But the phone only had Pig Latin on it so the watch couldn't utilize the functions. Those watches don't have the juice to run alone. There was no foreign language support on the Borgot code drop you gave me on the SD card either."

"Let me see that phone."

Huntington reluctantly handed it over.

I hadn't done any of the foreign language testing, but I knew how to activate the translation service, at least in theory. I said the words and typed in the proper letters. "Borgot, Spanish."

"Si, estamos para servirle," the phone replied.

My hand shook slightly. "Where is the bathroom?"

¿Dónde está el baño?

I shook my head in amazement. "This is weird. Very weird."

Radar tilted his head. "That sounds like the proper translation."

I nodded. "It is. But the translation code hasn't been loaded on any of the test phones at Borgot."

Mark raised his eyebrows.

"It isn't even supposed to *exist* yet." I explained about the arguments and scheduling. "Roscoe said some of the Spanish had been coded, but not enough to test. Howard said if we don't have language support, we have nothing patentable. None of the languages other than Pig Latin has been loaded on our official test phones, or I'd have known about it. Just how much Spanish was on Joe's smartwatch?" I asked.

Radar retrieved his jacket from the couch and dug around in the pockets. He finally extracted Joe's smartwatch. After a bit of tapping, he verified his earlier claim. "There's no actual way to start the apps on the watch, not without phone support, but there are two icons, one for Spanish and one for Italian. There was Pig Latin and a British voice versus an American one on his phone, but no Spanish, no Italian."

"None of the Borgot plans have a British voice. The actor we hired to do some of the voice impression is all-American phrasing. Borgot's translation plans call for everyday phrases and travel guide phrases, along with a kind of artificial intelligence to offer answers to oddball questions, but supposedly none of that code is ready to be tested except in English."

Radar tapped the watch face with one finger. "Smartwatches are all the rage. A watch that works with a phone to offer translations would be very useful. For a business traveler, it could save time and make him look smarter. A guy could just ask his question without even taking his phone out. The watch spits out the translation, and he's in business."

"But Borgot is only producing a phone that will someday offer translations. It doesn't work yet!"

"Looks to me like someone is leapfrogging over Borgot," Radar said. "They got their hands on the basic Borgot code and are adding languages and watch support."

I picked up the prototype smartwatch. "A gang of bikers is coding a watch to work with Borgot's phone? But how are they planning to get the watch to market?"

Huntington narrowed his eyes. "They caught the two in the Silverado. I'll find out if they had watches on them." He made a phone call.

"Cary had access to the code and so did Joe. But neither one of them was writing code, so who added the ability for Spanish? And then who coded the watch Joe was wearing to work with the phones? Anyone could steal the code once Kovid or Roscoe checked it into the main build machine. The problem is, there isn't finished code there. The code is barely *started* for most of the languages."

Huntington hung up. "No smartwatches on the Silverado crew or Joe's mother. This looks like it could be a separate crime. The bikers just wanted untraceable free minutes and disposable phones that weren't tied to them."

"Joe was stealing the phones for the gang, but he must have known about the translation code as well because he owned a watch that had some of the translations working," I said.

Mark agreed. "Looks to me like Joe was delivering code and phones, but not necessarily to the same people. Cary had to be involved also or he wouldn't have ended up dead in your garden."

I nodded. "Cary wasn't the type to get his hands dirty. He probably hired Joe as the delivery person. After Joe died, I heard Cary talking to someone on his phone. I think he was looking for Joe's watch. It must have fallen off, and Cary was supposed to recover it."

Mark grunted. "The more important question is what got Joe and Cary killed? Selling code to work with a watch or selling the phones to a biker gang so they could commit crimes?"

"The gang wouldn't kill Joe," I guessed. "He was their ticket to the phones. Joe's mom even said she'd tried to explain she couldn't obtain more phones. And since at least some of these phones have code meant to work with a smartwatch, they were probably not even headed to the gang. Joe must have intended to deliver them somewhere else."

Huntington nodded. "If the gang had killed Joe, they would already have known that Joe was dead and couldn't get more phones."

"And if Cary was a secondary source for the phones, killing him wouldn't help the bikers either," Mark said.

We stared at the watch. "It had to be the watch," I muttered. "Something to do with the language translations and making it work with a watch got them both murdered."

Mark picked up the phone from Wanda's stash. "The watch is a step above what Borgot intended to sell. But who is writing the language translations and making it work with this watch? And how are they planning to continue the operation without Cary or Joe?"

I looked at Radar hopefully.

He shrugged. "The bits we have seen are not that close to completion, but we're only getting pieces here and there. The code on the phones that Joe's mom had is obviously further along than any of the code you've seen at Borgot. My guess is that if they can get a few more tweaks, they are probably in business."

Huntington paced and grumbled. "Anyone could be stealing that code."

"Not just anyone," I disagreed. "Whoever is doing this has to be coding the languages ahead of schedule and getting it to work with the smartwatches. All the code goes through Roscoe and Kovid. There are a few junior engineers and a couple of real language experts, but their modules are integrated with everything Roscoe or Kovid do."

"You think one of them killed off Cary and Joe?"

"I can't imagine either Roscoe or Kovid willingly cooperating with Joe in the first place! Kovid did admit he put the Pig Latin in there, but he did that as a joke. Maybe he's been secretly working on the other languages too. But how do we prove it?"

Useful suggestions were in short supply. Even if Radar hacked into Borgot or I let him use my account, whoever was stealing code wasn't stupid enough to do it under their own account. They had to be delivering code via the SD cards —and that meant there was no tracing it back to an email account or work account. The phones were stolen, so there was no tracing the units back to whoever was doing the code.

Most worrisome of all was that whoever was behind all this was a murderer who had already buried one body in my backyard. I really didn't want to be the next victim.

Chapter 26

It was late by the time everyone departed. Thankfully Mark stayed. He called his mother to give her an update and then turned to me with a brooding expression. "I didn't find it amusing when someone took shots at you in the Panamera."

Was he blaming me or complaining in general? "I wasn't thrilled either. Nor was I very happy when you drove between me and the bullets on a *motorcycle*. You were in more danger than me!"

"Huntington should never have involved you."

"Or you, for that matter."

His eyes narrowed. "There's no arguing with you, is there?"

Since we were arguing, even though I wasn't certain why, he was obviously wrong.

He ended the argument by striding over and kissing me.

If he didn't want to discuss my involvement anymore, who was I to argue? I could redirect my worry every bit as much as he could. I squeezed his broad shoulders, knowing he hadn't been hit, but needing the reassurance of touching him.

His hand traveled under my shirt across my back to my bra clasp.

It didn't take me long to remember I was wearing the bra I'd sewn myself. The clasp was wedged on there crooked and triple sewed around the little hooks. Instead of melting from the sheer bliss of being with Mark, I was getting downright hot from the embarrassed blush that crept up my face, starting in the vicinity of the damn bra.

His lips were still on mine, but his concentration was obviously elsewhere. He had both hands involved now, trying to discern the nature of the bra clasp. At this rate, I'd be out of that bra by the time he was sixty.

Finally he pulled back, panting either with passion or from the effort of twisting the bra, the clasp and me underneath it all. "Do you have a lock on this thing or what?"

"Well, no, but I sewed it myself," I gasped out.

He closed his eyes.

"Except for the part your mother helped me with."

My words elicited a strangled protest combined with a grunt. "Let's not mention my mother when we're engaged in—do I need to find pliers to pry this off, or what?"

I reached back to study the problem. "I think you may have twisted the hook thingies more when you pulled on it."

"Maybe my mother did this on purpose."

"I did the hooks!" I protested. "But not on purpose. Well, not—"

Mark's sigh could have blown the bra off if it hadn't been sewn so tightly. He grabbed my shirt and pulled it off over my head, ripping the seams in the process.

"There's more than one way to peel a banana," he said, lifting the bra from the bottom and squishing my boobs down with the elastic. He kissed me again and worked his way down to make sure that any possible injuries were given proper attention while he carefully extracted me from the contraption.

It was possible I'd never have gotten out of the bra without his help.

Chapter 27

With all the excitement of delivering pillowcases, I had completely forgotten Monique's promise of a team building exercise, but there was the email first thing the next morning, demanding my presence in the break room. "Like we don't have enough work to do," I muttered. I grabbed one of the test phones, assuming she had thought up some brilliant way to group test in order to speed up the schedule. "It won't work," I told the phone. "But new managers always think they have a better plan."

There were already people milling in the break room, mostly huddled behind the counter or wedged against the fridge. There were two junior engineers, a lady from marketing, and an older guy who was part of the test team. He was a rickety fellow, and so far as I knew, didn't own a single t-shirt that wasn't torn in at least three places. Sometimes he even wore a shirt with one sleeve ripped completely off.

What was John, the CEO, doing here with us peons? And the one secretary in the whole company, Kay, was here, too. Watching them test phones would be interesting.

Roscoe was pointedly eating a poptart and ignoring an untouched plate piled high with rice cakes. Howard stood more in the open, staring at the far wall of the break room. He was yanking on the top of his dress shirt as though worried he had forgotten his tie, but Borgot was very casual. No one wore ties, not even the lawyers.

My eyes followed his stare. Along the far wall there was a long beam, waist high, supported by two Y supports on either end. A black guy in a black leotard was stretching along the length. He straightened, bounced on his toes and then lifted one muscular arm in a very convincing...ballet pose.

"Dear God, no," I muttered, closing my eyes. I swung around hard and promptly hit Kovid square in the chest with my first step to freedom.

He was rooted to the spot, his mouth hanging wide, staring at the ballet beam and Mr. Stretch. Kovid grabbed my arm in an ineffective attempt to steady me while he sputtered an apology. "Sorry. I didn't see you."

"No problem. A ballet beam in an engineering company isn't just riveting, it's scary."

Mr. Stretch stopped holding his ridiculous pose and called out, "Free your mind! Your body! You will be at one with your code."

"At one with code?" I sneered.

Kovid's eyes bulged. "I don't want to be—"

We both hightailed it for the stairwell, bumping shoulders and promptly running smack into Lawrence. "It's a good idea," Lawrence said, patting his full head of blonde hair, a direct contrast to Mr. Stretch who sported dark hair that capped his head like a second skin. "This guy did some work at another company I worked for. Had an amazing effect on employee moral. Work output increased dramatically."

"What, when you promised you wouldn't hire a ballet teacher ever again if they made the shipment date?" I blurted out.

He snorted. "If it works, it works. If we don't get this product to market soon, we'll all be on the street looking for a job. Startups don't have the luxury of falling back on old income. Come on, you two. Give it a try."

I didn't report to Lawrence. I opened my mouth to tell him so when Monique materialized from behind him. "How bad can it be?" She stepped sideways, right in front of me, her gaze determined. Of course, she wore her purple spandex pants, the ones with the yellow smiling, winking icon on her butt. Nothing like being prepared.

I had on jeans. So did every other engineer in the place except for the IT guy. He wore shorts even when it was twenty degrees outside. He had probably read the emails that arranged this disaster because he was nowhere to be seen.

Howard mumbled something about "idiotic, waste of..." but then Lawrence turned his eagle-eyed stare on him. Howard slugged back a drink of coffee and promptly choked. He used it as an excuse to head for the men's bathroom, coughing and gagging the entire time as though he might die any second.

Great. Now I couldn't use choking as an excuse. Kovid and I eyed each other. There were only so many excuses. Would he fake a heart attack before I did? Was I that desperate?

Mr. Stretch called out, "Everyone line up! We'll limber up first. No one has to go on their toes. Nothing too difficult for beginners!"

Yes, I was that desperate.

Monique grabbed my arm and dragged me backwards to the ballet bar. "Will you just participate already?" she hissed in my ear. "We can't expect the guys to do this if we don't. And Lawrence said it worked miracles at his last company. We need a miracle!"

She was right about the miracle part, but I doubted we were saying the same prayer.

My thoughts on participating did a one-eighty when I spotted Mr. Stretch's gym bag in the corner by the end of the pole supporting the ballet beam. The nylon bag was a light blue with yellow stripes, zipped up tight. The phone sitting on top of it was black—just like all the other Borgot prototypes. I wouldn't have noticed it there except for the fact that a lot of Borgot phones had been turning up where they had no business being.

What was he doing with one of our phones? It couldn't be part of his pay package.

My gaze swung around wildly, wondering who had set it there. Or had he stolen it? Not likely. He wouldn't leave it in plain view if he had filched it off a desk. But sitting where it was, it would be very easy for him to pick up and nonchalantly walk out with it. What then?

I needed that phone. Mr. Stretch, who was now introducing himself as Clint Lewis, needed to be followed. I couldn't follow him, but maybe I could steal the stolen phone. I never carried a phone on my belt, but I had brought one of the test phones, under the very mistaken assumption that the team building exercise might include actual work or something that would forward the company objectives.

I scooted over to the beam, my sudden enthusiasm propelling me to the front of the class. With a determined grunt, I propped my leg up on the bar. "Ow." My plan to grab the contraband during a stretch needed a serious adjustment. The seams of my jeans barely allowed for this position. My leg didn't feel so lucky and leaning over without stretchier pants was impossible.

Clint twirled around and clapped his hands at me. "Excellent. Excellent!" Ballet was obviously a muscle builder because the guy was built like a truck.

Thankfully, Monique took up a graceful position behind me. I'll bet her smiling butt pants were something to behold from the other side. I closed my eyes. Once again, Huntington owed me a raise.

I wished Mark's mom, LeAnn, was here. Between the two of us, we could manage a distraction long enough to ensure one of us could retrieve the phone. Plus, if she was here, maybe she could somehow shut Clint up. He was giving instructions at the top of his sing-song voice while spinning around the group helping "position" everyone.

When he started an old fashioned boom box playing the sound track from "Flashdance," I dropped my leg and leaned over, intending to fake a cramp. Unfortunately, my thigh cooperated a little too realistically. "Aaaargh."

I sat down hard. The phone was within reach, but Clint rushed over to push against the toe of my sneaker. I glared at him. The cramp wasn't in my calf. There was no way I was telling him that the side of my thigh was the problem.

I squawked and scooted back, hitting his bag.

"Oh Sedona, quit being such a prima donna," Monique yodeled. "This isn't hard at all, is it guys?"

What guys? The CEO was standing at the very end of the beam with Lawrence. He was leaned against it casually as though that counted as exercise. Kovid gripped the bar with both hands and looked like he was hoping to snap it with his bare hands.

Roscoe faced the CEO and Lawrence. He was in full spout mode about his great code. Two others had taken positions at the beam; one was our overweight project coordinator, but he merely stared at the beam as though it would exercise itself. Monique's replacement in marketing, Heather, was pretending to stretch near the snack counter while she talked to the CEO's secretary, Kay. Kay wore pretty red heels so apparently she was exempt.

"This is insane," I muttered. Clint still knelt nearby, ready to offer help I didn't want. From this close, his bulging arm muscles were even more evident —a threat if there ever was one. I scooted away another scoot. "I'm fine. I'll recover in a minute. You just go on herding the insane."

Hazel eyes, hinting at a mixed heritage, flashed laughter and far more intelligence at that moment than the quirky, hyperactive ballet teacher he was playing at. Perhaps he was laughing at me, or perhaps at the fact that he was getting paid, who knows how much, to coerce a bunch of gangly engineers into standing next to a ballet beam. We came to an agreement sitting there, me with a snarl and he with a grin.

With a nod that said he would leave me alone, he stood to usher Heather to the beam. Kay was used to ignoring pesky, inane requests. She gave him a steely-eyed glare and while pretending to finger the crimson garnet necklace she wore, she flipped him off. Her dark brown ponytail wagged a dismissal as she pranced off down the hall, the sound of her red heels lost underneath the music. Not even her boss was willing to suggest she stay.

Kovid gladly stepped back from the bar to make room for Heather. The fat project coordinator behind Kovid gasped in alarm, wiped his brow and rushed the snack counter. Instinctively, he grabbed a rice cake and stuffed it in his mouth. Then, with a garbled gag he darted away.

While everyone watched him enviously, I shoved the Borgot phone in my back pocket.

I rolled to a standing position, dropping my own Borgot test phone near the bag.

Clint called out another set of instructions that was soundly ignored by one and all.

I limped to the other side of Monique.

The CEO tired of Roscoe shouting above the music. He gave the beam a friendly pat, waved at us and headed down the hallway with a, "Good work, keep it going."

Lawrence muttered something about, "This really did help at our old company, although I don't see how."

"Yeah, you should have thought of that before you hired this guy," I grumbled darkly.

Clint was now dancing with Monique. "You want to stretch your arms when you do this," he called out. "Everyone grab a partner."

"Anyone touches me, dies," I promised.

With Monique occupied, the CEO gone and no one closing in, I bolted for the stairwell like the devil was on my tail.

Radar needed to see this phone.

Chapter 28

I hit the first floor, raced to the opposite end of the building and took the stairs back up. Luckily, everyone was hiding from everyone else because no one wanted to be dragged to the break room where music was still blaring. I stayed low, collected my backpack and scurried back out. From now on I'd carry my car keys in my pocket.

I drove out of the parking lot, afraid someone might follow me. After several checks in the rear view mirror, I pulled into the first available gas station to call Mark and Radar.

"I don't know if Clint left Borgot yet," I told Mark. "It might be interesting to see where he takes that phone or find out if he keeps it."

"What does he look like?"

"He's a black guy in black tights. How many of them can there be coming out of Borgot?"

Mark laughed. "Last name Lewis?" he verified.

"That's what he said."

"Okay, I'm on my way."

Radar showed up shortly after I arrived at home. He had barely sat down at the kitchen table when he stopped to rub his hands together gleefully. "This has an SD card in it and there's code on it, just like your test units."

"I'm going to assume you mean the units I gave to you, not test units you had no business looking at."

He just grinned and held up the small card he had taken from the phone I had just retrieved from Clint Lewis. "This phone is not only running the latest translation code that includes Spanish and Italian, the storage card has the raw computer code, module by module."

"And whoever has that storage card can import it anywhere—like another phone."

He nodded. "And sell it as their very own code or add the code needed to work with a smartwatch."

There was a quick tap at the front door, followed by Mark coming in. Since we weren't expecting anyone else, he locked it behind him.

"Did you find him?" I asked Mark before he even unzipped his jacket.

"I found a Clint Lewis. He runs a karate dojo downtown. According to the website, he's an ex-marine."

"What?"

He nodded. "The ballet must be a side thing."

The guy had been in good shape. And that second or two when our eyes met after I fell...maybe Mr. Lewis was more than he appeared to be. "Did you catch him leaving the building?"

Mark shook his head. "No, but since I know where he works, I can question him later."

"That's a good idea. We can ask him what he was doing with the phone."

Mark ignored my hint and focused on Radar. "What did you find?"

Radar relayed the information. "The storage card in this phone contains the code for the Borgot assistant and translation modules. There's nothing to support a smartwatch, but the person on the other end could be adding that code. Once the smartwatch code modules are added, presto, you not only beat Borgot to market with more translation features, you have a smartwatch that supports translations as well."

"Joe must have been delivering code drops, and he somehow wrapped his slimy hands around one of the smartwatches," I said.

Radar nodded. "Someone also added the smartwatch code to his personal phone, the one you ended up with, which is why it worked with the watch. The drops weren't perfectly synched because his phone didn't have the language modules updated." He turned back to the phone. "Give me a few more minutes with this thing," he said.

It took him longer than a few minutes, but the results were what we expected. "This looks like close to the final code drop. The Spanish translations are much more complete. This could be good enough for someone to use in production, although I obviously can't test it thoroughly, and the only watch we have is an early prototype."

"I say we have a little chat with Clint," I suggested. "Let's find out what he knows. Maybe he is coding the watch part of this project, and needed the latest language modules. Without Joe or Cary, he had to go in and pick up the code himself."

Mark sighed.

Radar stood. "You guys go ahead. I want to take this home and delve into the code. I'll test it more to see how well it works with Joe's smartwatch. I may have better luck getting it to work with one of mine, but either way, this raw code is very valuable."

Radar followed us out. I was pleased to see that Mark had driven his SUV and not one of the motorcycles. It would be easier for him to take me along to talk to Clint.

***

Clint lived above his karate dojo studio. I had expected Mark to argue with me when I insisted on coming along, but as we climbed in his SUV all he said was, "You know, Steve wouldn't have even told you he found this Clint guy, never mind taken you along to question him."

"I'm not dating Steve," I replied. "And neither are you."

He drove in silence for a while. "He keeps hiring you."

"That is a problem," I agreed.

Denton wasn't that large and nothing was terribly far. The dojo was a few blocks over from Abba's studio, the one where I had been a member. Given the fact someone disliked me enough to bury a dead guy in my yard, I should probably still be attending karate practice regularly.

The sign on Clint's dojo door listed the first afternoon class starting at five. I had taken karate long enough to recognize the validity of the hours. One morning class for pros, one for beginners who were people like me—not really all that good at karate, but needed a few self-defense moves and the exercise. Evening was a repeat for various levels of expertise.

The front door was locked, but another sign requested, "deliveries in the back."

We walked around to an alley that was wide enough for a truck, found the door, and rang a bell.

Whoever was upstairs buzzed the door open.

A very short hallway directly in front of us led to a door that probably led to the dojo and the front of the building. We tried the door first, but it was locked so Mark opted for the stairs on our right. He took them two at a time ahead of me, his sneakers never scuffing enough to make a sound. The only time I was that quiet was barefoot and on carpet. I exerted an effort to stifle what felt like a clumsy stomp.

Clint opened the door after the first knock. He was vastly more manly in sweatpants and a tight black t-shirt. He was shorter than Mark by at least six inches and where Mark had a fluid grace, Clint exhibited more of a stone wall strength.

He assessed Mark quietly, without a smile.

That changed when he noticed me on the landing next to Mark. His lips quirked sideways into a half grin. "Don't tell me you're mad about falling off that beam and dragged your boyfriend here to beat me up."

I rolled my eyes. "Hardly."

"She'd have done that herself if necessary," Mark contributed. "She attacked me even though I had a gun."

While that was true, the circumstances had been less dangerous than Mark implied. I do believe Mark was giving Clint a subtle warning that may have been more territorial than protective.

Clint's eyebrows raised. "Why do I believe that?" He folded his arms across his broad chest. "Okay, so you aren't here to bust me up, and you aren't the UPS package I was expecting. And if you carry a gun, and she's capable of taking care of herself, how can I help you?"

Mark held up the Borgot phone minus the SD card. "This little item. Recognize it?"

Clint met his stare silently.

"It seems odd that an ex-marine would be giving ballet lessons to a room full of geeks, especially when that same man owns his own karate dojo. Maybe there was more to that job than first met the eye," Mark said.

Clint didn't flinch. "My contracts are private. I don't share details. I'm afraid you'll have to find your answers somewhere else."

Clint didn't seem all that upset about us having the phone or the code. "Contracts" implied he was working for someone else. Was it possible he didn't realize I had switched the phone out? Maybe he was Joe's replacement, a delivery service. "Did the person you delivered the phone to complain?" I asked.

His gaze switched to me, but only for a second. He knew the real threat. Well, he thought he did. Mark was right though. I had a tendency to be a wild card.

"Why would they complain?" Clint asked.

"Because it was the wrong phone," I replied.

Mark gave a tiny grunt of exasperation. Giving up details to the bad guys was probably not the way he normally went about his undercover work.

"It was the wrong phone?" The question didn't rate another glance my way, but Clint raised both eyebrows.

I nodded. "Wrong one. Didn't you notice?"

Now his eyes strayed to me and stayed there. "It wasn't my phone. I had never seen it before and don't expect to see it again."

"How often do you hire out to, erm, teach ballet and deliver stolen contraband? Wouldn't it have been a lot easier to just hire out as a karate instructor?"

"Too threatening." He shook his head then as if it occurred to him that he had not intended to answer questions. "You may as well come in." He stepped back, letting Mark squeeze sideways through the opening. The space was plenty big enough for me.

The room was Japanese sparse, with a tatami mat covering most of the floor, a futon couch, a wooden-framed chair and a coffee table sporting a bonsai plant in the center. A fountain running over four perfectly round stones sat in an art alcove along one wall, explaining the very slight sound of running water. Clint didn't look the least bit Japanese, but the décor fit his contained and calm personality.

"Have a seat," he invited.

Mark declined. The two of them stared at each other, still assessing or threatening or whatever guy thing they were doing.

"Karate would have worked out better at Borgot," I said.

"Probably, but the email asked me for the same stunt I had done at Clockworks, so that's what I did. It's a long story."

To cover up my interest in a company called Clockworks that might have something to do with smartwatches, I plopped down on the futon couch. "Oh, we have time," I said, cheerfully.

He sighed. "I could have guessed that." His drop into the chair across from me was much more graceful and controlled than my own. "Basically, my girlfriend started a yoga business about a year ago after she saw an article that said HP hired a dance troupe for inspiration. She now hires out as a yoga instructor to companies that want unusual team building exercises."

"HP? The big computer company hired a dance troupe?"

"Yeah. Go figure. My wife, Keiko, started offering the yoga inspirational exercises at companies on a lark. I never thought it would take off." He smiled and shook his head. "The ballet thing was because I lost a bet we made on the topic. It was a one-time thing, but then a couple of weeks ago, an email came in asking if I could do the same routine at Borgot."

"You lost a second bet?" Mark took a seat on the edge of the couch next to me.

"No, I'm not that dumb." He rubbed his hand across the stubble that was his hair. "But the first job at Clockworks paid twenty thousand dollars even though it was a ballet ad I put up on her website as a joke. A guy I'd never heard of sent me an email two weeks ago telling me he had heard about me from a friend at Clockworks where I did the first ballet demo. I wrote back and said the price had gone up to forty. Idiots said yes. What the hell could I do?" He spread his hands. "My military severance is basically healthcare. I wasn't in long enough to earn a giant pension. I do okay, but not forty thousand dollars for a morning okay. Who does?"

"That would convince me to wear tights," I said, "even ugly ones."

Mark's lips twitched because me wearing tights was not quite the same as an ex-marine wearing tights.

"Who hired you and who asked you to deliver the phone?"

He stared at us for a while without answering, but he'd already come this far. "After the damn ballet lessons were set up, the same guy emailed me again. Larry. He asked if I could drop a phone off at Clockworks for our mutual friend."

"Lawrence Gifford?" Lawrence was behind the thefts? He was a lawyer, not a coder. Then again, lawyers did have a slimy reputation. Maybe his salary wasn't enough. He'd know all the rules when it came to selling to two sides of the same fence. Maybe he planned on representing himself if he got caught.

"That's the guy. Apparently he used to work at Clockworks and asked his contact there for my info. I didn't ask too many questions, not with an offer on the table."

"The phone delivery didn't sound fishy to you?" Mark asked.

Clint shrugged. "Not until you two showed up. How do you figure schlepping a phone to someone is weirder than being asked to teach a two-hour lesson in ballet for forty grand? Larry thought I was buddies with some friend of his at Clockworks. He sent me an email the morning of the lesson asking if I could drop a phone there when I was done. I sure as hell didn't care one way or the other."

Mark sat back. "And you didn't feel a need to let on that you weren't close friends with anyone at Clockworks because supposedly that referral had just netted you a lot of money."

"That about sums it up."

"Once Lawrence handed you a phone, you took the phone to Clockworks?" I prodded.

He shook his head. "No one gave me the phone. I was setting things up in the break room. People were coming and going. Believe me, I didn't wear those crazy tights outside of that building. You walk around in something like that, it can get you killed. I was in the bathroom changing into the ballet getup when someone left the phone on my bag."

I groaned. "It had to be Lawrence, though, right?" I looked at Mark.

"A good hacker could borrow his email," he pointed out.

Radar had certainly taught us that much. But Lawrence had worked both places. He'd know the players there and maybe he had taken the job with the intent to steal Borgot's code and sell it back to his old employer.

Clint pulled out an iPhone and swished a few pages. He held up the email. I read Lawrence's email for myself.

"Did you meet the guy at Clockworks at least?" I knew the answer before he started shaking his head. Whoever was adding translation code and working this thing had been very careful not to be seen with the phones and had avoided delivering anything in person.

"I left it at the front desk at Clockworks," Clint admitted.

"And no one contacted you to complain it was the wrong phone?"

It was Clint's turn to sit back. "What's wrong with the phone I delivered, and why is the delivery a problem in the first place?"

I glanced at Mark, but fair was fair. "It's a prototype from Borgot. No one should be getting one of our phones. When I fell off the beam, I switched out the phone on your workout bag with a different phone. I wondered what you were doing with a prototype when you obviously don't work for Borgot."

"What's on the phone that is so valuable?"

"Code that a competitor might want for their own phone," Mark supplied. He left out the part about how that same phone code might also be helping bring a smartwatch to market.

The boys played cat and mouse with twenty questions a while longer, but we had our information.

We finally took our leave after Clint agreed to let us know if Lawrence or anyone from Clockworks or Borgot contacted him again.

As we exited the building out the back door a brown UPS truck pulled up.

"Good thing he was expecting a delivery," I said.

Mark smiled. "Or we'd have had to make our own luck."

Mark looked up Clockworks on his phone.

"The building will be closed already," I said, knowing that wasn't necessarily a deterrent for someone as skilled as Mark. "But it's a computer company. There could easily be engineers staying late."

He nodded. "I'll need time to scope it before we go in."

I was very pleased to hear the "we" in that sentence. "When?"

"I'll check the building security features out tomorrow while you're at work. Late afternoon is usually a good time to visit. People are in a rush to get home, and they aren't paying attention to anyone who is entering or leaving. If the cameras aren't actively monitored, I can probably disable them for a short time, but we'll just be two people with a late appointment. A single guy like me would be more suspicious. With you along, we'll either look like co-workers or a random couple heading in and then out."

"Bonnie and Clyde were hoodlums together," I said.

He flashed a grin at me. "We won't be there to steal anything. We'll just take a look around. If we need someone to pretend to offer a business deal to obtain more information, we'll send in Steve."

"Okay," I agreed. Huntington was by far the better choice if a snooty businessman were required.

Chapter 29

If you ask me, ballet lessons were lower than the bar should be when it came to work obligations. And once you'd done that much at the behest of a company, surely they should leave you alone, at least for a few days. But this was Borgot, and we had a murderer in our midst and two unscheduled deaths on our tab.

The email was brief and provided driving directions along with the time of Joe Black's funeral scheduled for the afternoon.

"How about I show my dedication to my career and *not* attend?" I grumbled.

The last line, "We'll see everyone there," left no doubt that our attendance was mandatory.

I raised my eyes skyward, but instead of lightning, all I got was fluorescent bulbs. "Huntington, I demand a raise." Even though the part of the case he'd hired me for was probably solved now that Wanda Black had been arrested, surely attending the funeral of someone I didn't even like was call for a bonus or a permanent raise.

"I have religious reasons for not attending." I said it out loud to see how the excuse sounded. Lame. There were very likely some good religious excuses, but being Catholic didn't provide a single one. Catholics were big on funerals and pomp and everyone knew it.

I'd have to think of something else or hope for an inland hurricane. I texted Mark and let him know about the funeral. It might mean we'd have to shift the time for checking out Clockworks.

My cell phone buzzed almost immediately. I was expecting Mark, but it was his mother, LeAnn.

"Are we still supposed to attend the sewing circle tonight?" she asked.

I had completely forgotten about sewing. Imagine that. "We probably don't need to go. Surely that part of the case is resolved now that we know how phones were being used in robberies. And since I'm not likely to win the quilting contest, there's no point in my showing up again."

She laughed. "Not this year, but maybe next."

"I have to be at a funeral this afternoon anyway. It's the one for Joe. It doesn't start until four. I could leave there early if you think we should still show up to sew." Sewing beat a funeral. Not by much, but enough.

"You're kidding, right? Joe's funeral is the perfect opportunity to uncover his accomplices or the murderer! The killer always attends the funeral."

"He does? What if he's already dead?" My pet theory was that Cary had somehow offed Joe before the mafia bosses got to him.

"Could be," she agreed. "I'll meet you there. Give me the address."

Reluctantly, I complied, but what harm could there be in having her there? And I hadn't exactly involved her. Huntington was still responsible for that little piece of mayhem.

Monique stopped by to make sure I understood my presence at the funeral was required and also to share her happy news. "I bought the sculpture," she whispered dramatically, her hand over her heart. "It will be delivered next week. Rohit—you remember, the guy who came over to help—kept the sculpture to prepare it."

"Prepare it?"

"He's planting moss along the bottom and adding complete landscape details to it! I had to pay extra for the watering system, but he threw in the plants for free. It's going to be so gorgeous. I'll email you a picture of some of the flowers I've chosen. I wanted roses, but Rohit said they'd grow too large and be messy. What do you think?"

Since it would be impolite to point out that the thing was a standing monument to ugly and couldn't get much worse, I swallowed hard and searched for diplomacy. "The owner of the nursery swears by Rohit's expertise. Plant a climbing rosebush nearby, maybe?" And hope it eventually hid the sculpture from view.

"Oooh, that's a good idea. I'll ask him about it."

"Yay, verily," I muttered under my breath. "Verily? Since when do I say verily?" I stared at my test phone with consternation. "Stupid phone."

Kovid overheard my remark since he was in my doorway with more code on an SD card. "What's wrong with your phone?"

"Did you code it to use the word verily?"

He shrugged. "Maybe. There's an extensive dictionary, and the algorithm can choose from multiple answers."

"Hmph." I accepted the SD card from Kovid. "Is there support for Spanish on here?" I asked innocently.

"Of course not. Marketing is still pushing for it, but there's no way we can squeeze that in."

"What about just loading the dictionary? It would be crude—"

He shook his head vehemently. "It would be pointless. We haven't programmed the phone to respond to even single word translation."

"How long would it take to just add a raw dictionary translation? If I said 'water,' couldn't it say 'agua'?"

"Whose side are you on, anyway? You want to try and test all that? Even if we shoved that kind of mess into the code, you'd have to do extensive testing. And we'd be selling it to the customer as almost pure guesswork. It wouldn't be a voice assistant, it would be more like a random Google search. The translation could range from almost correct, to jumbled meaningless words, to a full blown ad."

Kovid did not appear to be coding anything on the side. "I guess we have to be more clever about the exact phrases we choose to translate," I said.

He nodded. "The first phrases will be the types of things you see in travel books like 'Where is the best restaurant?' or 'Where is my hotel?' The idea isn't just raw words translated. If we drop a dictionary in there, we can hardly market the idea of the translations being part of a personal assistant."

"I wonder if the translated words would sell if you hid it behind a special door. Then let early customers test it."

He rolled his eyes. "Now you sound like marketing and Cary combined. Customers don't want a 'test' phone! They want a working product."

"Okay, okay." I loaded the new code on my three phones, but instead of starting tests, I visited Roscoe. My plan was to play the same game with him, only butter up his ego because he was the kind of programmer who required that sort of thing or he wouldn't even agree to talk to a mere plebeian like myself.

Roscoe and Kovid were both smart enough to hack into Lawrence's email and set up the contact with Clint to pass along a new drop of code. They didn't need Lawrence, only his email.

I leaned against the doorway to Roscoe's cube. "You know how you were telling us about your super efficient code? Could you drop a Spanish to English raw dictionary in the code in a short time?"

He didn't bother to stop typing. "I can do *anything* I'm paid to do. But if you want quality, you have to wait. We're not robots, we're engineers. You want good code, you hire the best and let them do their job."

Blah, blah, blah. He had barely glanced over at me the whole time he was delivering his speech. "Well, what if the dictionary was dropped in but hidden? There are always blogs out there that dissect every electronic gadget released. What if you snuck something in there like that for them to discover? If it wasn't a confirmed feature, it wouldn't have to be perfect, but it could gain some notoriety if the right blogs discovered it and began talking about it. Then when we officially add the extra glamor of the assistant delivering knowledgeable answers in several languages, it could be a big hit."

"Or a complete flop. You're just Miss Idea, aren't you? I guess you haven't bothered to run this by Lawrence to see if it's patentable?"

I blinked. "Uhm, well, no."

He snorted. "Well, it's not. Tossing a dictionary in there just plays our hand early. No way is it patentable."

I stared at him as he turned back to his computer screen. He wasn't the type to lift a finger to do any extra work, but if something was patentable, he might hire out to the highest bidder.

As I stomped away, I heard a "hiisst" from another cubicle. I turned around and peered through the opening.

Howard reached up as though to adjust a tie, but he was wearing a blue polo shirt with gray khakis. "He's right. Not patentable. If the way to access the Spanish dictionary were clever enough, we could possibly patent that, but you have to have something to bank on, something that is good enough to keep investors interested. If you want to run an idea by Lawrence or myself, it really helps if you have the basic code in place along with a complete diagram of the engineering."

I sighed. If I had the code in place, maybe I'd sell it upriver and not bother with these people. "Yeah, thanks, I'll get right on that." I didn't bother to tell him I wasn't gunning for a patent, but the thought made me curious. "If Borgot gets a patent, does your name go on it automatically as the lawyer filing it?"

He blinked a little owl blink and huffed out a sigh. "Only the *inventors* belong on the patent." Red crept up his neck. "Just testing the invention doesn't count either."

I turned away before he got any angrier, but his comment made me wonder how Lawrence had gotten on a patent. He had one; I remembered seeing it listed when I looked up the executive names. But selling our code upriver—or was it downriver? Either direction wouldn't help Lawrence or Howard get on a patent. Maybe Lawrence didn't want another patent so he now sold his ideas to the highest bidder?

Instead of starting a test, I pounced on Paul, the IT guy, because he foolishly happened to walk by. "Did you get started in this business as a programmer?"

He hiked up his khaki shorts with one hand and frowned at me. He hadn't shaved that morning, and possibly not the morning before that. "Yeah, right. Cary already offered me a programming job. I'm not into that stuff. I'm not doing ballet either. Look, if you people want programmers, drop the hiring freeze and hire some programmers. I don't care if they make more money, and there is no job that pays well enough for me to dance around with my co-workers."

"You got that right," I nodded my agreement as he stomped off. If his hating the idea of being a programmer was a ruse, he had managed to sound as put off with it as with ballet lessons.

I visited the two other testers in my group and three marketing people. I even asked Heather, Monique's replacement as the head of marketing, about programming. She didn't know what I meant. She just started complaining about her DVD player not recording her shows properly.

It made sense to talk to Lawrence and find out whether he'd ever been a programmer. His name and address had been on the email that set up the ballet lessons and the phone drop. But what if he was guilty? Would I be showing my hand by questioning him? And I bet Monique had access to his email. Howard probably had access to it too. Monique had said she was planning on setting up the team building exercise. Maybe the two of them were in cahoots to sell and market Borgot code to thieves.

Of course, Monique didn't sit still long enough to code. If she needed an alibi for just about anything, including the murders, she could turn in her cell phone records. With all the phone calls she made, there wasn't any time left over to write code. Larry was out of the office more than in, but there was no telling what he was working on when prying eyes weren't around.

I passed by his cube twice, but he wasn't in. Maybe the smart thing to do was to ask Monique if Larry had a programming background. The only problem with that plan was that she was yakking on her cell when I waltzed by.

These questions were a waste of my time. Even if someone admitted they knew how to code, we still had to prove that same someone was adding to the Borgot code and selling it to Clockworks.

I settled down to work for several hours, but it was very hard to concentrate. Near the end of the day I made another round of the cubes, inspecting the name tags on each one, trying to figure out who might be adding extra code to the Borgot phones.

I paused near the cube of the one other person who probably had access to most of our email accounts. I stuck my head in. Kay set up meetings on behalf of several people at the company even though she reported directly to the CEO.

She gave me one of her raised eyebrow sneers and chuckled when I casually asked her if she spoke Spanish or knew how to code. "I should have gotten my degree in programming," she said agreeably. "Instead, I waitressed my way through college and busted my butt to earn a geology degree. Yet, here I am." She spread her arms wide to indicate her cubicle. Not even the admin for the CEO had an office at Borgot. Granted, her space was twice the size of mine, and she had somehow managed to have the walls done in a paisley fabric instead of corporate gray, but we were all rats in the same maze, no matter how you decorated it.

"We need all the help we can get with this phone," I said. "There's got to be someone who can help with the code."

I waited, but she didn't bite. If she knew of anyone harboring secret skills, she wasn't sharing.

As I turned to go, she asked, "You leaving for the funeral now?"

I sighed. "Is it four already?"

"Three-fifteen. Some managers might have mentioned they'd like me to write down names." While I processed her hint, she removed her heels and extracted flats from a large tote bag. She unclipped an amethyst pendant from her silver chain, leaving the subdued silver necklace as her only jewelry. The red shoes had brightened up a dark pantsuit. With the black penny loafers replacing the heels, she was now perfectly dressed in funeral attire.

"Seriously?" I asked. "You're jotting down roll call?"

She nodded. "No joke. If there had been any geology job out there that paid, I'd be hunting and cataloging rocks. Instead I work with people who have their heads full of pebbles, and I get to catalog infractions." She picked up her computer tablet and stashed it in a black purse. The red tote with her heels went under the desk.

I shuffled out. I didn't care about my name being on a list for missing Joe Black's funeral. If I hadn't told LeAnn I'd be there, I might have skipped just to be contrary.

***

I waited outside the funeral home for as long as possible, but LeAnn was a no-show. The sedate little building was shaped to resemble a chapel with steps leading up to large double doors. The guy posted at the door was the size of a tank, decked out in a leather vest and motorcycle chaps. Tats circled one arm, crooked teeth poked from beneath his upper lip, and he either forgot to comb his hair or it had recently been on fire, making it impossible to force the stray knotted bits down over the various bald patches. Maybe he'd been in a fight and someone had pulled clumps out. The gold hoop earring in his right ear looked as though it had been yanked on a number of times because that earlobe was long and distorted, almost double the size of his left ear. He had not shaved in days, and the speckled stubble was mottled gray and black. If he were competing for the world's ugliest dog title he'd lose, but only because at his feet was a bulldog mix of some sort that had obviously won the title.

When I reached the top step he put his hand on the doorknob. "You here for Joe or his ma?" he growled out.

"What?" I stuttered, backing down a step. While I contemplated running away, LeAnn appeared behind me and grabbed my arm, panting.

"Yes," she gasped out.

His beady gaze drifted to her. She met his stare with bravery that had to come from having survived childbirth and the raising of children. Or insanity.

My feet shuffled, but LeAnn held steady, albeit breathing hard.

"Joe's side on the left. His ma on the right," the man holding the doorknob declared.

"It's divided? Like a wedding?" I sputtered.

LeAnn cocked her head sideways and gave him a respectful nod. It was easy to be respectful when the guy towered over us by two feet and had us by a yard on either side. He was either carrying a retractable whip or a baton on his hip, and he kept his hand near it, hooked in a pocket.

"Your dog is adorable," LeAnn said. "Is it okay if I pat her on the head?"

Tank's eyes lit up, and he showed more crooked teeth than an aging dinosaur. "Harley. She's more'n happy to say hello."

LeAnn matched his smile, if not his teeth, and crouched down to greet Harley. "We're in Wanda's sewing group," she said. The dog showed her approval by trying to wag half her butt off. The slobbering growling noises she made were either because LeAnn represented a tasty snack or because Harley was very enthusiastic about being petted.

I double checked to make sure Tank wasn't any closer to drawing his baton weapon and offered my fingers to Harley for a sniff. The mutt, who had four different colored paws, made more gurgles and accepted a petting from me as well.

"Wanda's a good egg," Tank said. "Her son got her in with the wrong crowd. We take care of our own."

Harley looked up and whined at the threat in her owner's voice.

"Weren't some members of your own gang the ones who introduced Joe to—" I started.

"Fleet. We have a fleet, not a gang." His finger jabbed at me to emphasize his point. "And those kids were Joe's friends, not his ma's."

I nodded my agreement before he loomed any closer. "Well, sure."

Without further stalling, we scooted past. Most Borgot employees sat on the left. That alone would have convinced me to take the right side, but LeAnn had already declared our loyalties. She parked us directly behind Joe's "ma," much closer than I'd have ever sat on my own. Of course, had I come on my own, after seeing Tank I might have claimed a robbery was in progress and left.

Wanda sat in the first row, her ankle monitor almost completely hidden by jeans that had torn seams at the bottoms to make room for boots. She wasn't wearing her motorcycle boots today; they probably didn't allow it because the ankle monitor would never have fit.

The funeral home was dead cold. I shook that thought from my head. I was sweating profusely, which was ridiculous given the freezing drafts in the place. Were they running the air conditioner this early in the springtime? Maybe they did it so the bodies wouldn't smell. I choked back that thought as well, focusing instead on the scent of flowers. The only problem was there was a noticeable lack of blooms near the casket. Two tall stands of lilies shouted, "standard funeral home provision." A smallish vase near the pulpit had a card bearing Borgot's logo. Well, thank God someone had thought of flowers. I certainly hadn't, and it didn't look as though Joe had many friends.

Everyone on this side of the aisle, excluding ourselves, was dressed in mostly black leather and tight jeans with boots, or a combination of the two. They all took up two seats because a helmet was placed next to each person.

My cell phone buzzed. It took me a few extra-long seconds to extract it from my jacket pocket. For the first time, I envied Radar and his smartwatch. If I had one, I could have discretely glanced at the watch to see who was calling and possibly sent a response without ever showing my phone. It was bad form to pull out a cell during a funeral, although technically the funeral hadn't started yet. LeAnn was busy on her phone too so it was probably acceptable, at least until things got started.

Checking my phone, I saw the text was from her.

"I arrived early," she texted. "Put large black watch on his arm."

His. Arm. I glanced at the casket, my eyes wide. She had put a watch on Joe's arm? Was she crazy?

My phone buzzed again. "Can't see the watch clearly without pushing sleeve up," she texted.

I swallowed hard, wanting to ask just how she had managed this task, but the answer arrived without any prodding.

"Showed up early, but had to duck in a closet and hide until the coast was clear."

I closed my eyes momentarily and then typed, "We aren't planning on mentioning this to Mark, right?"

"Already texted him."

I looked up to find her grinning at me, her face flushed with pride or from whatever Mark had texted in return. I gave her a nod. She was a brave woman.

She texted me again. "We'll keep our eyes glued to the subject. Catch anyone fiddling with sleeve."

I wasn't gluing anything to that idiot. I'd had more than enough of Joe.

LeAnn put her cell inside her voluminous canvas bag. She then extracted a neat pile of kerchiefs. There was a pink one with delicate lace on the edges, a blue one that looked more practical and two nice big white ones. She tapped Wanda on the shoulder and handed her the stack. "From the sewing girls," she whispered. "Made them this morning."

Wanda turned and blinked at us. When recognition dawned, her jaw dropped. She worked it back up, but it fell again. We were the reason she was in jail, but our cover was good. No way would anyone think we had pulled off that arrest on purpose, because it certainly hadn't gone as planned.

Wanda finally reached up a tentative hand and accepted the hankies. She fingered them for a moment or two before nodding her thanks and turning back around.

LeAnn whipped another two out of her bag and handed one to me. It was a very soft cotton in a flower print. The edges were perfectly finished. I wasn't about to cry over Joe, but the hankies were nice enough to bring a tear to my eye.

Just as I relaxed back in my seat, Tank rolled through the middle aisle and took the three seats next to Wanda. One was for his helmet, the other was for his dog.

Mark sat down next to me as the funeral director took the mic.

Chapter 30

Joe's mother didn't offer a eulogy, and who could blame her? It wouldn't sound good to say, "My son got himself killed, and his criminal activities got me arrested."

When LeAnn offered Mark a kerchief, he rolled his eyes and shook his head sharply. I covered up a laugh by pretending to sneeze.

The funeral director intoned peaceful cliches about "moving on" and read a poem about hills and valleys and journeys. The whole presentation would have been more successful had the guy not borne a striking resemblance to Ichabod Crane right before he lost his head.

I shifted in my seat in order to scan the room behind me.

The Borgot employees were stacked together like dominoes ready to fall. Roscoe was definitely typing on a tablet. Lawrence wore an impressive dark blue wool suit that went well with Monique's subdued pantsuit. She dressed it up with extremely high heels and a small nose stud. We all had to be grateful that there was probably nothing painted on her butt.

Howard must have called in reinforcements because he was sitting near a couple of guys I had never seen before. The three of them looked like a lineup for an Eddie Bauer flyer, casual professional. Then again, maybe the two unknowns were with Paul, the IT guy. He was in the same row dressed in his shorts and ever-present sandals with socks. He probably didn't own anything other than eight sets of the same. He reminded me of Radar when we first met; uncomfortable in the light of day with a touch of panic about him. Kovid wasn't much better, fidgeting and earning a glare from Heather and Kay at the same time. I doubt he noticed or cared.

The surprise attendant was Clint, our mysterious ballerina ex-marine. He sat near the back on our side, next to two of the ladies from the sewing group. Barb, the owner of the shop, was too nice a person to miss the funeral. The rest of the chairs were peppered with the motorcycle gang, er, fleet members.

I completely expected to see Detective Saunders and Adrian standing at the back of the room, and they didn't disappoint. Saunders grimaced an accusatory stare in my direction. I wrinkled my nose and turned around lest he decide I was obviously the perpetrator because I dared peek at the other attendees.

When it came time for us to offer condolences and respect at the casket, I kept myself planted. Not only did I not want to greet Wanda, I had nothing to offer that casket. Besides, it was my duty to watch for anyone who might show an interest in a half-hidden watch.

Mark squeezed my wrist, and whispered, "Stay put." He found a place against the wall where he could keep track of people offering their respects.

Tank must have been expecting trouble or perhaps he just enjoyed scaring people because he stood to the left of Wanda as though he was her personal bodyguard. His stance blocked LeAnn's view and part of mine.

Undeterred, she hopped over my legs to Mark's abandoned seat.

We watched. Mark watched. The policemen watched us all. Joe's mother kept her composure, but her hands shook when she accepted the clasps from some of her friends. Borgot employees streamed past almost as a single entity. Roscoe didn't even pretend to pay his respects to the casket; both he and Kovid bolted down the center aisle without looking back.

Lawrence and Monique minced their way past, heads mostly down. The rest of the group seemed to end up in front of the casket at the same time, blocked by Lawrence who had to stop suddenly because Harley had shuffled into the center aisle. The dog sniffed studiously at his shoes and may have drooled on them because Lawrence jumped back, bumping Monique. She hit Howard. For a few moments, everyone was shifting and shuffling, searching for personal space.

Lawrence finally edged around the dog, but Monique was having a harder time of it in her high heels.

I glanced at Mark. He was surveying those left in front of the casket. Good. With so many people standing there, it was impossible for me to see what any one individual might try.

Tank finally realized Harley was blocking traffic. He patted the side of his chaps and Harley lifted her head. She gave a quiet woof rumble and dragged her rolls back over.

The dam broke.

When all had cleared, Joe was still in his casket. If anyone had tampered with him, I couldn't tell. LeAnn slumped beside me in frustration.

The rest of the line went through smoothly. Before I had a chance to decide whether it was necessary to offer further condolences, Tank stepped up, raised his hand and closed the casket. It slammed shut rather hard, a ponderous, final thud.

Tank's friends were prepared. Without further ado, they marched Joe down the aisle and outside.

The detectives remained by the doors, watching us stragglers.

I let the casket get a head start and then stood. LeAnn was right behind me.

Ichabod disappeared through a side door.

Mark and LeAnn flanked me, which meant I didn't have to pretend to stop and talk to the detectives. They followed us right out, though.

The bright sunlight had me blinking tears that I hadn't managed for Joe. I sucked in a lungful of fresh air, one that wasn't canned and wasn't as cold as the frozen air inside the viewing room. We stood with a few others on various levels of the steps, waiting for the crowd to disperse.

Tank and the other pall bearers slid the casket into the back of a hearse. The young driver, in an ill-fitting black suit, hurried behind the wheel and slammed the door. The bang of that door was too reminiscent of the casket closing. The boom silenced the already subdued crowd.

We all watched as the long black car shot away from the curb.

"We don't have to visit the gravesite, right?" I whispered.

"There's usually a ceremony there. We probably should," LeAnn replied.

"That driver left in a hurry," Mark said, sounding puzzled. "Doesn't at least one family member usually travel in the hearse?" We all looked around for Joe's mother, but she hadn't come out yet. "He could have at least waited for the pall bearers to get in their vehicles."

"You mean on their motorcycles," I corrected.

"Whatever."

The hearse was already well down the road. It turned at the stop sign and sped out of sight.

We started down the steps again. From behind us, Ichabod burst out the doors.

"Are the police here? Is anyone an official with the police department?" he gasped out. His adam's apple bobbed as if it were diving after a lottery dunk. Long, bony fingers wiped sweat from his forehead.

Adrian snapped around. "What's the problem?"

Ichabod pointed down the road, but the hearse had already disappeared from view. "My driver was in the back room, tied up! I stopped to untie him, but someone just stole my hearse!"

Before Adrian could jump back up the two steps, Tank loosed a caveman roar. "Let's get'm, riders! No one disrespects our dead!"

I wasn't sure Joe was really one of them, especially since Tank had separated the crowd, but apparently it didn't matter to the clan of bikers at this particular moment. Leather and metal flashed.

Instead of following the cops, Mark followed Tank. He hopped on a bike that had a lightning bolt down the side. I recognized it and sucked in a worried breath.

LeAnn crossed her arms. "Well. That plan went to hell. This place is totally disorganized. It's no wonder someone stole the hearse. You should see the back room in this place. It's a miracle they get the right bodies in the right caskets. I've never seen such an unorganized mess. I just about died in that closet, it was so jammed with paperwork that should have been filed last decade." She stomped down the steps and then glanced back over her shoulder. "Are you coming?"

"Where are we going?" Gamely, I skipped down beside her.

She waved up the road. "They'll never catch him. Whoever it was will figure out the watch is a fake. We may as well go back to your place and wait for Mark to report."

I agreed. With Mark on the chase, we wouldn't be making it to Clockworks today.

In all the excitement, there hadn't been a chance to ask Clint who had invited him to the funeral of a guy he couldn't have met unless maybe Joe had worked at Clockworks. It was too late to ask now. Along with the rest of the revelers, he was long gone.

Chapter 31

LeAnn headed for the sewing table as soon as we arrived at my place. I headed for the kitchen. To each their own unwinding mechanism.

While I concocted a chocolate mousse pie to calm down, she held up one end of the tank top I had cut out. She flipped it and studied it from the other end, but that didn't seem to provide any additional clues.

"Tank top," I said. "I cut the pattern from one I found on the web. Well, it was a t-shirt, but I messed it up."

"The stretch has to go right to left, not up and down. You'll never get this on."

I didn't tell her that I never planned to finish it, especially since that part of the case was solved. "Yeah. Probably." I left her to her hobby and attended mine.

The pie was in the fridge setting up by the time Mark arrived. Dusk was already darkening corners of the yard outside.

LeAnn had helpfully sorted all the thread and fabrics by color. Neat little stacks had been stowed in bags she must have sewn while I cooked. "Thanks," I said.

She shook out the tank top, eyed me and then the top. "I think it will fit."

I hadn't even noticed the tank, but I smiled and accepted it before addressing Mark. "The driver escaped, didn't he?"

"Clean as a whistle. He didn't drive far before he ducked into a side road, pushed the casket out and liberated the watch." Mark turned his accusing gaze on his mother. "It might have been better if Joe hadn't been wearing a watch in the first place."

"Nonsense," I said. "It was a great plan. It just didn't happen quite as expected. It does prove that the guilty party was in attendance because someone noticed that watch and wanted it."

"Don't worry, dear." LeAnn stood on her tiptoes and kissed his cheek. "I wasn't at risk and neither was Sedona. I didn't tell her what I was up to."

He glanced at me. I nodded. I hadn't had any idea she had planned to add a watch to Joe.

"I have to get home," she said. "I was hoping you'd run the guy to ground. Do you think the pie is ready?" she asked me.

It wasn't, but mousse was just as good lumped in a container for later as it was firmed up. I boxed up a generous piece.

After LeAnn left, Mark helped himself to a piece of the soft pie. "If she had invited you along to sneak that watch on the corpse, you'd have gone, wouldn't you?"

I pretended to ponder the question, my eyes sliding up and down. I drummed my fingers on the table. "You know how women sometimes ask whether a particular outfit makes their butt look fat?"

He blinked and then frowned. "Yeah, why?"

"You know how you're smart enough to avoid or not answer that kind of question?"

He nodded.

I nodded. "Me too," I said.

The confusion on his face cleared. He grunted and shook his head. "I think that's a yes. But I knew that before I asked."

The phone Radar and Turbo had left sitting on my counter beeped.

I about jumped out of my skin. Mark went for his gun. He positioned himself next to the back door in the blink of an eye. "Can you shut the security features off?" he asked quietly. "Before Miley starts dancing out there?"

With the lights on in the kitchen, it was impossible to see anything in the dark yard outside. I crab-crawled to the phone on the kitchen counter. The watch had lit up and "Security Breach" showed on the face.

Luckily, per my request, there was a list of instructions taped to the phone. Unluckily, the phone emitted a second warning beep. Hurriedly, I read through the instructions and figured out what to press to disable the various features. I punched each icon and then selected "disable," while Mark attempted to see out the bedroom window.

He was back by the door very quickly. "Can you turn on the floodlights without any of the water or dancing? On the count of three?" He crouched, one hand on the knob.

I sat, cross-legged and scanned the list. "Okay, on three. Start counting."

Luckily, I recognized the floodlight icon. By the time he would have said four, the floodlights came on, and he had rolled out the door, coming up ready to fire.

Somehow, Miley must have also come on because the sudden noise from out back was very loud. "Crap." Had I not disabled her? Frantically, I punched the disable for the robot, but the chatter and screaming hoots continued at full pitch.

Mark rolled back inside the door and slammed it shut. He stayed on the floor, breathing harder than normal.

"Are you hurt?" I dropped the phone and scurried over, frantic.

"Ra...ccoons."

"What?"

"Raccoons," he repeated. "Those damn things are worse than rabid dogs. I didn't want to have to shoot them."

I stretched up in order to peek through the window. Sure enough, the floodlights illuminated three raccoons the size of small German Shepherds scampering about the backyard. They were responsible for the shrill noises, not Miley.

While I watched, one returned to excavating the garden. Blast his hide, there was already a hole large enough for me to fall into and be swallowed. There were two smaller holes nearby and enough other spots to make the whole plot resemble a whack-a-mole game.

"Beasts." I dove for the phone again.

"Miley might be enough to frighten them off," Mark said, standing so he could watch.

"They'd probably just tear her arms off. Radar made the thing so that the arms and legs detach easily. They can be replaced with other tools."

"How do you know that?"

I held up the list. "Precise instructions." I punched in the manual start for the last icon. The sprinklers, which were more like blasts from a paintball gun, gushed.

The raccoons bellowed more protests, but they did leave. Mark watched them waddle away, noting that one climbed the fence and the other two wedged through a spot behind a bush. "I'll fix that fence in the morning. But it might not keep them out."

I worked on shutting off the security features before my neighbor called.

Chapter 32

Next morning, before I even got out of bed, Mark propositioned me. "Too bad you have to go to work," he said. Unfortunately, he was not snuggled suggestively next to me. He stared up at the ceiling with his hands behind his head.

"Hmm. What did you have in mind?"

"I want to check out the Clockworks place this morning. I haven't had much time for research, but I've checked the security on the place. There's enough traffic and more than one company in the building. We can blend in easily." He grabbed his phone from above his head where it rested on my bookcase headboard and began typing.

"Good idea. I'll text in sick, indigestion from rice cakes."

He stopped swiping at his phone. "What rice cakes?"

"They served some at the ballet lessons the other day, and they've been sitting on the counter in the break room ever since."

He lifted up on one elbow and scanned my face. "You didn't eat rice cakes."

"Of course not."

"This job isn't working out very well for you, is it?"

"How can it possibly last? Two people were murdered the same week, someone is selling the bread and butter code to another company, and the lead lawyer is ordering ballet lessons for the programmers."

"When you put it that way, it doesn't sound much like a dream job."

I shrugged. "I can find another one."

"Maybe we should stop finding you jobs and let you actually find your own."

I grinned. "There's an idea."

He looked down and studied his phone for a few more seconds. "Did you know Clockworks is out by Dave's Garden?"

I started to shake my head, but changed my mind. "I wonder if it's in the new office building across the street. There's a huge fancy clock with the building directory underneath."

He nodded. "That's the place. Top floor. The news cycle I just checked says it has gone bankrupt. It will be interesting to see who still works there or who has been picking up phones. The location would make it very easy for someone from Clockworks to have met Joe at Dave's Garden during a garden meeting. Anyone from that building could walk across the road and pick up a phone with rogue code on it."

"And who would notice such a clandestine meeting, especially if it took place during a legitimate lunch break?" I hopped out of bed, made my excuses to work via text, and showered.

* * *

Had I been nosing about Clockworks for information by myself, I'd have stopped at the reception desk first and nervously asked a bunch of nosy questions about the company. It was vastly more fun to watch Mark in action. He barely glanced at the reception desk, other than to give the guy sitting there a short nod. He didn't keep his head down to avoid the cameras, nor did he change his smooth stride. He didn't try to appear "important businessman" even though it was a look he could pull off if he cared to.

He just strode to the elevators without checking the directory, like he'd been here before and had no interest in anything special.

When the door closed behind us, he put his arm around me and pretended to nuzzle my neck. "There is a back exit if you walk past the elevators. If we leave in a hurry, we take that route."

I had seen the doors. Mark was rubbing off on me in more ways than one.

When the bell chimed for three, we exited. In front of us, there was a glass door, locked. Behind it, there were other solid doors that likely led to offices. Light from a big window at the end of the hall lit the place. Maybe because Clockworks was supposedly bankrupt, only every other fluorescent light was illuminated.

Mark patted his pockets. There was a badge scanner to the right of the door. The scanner light was off. I wasn't surprised when Mark pulled out his keys, the ones with his lock picks. He made it look as though he was trying more than one key while he picked the lock. Then, very politely, he held the door for me. He was always prepared.

I started counting the minutes. If the guard behind the reception desk was watching camera monitors, he'd have seen us enter. He probably couldn't tell a pick from a key on the camera feed, and Mark was quick with the lock picks.

My heart still beat faster. Maybe I should have stayed downstairs and chatted with the guy while Mark came up here to see what he could learn. "When you said Clockworks went bankrupt, I didn't expect the place to be completely shut down." I kept my voice very low.

"Me either. Not with phones being delivered to the reception desk."

There were no visible cameras inside the area, but the doors were locked, two pairs on either side of the hallway. Mark unlocked the first and we slipped inside. There was an open space that had partially torn down cubicles with a few offices along the outside wall.

I checked the office doors. They weren't locked, but the rooms were empty except for giant dustballs drifting aimlessly.

We checked the area in silence, opening the remaining cubicle desks to look for remnants and glancing at the squiggles on the white boards. The few pens and paperclips left were not the types of things that offered extensive clues.

We exited. I checked the bathrooms while Mark opened one of the doors on the other side of the main hallway. The remaining door at the far end was a fire exit stairwell. Mark pointed to it to make sure I saw it.

The other side of the office hallway wasn't as empty as the first area, but the equipment made little sense. While there were two laptops sitting on a table, the rest of the place looked like a wizard's laboratory. Two giant five-gallon office water bottles contained some kind of brown murky sludge. If it was meant to be fresh water for the office, it had gone seriously bad. The place had a musty smell, almost like bread, or maybe there were questionable contents leaking from the fridge against the wall.

"Beer brewing," Mark said quietly, but not without a slight question in his voice.

Now that he pointed that out, I noted the case of empty beer bottles and what looked suspiciously like a keg. My mind had associated those items with one hell of an office party, not brewing.

I headed for the computers, bumping the one laptop so that it came out of sleep mode. On the table with the two laptops, five watches and three Borgot phones were scattered about. The watches were replicas of the one Joe had worn, but only one had a band. It was a silicone band unlike the worn leather one on Joe's watch.

Had Joe somehow gotten in here, and stolen the watch when he dropped off code?

The Borgot phones made sense. Smartwatches worked with a phone—showing who was calling, showing text messages, and if whoever ran this place had any say, the smartwatch would run Borgot's translation programs. The table also contained an iPhone and a Samsung phone. Whoever was working on this project wanted the translation code to work on more than just Borgot phones.

Since the computer was sitting there, I used it to do a quick search on Clockworks while Mark finished searching and took inventory of the rest of the place to make sure we hadn't missed anything.

The place certainly looked as though someone was using the empty building to finish the smartwatch project. I didn't see how they thought they could manufacture the things with two or three test watches, but then, not being of a criminal mind, there were probably a lot of things about stealing programming code that I didn't understand.

The internet told me that Clockworks hadn't been a public company. It was a startup funded by the usual "angel" investors. The venture capitalists hadn't given it more than two years before funding dried up. The company had disbanded at the end of last year.

At least one employee hadn't given up on the idea of a smartwatch. Now that the project lacked legit funding and engineers, that someone had decided to just steal the code from Borgot and brew beer in the extra space.

I wrinkled my nose. The smell of yeast and whatnot wasn't really unpleasant, but there was definitely an odor to it. The equipment took up more room than the laptop and watches. Maybe Joe had been in on the beer stuff, and when he moved back in with his mother, he couldn't take it with him so he moved it here.

I frowned. Joe didn't have the experience or ambition to brew beer. You had to know how to follow specific recipes and buy the grains and hops and...hops.

Mark caught my wide-eyed stare. He moved closer in a hurry.

"You need hops for beer, right?" I asked quietly.

"Yeah, why?" he whispered back.

"I think I know who is working here on the sly."

Chapter 33

We drove straight over to Dave's Garden. My heart was racing. Was Dave's new assistant guilty of murder? Would he shoot us in broad daylight?

I wiped one sweaty palm down my jeans as Mark pulled the SUV into the parking lot. Dave's Garden opened early. It should be easy for Mark to get a good look at Rohit.

"Rohit is definitely the guy who talked Dave into carrying brewery supplies," I said. "Dave also mentioned he was lucky to have been able to hire him because he had been laid off at the end of last year. The timing fits."

"Show me who he is, and I'll stake out Clockworks for a few days. If I don't see this guy come and go into the Clockworks area, I can add a camera. Now that we know the place is supposed to be closed down, whoever is working in there is pretty obviously the guilty party."

I waited for Mark to join me on my side of the SUV. We both studied the garden center from the parking lot. There were plenty of exits since most of the place was outdoors, but the area was a maze of plants, trellises, the main building and two greenhouses.

"They know me here," I said. "I'll buy a plant and talk to Rohit. I'll keep him talking long enough so that he's distracted, and you can memorize what he looks like."

Mark finally took his eyes off the landscaping in front of us. "Talk to him about what?"

"I'll make something up about gardening. You can watch the exchange without him ever seeing you. That way he won't be suspicious later if he sees you watching the building."

"He won't see me."

When Mark worked undercover, he gave blending in a whole new meaning. He'd been disguised as a creepy thug the first time I'd seen him. "Wouldn't it be better if he didn't see you at all? Not that we can use Huntington to play at being a venture capitalist since Clockworks is already defunct, but your brother does look like you."

Mark nodded perfunctorily. "Okay. I'll wander around. I assume if you talk to the older guy you told me about I'm to know that is Dave and not Rohit?"

I nodded. "I'll try to just corner Rohit, but Dave does have some plants on order for me so if he sees me, he's likely to come over. He'll be the one in the farmer coverall things." I did another scan, but didn't see either man. The outside booth was empty. This early on a work day, there weren't many customers around either.

"Rohit was in shorts when I saw him last time, but it was much later in the day." The breeze was cool, and I was glad to be wearing jeans. I could have used a jacket for my bare arms, but the goosebumps were more from nerves than cold.

We separated, and I took my time picking out the smallest blueberry bush available in a black quart-sized container. Dave was talking to a customer over in the tree section, waving the man toward the main building. I hurried to beat them. If Dave was helping customers, Rohit was likely inside at the checkout counter. There was often a part-time clerk on weekends, and I'd have to hope that person wasn't here now instead of Rohit.

I paused to the side of the doorway to let my eyes adjust to the inside light. I smiled. *Paydirt.*

Rohit was working the counter. His brown hair wasn't smashed down by sunglasses this time, but he still had the goatee. I noticed a watch on his arm. The face was big enough to be a smartwatch. My deep breath hitched a bit, but I sauntered up to the counter anyway. The blueberry bush was dripping muddy water, and it wasn't the variety I wanted, but Rohit wouldn't know that Dave had some others on order for me.

I handed the scrappy twigged plant to him to ring up, wondering how to get him to step outside so that Mark could get a look at him. "Hey, didn't you work at Clockworks across the street?" I thought my opening question was casual enough, but Rohit's eyes went wide. Maybe some criminals have a sixth sense that the game is up or maybe his guilty conscience burst like a dam.

He threw the bush at me, plastic pot and all. It caught me square in the chest, scratching my arms on the way down and liberally splattering muddy globs. "Hey!"

Dave froze in the side doorway where he was holding it open for the customer he'd been helping.

I lunged after Rohit, but he leaped for the front door, knocking over a shelf full of fish emulsion fertilizer. At least two of the plastic gallon containers burst as they hit the floor.

Knowing their contents, I jumped high and wide, hitting a rack of seeds. The seeds scattered, sounding like drops of rain against the concrete floor. From the seaweed stink of the leaking fish emulsion, the seeds would be well fertilized.

"Stop him!" I yelled to no one in particular.

Dave did nothing of the sort. He put his hands on his hips in exasperation and opened his mouth to say something. I had no idea what he bellowed. I hopped the mess on the floor and chased after Rohit out the front door.

I skidded to a halt as soon as I cleared the entrance. Mark was waiting behind the lineup of sculptures on the right. He'd catch Rohit easily before he made the parking lot.

Well, he would have except that Rohit glanced back at me and plowed right into the largest sculpture by the walkway. It was an ugly looking swan that was just sprouting green from whatever was trying to grow in the peat moss or straw.

Mark grabbed at Rohit. He got one arm and a lot of swan. The three of them danced an odd tripping waltz with Rohit's arm wrapped around the neck of the swan.

I dashed over to help, but the swan's neck snapped and Mark lost his grip against the struggling Rohit.

Rohit ran, yanking on sculptures to block our path as he went.

As I came even with Mark, Rohit nearly tripped us both with one particularly tall tangle of metal and plants. The towering monument was an ugly thing with green moss all along the bottom and pansies hanging from some sort of copper bucket. "Hey, isn't this the sculpture for Monique?" I grabbed at a blue octopus arm for balance as I tried to dodge it. There might have been strawberry vines poking out of the holes until my flailing hands ripped the octopus completely off the sculpture. The ceramic shattered on impact with the ground.

I was mad enough to grab a piece of strawberry plant dirt and throw it hard at Rohit, scoring a hit on the back of his head. "Stop!" I panted.

Mark didn't need any more of my help; he was faster and more agile. He closed in and locked a leg under one of Rohit's.

For a half a second, he held Rohit up by one arm and a handful of hair.

Rohit fell to his knees. Mark kept him there by twisting his head to one side and planting a foot on the back of one leg. The fight went out of Rohit on a gasp for air.

"I thought you were going to ask him a couple of innocent gardening questions," Mark said to me.

"I just asked if he ever worked at Clockworks!"

"Okay, okay, I give up!" Rohit pleaded. "I did it, I accepted the code, and I knew it was stolen. I knew it came from Borgot. Dave told me you hunt down crooks and thieves and to watch out for you. I knew when you asked about my old job that my ticket was punched."

I blinked. Dave had said he warned Rohit about me, but not because he thought Rohit was a crook. "Who gave you the Borgot code?" I demanded.

He sucked in deep lungfuls of air. "I don't know."

"Liar!"

He tried to shrug, but with his head twisted, he could barely move. "Clockworks was my dream. I worked my way through college selling beer and risking everything because I didn't have a license to sell booze. I tutored for half the departments, and I saved every penny! At first, the venture capitalists were hungry to join the company, but we couldn't stay on schedule, and there were always other companies after the venture capitalist money. When the money demanded I step aside so they could put in one of their own as CEO and control everything, I refused."

I caught Mark's eyes. "And they withheld the cash."

"There was no point in succeeding if I couldn't do it my way! And they wanted me out completely. Sure, they offered me a vice president job, but I knew what would happen. I'd seen it before."

He was right, of course. Venture capitalists tended to dump founders at the first opportunity. They didn't want big dreams; they wanted someone they could control. The consolation prize that was offered would quickly turn into a nudging towards the door and no job at all.

"If you don't know who was coding the phone and language parts, how did you get the code at all?" I asked.

Mark let up on his hold. Rohit collapsed down onto the dirt. He rolled over and sat up, but didn't try to stand. Instead he put his face in his hands, his shoulders shaking with dry sobs. One sandal had been knocked askew, but still dangled from his ankle by the top velcro strap.

I resented the fact that he hadn't collected nearly as much dirt on his person as me. "Well?" I demanded. "How did you get the code?"

It took him more than a few moments to collect himself, but eventually he started talking. "I was cleaning out the Clockworks office and selling off equipment when a package came in. It was an offer to keep delivering the phone end of the code that was needed to work with the watches we had started."

"For a price?"

He nodded. "A large price. Every cent I had left, and I had to start selling beer again just to keep eating. The only thing that was paid up was the yearly lease on the building because that payment was made right before the funding was yanked."

"What made you think you could use stolen code to finish the watches?" Mark asked.

"The phones and code I was given worked. The first drops on the SD cards weren't complete, but it was a big piece of what we had been missing when we'd designed the watches at Clockworks. With the code I was getting, I hoped...I dreamed that maybe I could get the watch to market after all."

"But how did you obtain code when you didn't know who was writing it in the first place?"

He shrugged. "I met Joe Black here at the garden center. He put the phone on the counter, I picked it up. He bought a roll of coconut fiber rolls that I had lined with money that was the payment for the code drops."

"You knew he wasn't the one writing the code?"

Rohit looked at me with his mouth gaping. "No way. I used to tutor in college. Are you saying Joe could write code?"

I shook my head. "No. I just wondered if you thought he could."

Rohit shook his head. "He didn't seem to know about the smartwatches at all until he stole one from me."

"How did he manage that?" Mark asked.

"I wore it to work. I did some of my testing during the day if things here were slow. The watch strap was already loose and somehow when I was rolling the coconut fiber, the watch fell off or got tangled in it. I didn't notice it until after Joe picked up the bundle. I wouldn't have even known he had found the watch, but he wore it when he came back in with the next drop of code!"

That sounded like Joe. Too stupid to cover his tracks even if blind luck sent him a gift.

"This would go easier on you if you turned evidence over and pleaded guilty," Mark said.

Rohit hung his head. "I'm too stupid for that. The only person I ever met in person was Joe. Even after the watch was stolen and I tried to get it back, I couldn't figure out who was behind the code."

"How did you try to retrieve it?" Had he murdered Joe in the attempt to get the watch back?

"Joe delivered phones and code back and forth. When I needed to request certain features or fixes to the language modules, I used the phones to leave instructions for the guy coding on the other end. In this case, I left a text message on every single Borgot phone I sent back. The message made it clear that the stolen watch wasn't part of the deal. No more payments unless I got the watch back."

"But you never did."

He shoulders couldn't slump any further, but he dropped his head. "I got a message back on another phone indicating the watch would be returned, but that never happened. Whoever he is, he's probably reverse engineering it and preparing to sell my end of the technology. His code is good. I know he has the ability."

"If the deal was working other than the stolen watch, what makes you so sure your original contact has turned on you?" I asked.

"The last drop of code didn't contain any of the language modules at all. It was old code that I had a long time ago." The bitterness in his voice was laced with defeat.

Ah, the complexity of thieves dealing with thieves. Rohit assumed a double-cross, when in fact, it was just incompetence. Well, and me, inserting myself in the phone exchange process. Rohit had gotten old code because I had taken the new code. The slightest feelings of pity stirred in my cold heart. "It wasn't a double-cross. Joe stole the watch on his own," I said. "He was wearing it when he was murdered."

Rohit's head shot up. "Murdered?"

"Not all was well on the other end. That's why the phones have been delivered differently the last couple of drops. But Mark is right. You'd best turn over what you know and hope whoever is on the other end doesn't try to pin the murders on you."

"Murders?" His voice was little more than a croaking sound.

Mark hauled Rohit to his feet just in time. Police lights, red, white and blue, flashed in the parking lot. At least they hadn't turned on the sirens.

Dave stood at the entrance of his store, his arms folded. His glare was reserved for me, which was completely unfair. It wasn't my fault he had hired a thief.

Chapter 34

It took a while to get cleaned up. While I showered, Mark called Radar and Huntington to give them the latest news.

"Delivering code via the phone SD card means we still don't know who wrote those extra modules and sold them to Rohit," Mark said when he got off the phone. "Whoever is doing this has been very careful to cover all their tracks."

"Which means the real perp is still working at Borgot. Once that person figures out there is no one on the other end to work on the code or the watch, he'll probably just look for another buyer."

Mark nodded. "He may already be doing that. Steve has inserted himself into a venture capitalist meeting at Borgot tomorrow. He plans to find out whether or not anyone at Borgot has started talking about buying the language modules instead of coding them in-house. He'll also ask if Borgot is planning to add a watch to the phone products. Whoever coded those languages isn't going to be satisfied with just selling pieces to Rohit on the side, especially now that he's been arrested. He's going to need a new customer."

"And who could be an easier customer than Borgot? They're desperate for the code to make their ship date."

"Let's hope so. If the guy tries to sell it to someone other than Borgot, it's going to be a lot harder for us to track."

"Isn't Huntington too busy working on the burglary case to work on this?" Secretly, I'd been hoping that Huntington would drop out of the case. After all, he'd caught the perps he was after when we caught Joe's mother delivering unregistered Borgot phones to her biker friends. The murders and stolen Borgot code hadn't been part of his original case.

Mark shook his head. "He has plenty of time to help. His other clients were happy once the phone connection was discovered and severed. Borgot is the only place left to keep following the money trail. Some of the venture capitalists are probably the same ones who invested in Clockworks. Maybe one or more of them was in on selling Borgot code to Rohit."

Maybe. But I still had no idea how we could catch the programmer in the act.

* * *

Normally, I didn't care a whit about venture capitalists or angel investors as they were also called. They funded a lot of startups, including Borgot. As a test engineer, I'd never been required to attend the meetings when a new investor was interested or an active investor required an update. I understood the necessity of them, especially after we listened to Rohit's story, but I'd never had any real reason to pay close attention to their comings and goings.

When I pulled into the Borgot parking lot in the morning, I recognized Huntington's Viper. I sighed and headed up the stairs.

Chaos greeted me before I made it to my cube, but these days, unless someone pointed a gun at me, tantrums, ballerinas, and yelling engineers weren't even a reason to slow down. The platters of food, however, were enough to make me stop and stare.

Would it be rude to grab a carrot stick off one of the veggie trays as it floated past?

When a large cheese tray went by, I followed it. A guy in a white apron was in the break room flinging his hands up and down hard enough to shed his own skin. In a loud stage whisper, he bellowed at Monique and Kay. "I cannot be expected to cook under these conditions. I am a caterer. A full *chef caterer*. It says right on the contract that *you* provide a full kitchen! This is a water faucet and a coffee pot! Real chefs do not cook under these conditions."

I snagged a carrot from the tray on the counter. "We have a toaster oven," I offered helpfully.

He swung his burly body towards me. His curled lip revealed stunted canines that were thick and yellow like those of a woodchuck that had gone one too many rounds with ironwood.

I retrieved a paper plate from the cupboard and helped myself to cheese and crackers. If real investors were awaiting this spread, I might not have been so cavalier, but Huntington wouldn't be dumb enough to hand over money to this company.

Mr. Woodchuck gasped and made shooing motions at my audacity.

Roscoe, he who stole food on a regular basis and took it home, shouldered me away from the platter. "This is for the investors! And we're going to need these prepared ones since he," Roscoe jabbed a finger at Mr. Woodchuck, "refuses to cook up the dips and finger food without a real kitchen."

"Don't worry, I know how to snag from the spots where it won't be noticed," I explained to Roscoe. "I've made these trays before."

Roscoe spun around to face Monique. "You're supposed to manage Sedona. You tell her. We all know what happens when the venture capitalists back out. I'm not a big enough fool to hang around like I did at my last job."

The cheese froze on its way to my lips. "Your last job? Where did you work?"

"Hardly matters now, does it? If a startup doesn't get funding, it dies."
He turned to the chef. "And people like you don't get paid. So I suggest you
cook up something, full kitchen or no."

Oh, that set off the woodchuck. "Not get paid?" He lost his stage
whisper and any pretense of professionalism. Monique's shushing and
reassurances did nothing to halt his performance either. He untied his apron,
hissed out threats about lawyers and, "I'd better see the second half of my
payment."

I kept up a continuous scan for any sign of a Borgot phone on his person
or one being added to one of his food boxes. That last phone with the code
hadn't made it to its final destination. Maybe Woodchuck here was the next
train ticket. "What was on the menu?" I asked, helping myself to more cheese.
It was very good cheese.

"Sedona, will you stop eating all the food?" Before I could protest the
"all the food" comment, Monique ruined her own order by filching a sausage
stick from the meat tray. She came from a marketing background. If anyone
complained about missing food, she'd blame me. "Listen, Saul." When he
sputtered, she corrected herself. "Chef Saul. We can get you anything you need,
but there was nothing on the menu that had to be served hot."

With a final hand fling, he finally loosed himself from his apron. If the
phone was in one of the pockets, he wasn't leaving with it because he tossed the
huge white sheet down and stomped on it.

"John expects snacks throughout," Kay put in. "What exactly do you
intend to serve that requires a full kitchen?" She tapped frantically on her tablet.

"A full kitchen. It's in the contract. No kitchen, no food." With that
announcement, he sailed off down the hall to the elevators.

Kay scrolled here and there on the tablet. "I ordered salads, snacks and
finger sandwiches." More scrolling, during which time I inspected the contents
of the nearest box. "Damn. There is a clause in the contract about a full
kitchen."

"We have crackers, and if we put the M&Ms in a bowl, we can keep food
flowing," Monique said.

The box in front of me was full of avocados and a dry mix that smelled
and looked like one that could be turned into spinach dip. "Looks like he
planned guacamole? And some other dips." I scanned another box. "These are
cookie trays with dough already shaped out. The dough is plain...so he probably
has frosting around here somewhere. Cute. I think they are meant to be
phones." I grabbed one of the trays, marveling at the rack arrangements all
stacked neatly in a box. It was easy to slide a few cookies off onto tinfoil and
pop them into the toaster oven. "At six at a time, we can get enough of these
done in a half hour to make it look good. Someone find the icing. It will be in
one of those cake decorating bags, probably."

No one moved. Monique stared at me. Roscoe blinked. Kay finally
reached for a box. "He was supposed to take various items into the meeting

room in shifts, like a nine-course meal over the day. At least that's the way the brochure described it."

"It's early for cookies," Roscoe said. "Shouldn't you save those for the afternoon? We gotta keep these guys happy."

"Geez, how long are the investors hanging around?" I'd figured Huntington could ask his forty questions and be out of here in an hour.

Roscoe snorted at me again. "We're presenting, Sedona. This is an opportunity to sell ourselves so that we don't go down the drain!"

I grabbed an avocado and began peeling it. From the items in the box, this guacamole was going to be thinned with cream cheese. "Like your last company, right?"

"It wasn't my fault! My code was perfect. Borgot knew what it was doing when it picked the cream of the crop to come work here."

"I'm sure. Do you know anything about homebrewing beer?" I asked innocently. Maybe he knew Rohit. Maybe I could somehow get him to admit it.

His eyes widened. "You're going to brew beer for these guys?" He gazed down the hall towards the meeting room. "I never thought of that. Maybe that would be a good idea."

I didn't know much about beer brewing, but I was fairly certain it didn't happen in one morning. His line of thinking was not even close to mine. "No, I'm looking into beer and wine making, but beer brewing is cheaper."

Roscoe blinked at me. His bushy eyebrows came together while he tried to process my comment.

The first batch of cookies was done, so I removed the tray and tinfoil and started another tray. I inspected a few more boxes. There were several loaves of fresh bread, cucumbers and a giant jar of mayonnaise. "Hmm. Can we just put the mayo in a small bowl, slice the bread and let the investors make their own sandwiches from the meat tray?"

Before Roscoe could sputter out a complaint, I added, "No one really wants to eat cucumber sandwiches, Roscoe. Sure, they look nice on the platter, but I don't see any actual lunch here. The meat tray could easily be made into sandwiches. Or was a full lunch planned?"

Kay shook her head, her tablet still in her hand. "He was supposed to supply a light lunch, but he didn't specify exactly what that would be."

"Okay, let's go with toasted bagels, cream cheese and that fruit tray for breakfast." Instead of full bagels, there were pieces. "I'll toast the bagel wedges as soon as these cookies come out. The cheese and crackers can go with lunch."

Monique joined me in saying, "If I don't eat it all first." We grinned at each other. "It's good cheese," I told her.

Roscoe complained when I suggested that he and the other engineers would have to help serve, but I ignored him. It would be hard for me to serve with a straight face knowing Huntington was there to investigate, not drop millions. He probably had the money to invest, but only an idiot would put money into a company whose phones had just been used in robberies and kidnappings.   And that wasn't even counting the stolen code and murders. Yeah, we had it all at Borgot. I wouldn't ruin Roscoe's day by telling him, but we'd have a lot better luck if a mafia boss came along to buy us out.   Only someone with a criminal background would be interested in us now.

When it was Kovid's turn to cater in trays, I asked him where he used to work. "Clockworks, why?"

"I just wondered. Roscoe said something about Borgot having mined the best of the best."

Kovid nodded. "Yeah, we were both at Clockworks. Borgot was already up and running when we lost our investment backing. John and Cary were right there with job offers. There were a few other guys I wished they had hired before the hiring freeze."

I already knew that Lawrence had worked there, so I asked about some of the others instead. "Did Monique work there?"

"No. I saw her once or twice, but that was because she was dating Lawrence. Then when he got on here, she was hired shortly after."

We shared a knowing glance. "I wonder why Lawrence didn't just hire her at Clockworks too."

"Hiring had been shut down for a solid year over there. He couldn't have hired his own brother if he had wanted."

"I guess Cary and Joe must have worked there too."

"No. Cary did and he was already here when I was hired. Joe came after that. He wasn't at Clockworks. Are you going to give me that tray or take it in yourself?"

I handed him the tray. "I have to finish preparing the cookies." The cookies were all baked, but there were some that still needed icing.

It didn't take me long to finish them. Just for grins, I took the platter in myself. Huntington probably wouldn't be surprised to see me, but it might throw him off his game a little if he had to pretend not to know me.

When I entered the meeting room, the surprise was all mine. Huntington was there, businessman cool as usual, and sitting next to him, almost as calm and collected was Clint Lewis, the ex-marine ballet teacher.

Chapter 35

Mark and I met at Happy Family Chinese to compare notes. I ordered egg rolls even though I'd eaten plenty of food samples while prepping snacks for the investor's meeting. First things first. I told him about the multiple employees who had come from Clockworks. "Half of Borgot knew about the possibility of a smartwatch because they worked there. Any of them could have decided to supply the Borgot code so that Rohit could still bring a watch to market. If Rohit failed, whoever controlled the code would still have a job. Borgot would still have a product, albeit not as good as the one sold to Rohit."

He nodded. "Rohit, through his lawyer, supplied a list of employees and the final financials for Clockworks. I went through them today."

I didn't ask how he obtained that list. "Was Clint Lewis on the list of previous employees?"

"The karate guy?"

"Ballet, karate, whatever. Yes, him."

"No, why?"

"He was there today at the meeting. He was also at Joe Black's funeral."

Mark's eyes narrowed. "He walked into an investment meeting at Borgot after teaching ballet and delivering the wrong phone to Clockworks?"

"He didn't look the same, believe me. He had shaved his head completely, but grew in a nicely trimmed beard and mustache. There was a huge diamond earring in one ear as if he wanted everyone to notice he had money to throw at a project. He also wore funky rose-tinted glasses. They weren't sunglasses, but they looked like those kind that darken outside and never get completely light when you're inside. If we hadn't talked to him at his dojo face-to-face, I might not have recognized him as the ballet teacher. You take away the tights, add facial hair and put him in a suit, and he looked nothing like the guy prancing around our break area last week."

"Hmm."

I told him about Lawrence having a patent. "Most patent lawyers have to learn at least enough code to read and understand it; some of them probably start out as programmers or get pretty good at it. His fingerprints are all over this case. He could be programming the languages on the side. And maybe Clint wasn't so innocent when it came to the phone delivery. Maybe Lawrence hired both him and Cary so that he could stay in the background and look innocent."

"You think he also hired Joe?"

I shrugged. "It's more likely Cary hired him to do the deliveries because he thought such work was beneath him."

"But Cary ended up dead in your garden. You think Lawrence murdered both of them?"

I swallowed hard. My egg roll was not taking the edge off this conversation. "Lawrence is taller than either of them. He's in decent shape. We all worked together so suggesting a private conversation, one that lured someone to his death, wouldn't be impossible."

Mark nodded. "A woman didn't drag Joe into the bathroom or Cary into your garden."

I agreed. "Monique probably has access to Lawrence's email, and even though I think she'd stoop pretty low to get ahead, she couldn't have murdered either Joe or Cary on her own."

"She and Lawrence together?"

"It's possible. She was dating Lawrence when he was at Clockworks and got hired on with Borgot after he landed the job there. She could be the brains behind the operation." I shook my head. "I doubt it, though."

Mark smiled. "You're not dismissing your own sex, are you? Maybe she is smart enough."

I had overlooked a guilty woman before, but it wasn't because I was sexist. "She wears the words 'Doll Baby' on the back of her pants!"

He raised an eyebrow and laughed.

"Okay, it's possible she uses her sex as a distraction. It's possible she's smarter than she appears. But when would she have time to code languages? She's on the phone all day!"

"I'll look into her background anyway, just in case."

"Okay. And I'll make sure none of these people get behind me where I can't see them."

Mark sighed. "Good idea. And start looking for another job."

I nodded. That was another very good idea.

Chapter 36

I wasn't entirely surprised to see Huntington's Viper in the lot again on Friday morning. The venture capitalist meetings were supposedly over, but he could easily have set up a private meeting.

Trying not to be obvious about it, I scanned the parking lot for a motorcycle. There was no specific reason for Mark to be here, not really, but someone who worked inside this building was up to their neck in theft and murder.

The lack of a motorcycle in the lot didn't settle my nerves.

Once upstairs, I checked my email first just in case there was a notice about another venture capitalist meeting. There wasn't anything on the schedule for the wealthy donors, but there was a meeting for the rest of us tomorrow. Lawrence wanted everyone to attend a special seven a.m. Saturday meeting to discuss patents and what it would take to be named on one.

"As if." Since I didn't care about patents, I would definitely miss it.

I left my backpack in my cube, but kept my car keys and phone in my pocket. I considered carrying the backpack with me, but it would be too noticeable while I nosed around checking up on Huntington. If he was after additional information, the most logical place for him to be would be with the CEO, but Kay, our admin, informed me the boss was out for the day.

Two of the meeting rooms were in use. Barging in wasn't really an option.

I wandered through the maze, checking the cubicles, but Huntington wasn't likely to be digging into Borgot's financial health out in the open. There were no cookies or snacks left from yesterday's meeting so I couldn't pretend to drop by the meeting rooms with leftovers.

"Screw it." I grabbed a notepad and headed to the meeting rooms. I opened the door with my head down as though reading notes and then stopped quickly as soon as I had a foot inside.

The room was quiet, and to my surprise Howard was its only occupant. Before I could excuse myself, he started talking. "That's why you make the big bucks. Figure it out and make sure it's unique enough to patent." He reached around his laptop and hit the mute button on the teleconference phone before addressing me. "Don't tell me you are here to bug me about a patent because you won the contest for naming the phone assistant!"

I stopped in the process of stepping back. "What? No. Wrong meeting." I stepped away and pulled the door after me, but didn't close it fast enough.

"Well, your idea isn't good enough," he called after me. "Save your questions for tomorrow."

I slammed the door closed. Him and his stupid patents. I had completely forgotten the naming contest even though I had suggested the owner of the phones should be able to name the personal assistant voice themselves. Maybe I should have checked all my emails before looking for Huntington.

Before I could barge into the second meeting room, I noticed Lawrence glide into the elevator. Now that was interesting. He was our prime suspect, and he wasn't in the meeting with Huntington. And neither was John, the CEO.

Had Huntington's plan gone awry? Was he sitting in one of these rooms wasting time with innocent bystanders while Lawrence went about his nefarious business?

I hit the stairwell, knowing I could make it to the first floor before the elevator arrived. I really should have kept my pack. Maybe I should just start leaving it in the car.

If Lawrence was sneaking off to code languages, did that mean he had another buyer lined up? Rohit had been arrested and while it hadn't made the news, surely Lawrence would figure it out if he hadn't already.

I peeked through the small glass window on the stairwell door.

When Larry exited through the front door, I slid out of the stairwell and then waited at the front door until he hopped inside a yellow sports coupe.

There was no need to follow him. If he went somewhere to code, I'd only know his hideout, and it was likely his own home. If he met with someone, I'd have no way of knowing if they were new buyers of the code or just more hoods he happened to know.

Just as I retreated, Huntington's Viper edged out of its parking spot. He had to wait for two cars, but he turned in the same direction as Lawrence's yellow car.

Now how did Huntington think he could follow Lawrence discreetly in the Viper? If Lawrence was into cars at all, and from the looks of the yellow roadster it was probable, Lawrence would notice something as spiffy as the Viper tailing behind him.

I rolled my eyes, my speech for Huntington half formed when I noticed a black car pull out. The windows were not tinted.

Clint Lewis shot out onto the road even faster than Huntington and headed in the same direction.

I ran into the parking lot and jumped into my own car. I wasn't sure I'd gotten enough of a look at Clint's car to spot it outright again, but Huntington's Viper was an easy target. If I could glimpse that, I'd be able to follow without a problem.

A tiny Ford Fusion slammed on its brakes when I pulled out of the parking lot, but it was an overreaction. I had plenty of time to speed off ahead of it.

I took to the road like a professional racer, zipping into the far lane and gunning it. Driving Huntington's Porsche had spoiled me. The SUV, Mercedes or not, did not have the takeoff of his latest car. Maybe he had to drive the Viper because Detective Saunders hadn't released his Porsche yet.

I smiled an evil grin, not feeling the least bit sorry for Huntington. My glee was followed by a moment of panic before I finally caught sight of the Viper. The black car was still tailing behind it. Our entourage drove rapidly, but not overly so.

We took two turns before I was sure. If I had to bet money, we were headed for Alpine Hills where Monique said Lawrence lived. That wouldn't yield anything useful to me. I wondered if Huntington knew he was being followed? And did Clint know I was following *him*?

"This is ridiculous." My stray thoughts had me looking in my rear view mirror. Was I being followed? Was there anyone *left* to follow me?

I stayed on the trail long enough to verify we were headed to the ritzy part of town and then pulled into a gas station on Pine Ridge Parkway. I watched traffic for a full minute, but if someone was following me, I couldn't spot the tail.

My phone was relatively useless because I didn't have Huntington's number with me. I'd never called him on this phone. Then again, I did know his Alpine Hills condo number. He'd always set his phones to roll over to his cell.

I dialed the number. It rang, but he obviously wasn't at the condo. On the third ring it clicked and spattered. I smiled. The condo number was a land line so chances were good it was transferring the call.

He picked up on the seventh ring.

"Huntington? Sedona. Did you know you're being followed?"

"This isn't a good time," he said tersely.

He was almost always terse with me unless he was trying to convince me of the ease and benefit of some new job. "It's never a good time to be followed," I said. "Black car. I missed the brand because I didn't get close enough. Maybe an Infinity."

"I meant it wasn't a good time for me to talk," he muttered.

"Never good to talk while driving and following a suspect. The guy in the black car is Clint Lewis."

There was a long pause before he finally said, "The ballet guy?"

"Yup. Ex-marine, karate guy. He was at the investor meeting with you yesterday. Black guy with a trimmed beard. He's shorter than you by a foot."

"The guy sitting next to me?"

"That's the one."

"Why didn't you just say that?"

I rolled my eyes. My thinking patterns were never likely to match his. "Clint has been around a lot lately."

"Yeah. But is he following me or Lawrence? Gotta go."

"One more thing, Huntington. Lawrence lives in Alpine—" There was no point in finishing the sentence. He'd already cut the connection.

The only net positive was that if anyone looked for me at work, they'd assume I was in one of the meetings because my backpack was still in my cube.

With that happy thought, I drove back to work. As soon as I arrived I texted Mark to tell him about Clint and Huntington.

He texted back almost immediately. "Clint was following Lawrence. Steve pulled over. Clint kept going."

Interesting. "Was Lawrence headed home?"

"No. Had a tee time at Alpine Hills golf course."

A light went off in my brain. "Any chance Huntington noticed if John, the CEO of Borgot, was at the course?"

I waited impatiently, but I'd been dead on. When the response came, it was one word. "Affirmative."

Fiend. No wonder Lawrence had to schedule an early Saturday meeting for the rest of us. He was busy playing golf today.

I had another thought. "Did Clint join them on the course?"

"Negative."

Hmm. So why was he following Lawrence?

Chapter 37

I didn't think anything could ruin my Saturday until the phone rang at the ungodly hour of six-thirty. I looked at my phone. "It's Sean."

Mark opened one eye and sighed.

I mumbled something into the phone that didn't have 'good morning' in it.

Sean was unnecessarily terse. "You don't need to sew a baby bumper. Mom wants to do it, and I don't want to hurt her feelings by telling her you already offered."

Brenda and Huntington had done any and all offering when it came to baby bumpers, but I wasn't one to look a gift horse in the mouth, even if it was Sean making an excuse because he'd seen the awkward baby bibs on my table. "Great. I'm sure it will turn out perfect." I still didn't even know what a baby bumper *was* never mind how to make one. "I'm pretty busy anyway." Distracted by Mark getting up and heading to the shower, I nearly mentioned the case, but Sean would go ballistic if he had any inkling there was still a game afoot.

"Just don't bring up baby bumpers again," Sean instructed. "Don't mention baby bibs either. Ever."

"Sure, fine, whatever."

Sean grunted and hung up. No point in him faking pleasantries more than necessary.

Since Mark was already up and moving, I put coffee on. I wanted to check my bank account anyway.

Just as Howard had informed me, I had won the naming contest and a cool five thousand dollars had been sent to my bank account. I verified the amount had been deposited.

The money was definitely cause for a celebration. Oh sure, I'd have to save most of the bonus because the Borgot job wasn't likely to last, but it was a thrill to have won the prize.

Just as Mark came into the living room, the doorbell rang.

"This place is like a train station this morning," Mark said.

I opened the door to find Brenda on the stoop.

Brenda was slimming down from her pregnancy with remarkable speed. She was walking every day to make up for the fact she was on maternity leave and not doing rounds at her hospital job. Motherhood definitely agreed with her.

"Sedona," she cried, her big brown eyes holding back tears, "Sean says you can't do the baby bumper!" She wrung her hands.

"That was his opinion, yes. I didn't say I wasn't doing it." As soon as the words were uttered, I realized I had trapped myself. A few seconds ago, I had technically been relieved of the project because Sean had decided Mom should do it. "Wait," I said, looking at Mark for inspiration. He just shook his head at me and did not provide a new excuse.

"My mom is sewing one too," I blurted out. "She's better at it and faster."

Brenda flapped her hands. "I don't know how to sew either, but I thought between the two of us, we could figure it out. I left the baby with Sean. I didn't tell him I was coming over here, but we can do it! We'll sew it together, and won't he be surprised!"

If there was one thing in this world that was worse than me sewing, it had to be me trying to sew with Brenda.

"Oh, no." I shook my head vehemently. "There is no way we can sew anything that complex today." In desperation, I turned to Mark again.

"I'm not going to do it," was his response.

That hadn't been the kind of help I was hoping for. Neither was the beep of the alarm for the backyard. I started towards the kitchen, but the second and third warning beeps were much closer together this time.

Mark muttered something about it being too light outside for raccoons.

Whatever Radar and Turbo had improved, it wasn't the noise. The backyard exploded with the sound of a banshee attacking a ghost.

Brenda screamed.

Mark spun for the bedroom where he had left his gun. "You two stay here and get down!"

As if. "Brenda, hide behind the couch! Call 911 if anything goes wrong." I shadowed Mark as he positioned himself by the side of the back door.

"Shit!" He threw the bolt and the door wide in one motion as he crouched low.

That's when the shooting started.

I crawled backwards just as Mark took aim with one arm out the door and yelled, "Hold your fire!"

An arm came flying off the robot and slapped into his hand, knocking his gun onto the concrete and forcing him back. "Shit."

Through the opening, I could see Howard shooting at the scarecrow with wild abandon. Clint was barely recognizable because of all the blood, but he took a very precise swing at the guy standing behind him, connecting hard with his elbow.

The guy he hit was one of the ones who had been sitting near Howard at Joe's funeral. Clint's next blow smashed hard into his nose. The guy went down and didn't even twitch.

Before Clint could take further action, Howard turned and shot him.

Clint was already bleeding from one arm and now his leg blossomed dark red. His face contorted with pain. With superhuman determination he clawed his way towards Howard and the garden.

"That's right, you bastard!" Howard yelled. "I said I'd bury you here, and I will! No one steals from me!"

Mark edged his hand towards his gun.

"Howard?" I screamed the distraction before he could shoot again. "Why are you burying people in my backyard?"

He swung around and took a shot at the open doorway. I was already behind the wall and back down flat, but thankfully his gun was out of bullets. He squawked loud enough to be heard over the security alarms in my yard.

I hit the buttons on the control switch, leaving him screaming into the silence.

"Why aren't you at the patent meeting?" he sputtered.

"Why aren't you?" I yelled back.

"You stole my idea! You're going to pay."

I didn't have any idea what he was griping about. I pressed more buttons on the phone, but the robot was still flailing feverishly. The remaining arm windmilled around and around while the rest of the thing gyrated like a headless chicken.

Mark felt around the porch for his gun while staying mostly inside and keeping an eye on Howard.

Clint finally reached the garden. He grabbed wildly at the robot and yanked hard. A robot leg detached, pitching him sideways into the dirt.

Howard reached into his pocket.

Mark yelled, "Freeze, asshole!"

Howard ignored the order, pulled out a clip for the gun and would have been shot by Mark, except Clint swung the robot leg like a pro baseball player, nearly separating Howard from his head. "I don't...deliver..." He had to stop to gasp in two quick breaths. "Illegal shit for...shitheads." With a groan, Clint fell flat. He lay unmoving.

Howard clutched his head and groped around for his gun or the clip.

Mark and I both rushed him. Behind me, I could hear Brenda yelling.

Mark landed two punches before slamming Howard to the ground. A well-placed knee in his back kept him down.

I picked up the robot leg and held it ready to bash him in the head if he so much as wiggled. "What the hell are you doing here, Howard?"

Brenda rushed out with my medical kit in her hands. She went straight to Clint. "I swear, Sedona, I didn't know you were working another case and had people coming over."

The way she melded those two things together made my eyes cross. "Neither did I."

"No one steals from me and lives to tell about it," Howard bellowed. "First Joe thought he could steal one of the watches. Then it turns out Cary and he were stealing the phones and selling them to street thugs and cutting me out of the profit!"

"Those were Borgot phones, not your phones," I pointed out.

"They put the plan at risk! We could have all been rich. All Cary had to do was follow directions and get the code to Rohit. But no! Lazy asshole hired an even lazier asshole!"

"Why sell it to Rohit in the first place?"

"Rohit was the best there ever was. I can code. I had special tutoring because the law department required that we know programming for filing patents. Rohit could code anything. When he started his own business, I knew it would make money."

"You were friends?"

Howard snarled, "He wasn't in my league or he wouldn't have failed."

It took me a moment to make the connection, but his mention of the law department and learning to code was a big clue. "Rohit was your computer programming tutor in college, wasn't he?"

Howard's head twisted, but he didn't answer.

I pointed to the prone guy on the ground. He was also Howard's age. His hair was black. He didn't look it, but I guessed anyway. "He's Hispanic, isn't he?"

Howard's eyes flicked to his buddy. "Vince? He's Italian. Sosa's the Spanish expert."

"And they helped you code the languages. I bet Rohit tutored them too."

"Borgot wouldn't hire them, the idiots. I told Borgot they had nothing without the languages. These companies think they can stick any old crap out there and sell it, even with no new functionality."

I couldn't argue the point because it was often true. "So you sold the code to Rohit at Clockworks instead."

"We were so close to production when the venture capitalists yanked the funding at Clockworks. We were gonna be rich. And Borgot was raking in plenty of funding for a stupid phone! That watch is going to make way more money than just another stupid phone. When Rohit takes it to market, I'm going to be right there, funding it and getting my piece."

"Yeah, funding it with the money Rohit paid you for the modules you stole from Borgot and your two language experts."

He didn't have an answer for that, but he spit at me. "You're supposed to be at a patent meeting."

A meeting that would have left my house empty in the early morning hours so that another body could be buried here. A meeting supposedly planned by Lawrence, whose email was readily available to his assistant, Howard. "There is no meeting this morning, is there?"

Mark didn't give him a chance to answer. He pinned Howard's arm behind his back and yanked him to his knees. "Get some rope, Sedona, unless you happen to have handcuffs or strong tie wraps."

I headed for the porch, but had one more important question. "Why kill Joe and Cary?"

"Cary hired Joe, that was his problem," Howard grumbled.

"That left you with Cary as your problem."

"The idiot didn't even recover the stolen smartwatch. Claimed Joe wasn't wearing it. He probably stole it himself."

"Probably," I agreed, not about to admit that I had sat on the watch and then absconded with it. "Any special reason you picked my yard to dump Cary?"

Howard laughed, hysteria having parked and stayed. "During the code review, you blurted out my idea for letting the customer name the phone assistant. It was my idea, and I would have won if you hadn't yelled it out first in public! Cary was the perfect way to warn you that if you steal from me, you die!"

Cary's body had been a personal threat alright, even if I hadn't known what the warning was about. If I had managed to suggest a patentable idea, Howard probably would have moved me up the kill list because he believed all good ideas were his personal property.

"Did you call 911?" Mark demanded as he dragged Howard towards the house. On his way past the prone guy, he checked to make sure the guy was still out cold.

"Not yet." I leaned over and pushed Howard's gun further away from him even though the clip was empty and Mark had him immobilized. The gun had a silencer on the end, but it had been plenty loud anyway.

Brenda said, "I need an ambulance."

I picked up the robot leg and dragged it inside with me to call 911. No way was I going to stand around without a weapon of some sort.

Chapter 38

I dialed 911 and began answering questions over and over while dragging around the robot leg and hunting for duct tape or rope. I finally set the leg against the couch and went into the garage.

There was a roll of twine on a shelf with a whole host of gardening tools, including orange oil, seed packets, a small trowel and, yes, a list of instructions from Dad. I grabbed the twine.

"Are there shots still being fired?" the voice in my ear asked.

If I said no, were they planning on taking their time? "I need an ambulance," I repeated, scurrying out through the back door. I tossed Mark the twine and yanked a robot arm free in case I needed it. Radar had probably not intended the limbs as weaponry, but the arm was nice and heavy.

"I've stopped the bleeding," Brenda said. "He may still need a transfusion."

"I asked for an ambulance," I told her, ignoring the 911 operator squawking in my ear.

"Oh good. I called Sean. I told him to find a babysitter before he comes over and to bring my medical supplies." She continued bandaging Clint's leg. His eyes were open.

"She'll take good care of you," I told him. "Why did Howard shoot you? Are you working for him too?"

"No!" He closed his eyes and breathed steadily for a few breaths. "I got curious after your visit. I wondered about the phone and being asked to do a forty-thousand-dollar ballet lesson. I started poking around to see what I could learn about who sent me the original email."

I shook my head. "You shouldn't get involved in this investigation stuff. It's dangerous." I shot a pointed look at Brenda, but she was too busy to notice.

Clint glared up at me. "I had a buddy do some background checks for me, but nothing came up except on the dead guy, Joe. He had a record for petty theft and a hell of a lot of traffic tickets."

We knew that already and both Huntington brothers were more than capable of background checks. Even if they weren't, Radar could have gotten the information. I looked over at Howard and his cohort, Vince. "How'd you end up shot?"

Clint grunted. "Keiko has contracts with some big companies, so I've gotten to know a few bigwigs. One of the guys put in a good word for me at

Borgot, telling them I was a player looking to invest. I figured the investor meeting would let me meet Lawrence face-to-face and maybe find some clues to what was going on. But even using an alias and dressed in a suit, Howard recognized me."

"So did I."

"Yes, but you didn't come gunning for me. He decided I stole the code you took when you switched the phone out. He came to retrieve it."

"And you told him I had it?"

Clint closed his eyes again. "No. I have no idea why he dragged me here. He showed up with two other morons and shot me before stuffing me in the trunk of a car."

"Two guys?" I started to panic. "There's only one guy with him now."

"I kicked the other guy backwards down the stairs at my place. That's when I got myself shot the first time."

"They left the other guy there? Was he dead?"

Clint snorted. "I didn't check. We stepped over him on the way out. When they opened the trunk to let me out here, I planned to attack, but the guy with the gun stayed too far back." He indicated Howard with a twist of his head. "He ordered me to walk back here. From what he said, he thought I'd just lay down in my own grave and wait to be shot."

Fortunately, Howard hadn't known about Miley. She had startled him into firing early and often. She had also provided enough of a distraction to give Clint a chance to fight back.

Sirens finally broke through what had once been a quiet neighborhood. I checked my fence, but Mr. Jackson wasn't peering over. A smart man would cower behind his couch if he lived next to me.

I hurried inside, leaned the robot arm next to the leg and unlocked the front door. Thinking fast, I went back to retrieve Mark's gun. No need for it to be lying there on the back porch when the police arrived.

I tucked it safely away.

Mark dragged Howard inside. Since I wasn't listening to anything the lady said, I set the squawking phone down and helped Mark tie Howard to one of the kitchen chairs.

"There were two guys with Howard at the funeral," I said. "They must have been Vince and Sosa."

Howard laughed. "While you all stood there staring at the corpse, Sosa and Vince snuck around back and tied up the driver. Sosa slapped on the driver's jacket and Vince hid in the backseat."

"No wonder the hearse didn't wait for Joe's mother."

Mark shook his head. "And they drove off thinking they had the watch."

"If I'd known you put a fake on him, I'd have shot you first." He struggled against his ties to no avail.

I looked around for my robot arm. This guy deserved at least one more smack to the head. "Wouldn't all this have been easier if you'd just started your own company, hired people to do the work and paid them?"

"Sure, and get kicked out the second the real money gets involved. I saw what they did to Rohit."

Before either of us could reply, the front door slammed open. Sean came flying through the door. Behind him, we could see an ambulance pulling up to the curb.

The police followed very soon after.

Sean did a lot of yelling and swearing. Howard actually tried to hire him to be his lawyer.

"He charges more than you're worth," I said. "He only takes on *innocent* clients."

Sean didn't argue with me, but his eyes bulged. He made sure no one asked Brenda any questions. I thought he could have made the authorities leave me alone too, but all he did was glare at me while I gave my statement.

Chapter 39

It took another week for things to settle down at work. Rohit did own the code he had written, and he was willing to sell it to Borgot in exchange for leniency and a small amount of cash. Anything Howard had worked on while at Borgot belonged to Borgot, but his two friends had done most of the language coding. Sean had decided that he would represent Rohit, which made me proud, but also worried.

When Mark came over for dinner Friday night, he handed me a list. "Sosa and Vince both worked for Clockworks. Rohit tutored both of them as well as Howard for two years in college. Rohit was thrilled to have been able to hire them at Clockworks."

I scanned the list. "No wonder Howard hired Cary and Joe to do deliveries. Rohit knew him. He might not have agreed to the deal if he knew who was trying to bilk him."

"It would also have made it very easy to point the finger at Howard if things fell apart. Rohit not knowing that Howard was behind the code drops was extra insurance for Howard and the others." Mark handed me another sheet. "Howard was ready to file the patent on not only the languages, but the language use with the smartwatch. He didn't intend for Rohit to find out he intended to submit the paperwork before Rohit ever got the watch to market."

I groaned. "He was totally hung up on patents. Did he even list Sosa and Vince?"

"They were on the patent application, but Rohit wasn't. Howard was listed as the major contributor, taking full credit for the design, invention and most of the implementation even though he didn't code much of it."

"It should have listed him as the most warped. Who goes around stealing work and thinking they can patent it? Worse, he buried a dead guy in my yard just because I happened to have a good idea in a meeting!"

"And he planned to bury another one there. He seemed to think it would keep the police focused on you because you kept tripping over dead bodies. He expected you to be at work for the patent meeting."

I shook my head. "I wasn't that interested. Only someone as obsessed as he was would believe I'd go in for a patent meeting on a Saturday morning. And since everyone but me received a cancellation notice shortly after the original email was sent out, no one else would have been inconvenienced. If I had complained, my lone griping would have been ignored."

Mark grinned. "I find you impossible to ignore." He handed me the final package he was carrying. It was sloppily wrapped. It reminded me of my own wrapping skills, which ranged from that first very carefully wrapped Christmas gift to the last gift, the one that was rolled in wrinkled paper and secured with a lot of tape. On that scale, this gift was about the third one from the bottom.

I hefted it. "Clothes?"

"I ripped your shirt."

"Oh, well. It wasn't much of a shirt."

He grinned. "These are."

I tore the paper off. There were three soft and fluffy t-shirts inside. I shook one out. "Nice. Black is good." I held it up against my chest.

Mark reached over and unzipped a zipper under the left shoulder. "One pocket here and another large one down on the side." He lifted the end to show me. "You can carry your phone. Maybe I won't lose track of you if you actually carry your phone."

I inspected Mark from head to toe. His shirt was tucked in tight. There was no way to see if he had a hidden side pocket in his shirt. His jeans were snug against his very nice form.

He caught me checking him out, not that I had tried to hide it. He pulled me in for a kiss, guiding my hands to his hips. "You'll have to do quite a bit of searching to find out," he said.

His own hands were doing enough exploring that had I had anything in any shirt pocket, his questing hands would have discovered it.

When he finally allowed some air between us, he said, "Your new shirts should fit well, but you can take them off easily in an emergency."

I laughed. "Was that what we had? An emergency?"

He nodded, his eyes almost serious. "There was no time for scissors."

"I'm going to try one of these on." As focused as I was on Mark, it was no wonder I forgot about the robot piece hanging off the side of the couch. When I turned, my foot caught under one hard edge. The robot leg crashed to the carpet, forcing Mark to jump back.

I catapulted over it, my ankle twisting in the process. With a gasp, I stumbled free and fell into the recliner. The chair rocked back, threatening to flip me over the side. "Ow." I lifted my foot with a wince.

Mark sighed. "I'd ask if you hurt yourself, but it's kind of obvious." He picked up the robot parts and set them on the couch. "We need to get rid of this thing before your friends think up any other ideas." Kneeling next to me, he unlaced my shoe. "You need a keeper."

I sniffled, but the sharp pain was already receding. "I already have one." What was he if not my keeper? He was taking care of my foot, wasn't he?

He looked up at me. "A permanent one. Like a shadow, a..." His voice trailed off when we both realized at the same time that he was kneeling in front of me on one knee while holding my foot. He should have been holding my hand, not my foot, and a permanent keeper sort of implied a permanent relationship. Almost like, maybe marriage.

I trained my gaze on my hands, my fingers suddenly clenched in my lap.

"Why aren't you looking at me?" He reached up and bumped my chin gently.

I peeked at him.

"Well?"

"Well, what?" I caught his eyes and held there.

"I wonder what it would be like." He finished untying my shoe and eased it off.

I barely felt any pain in my foot. "Could be an interesting life."

He grinned and captured my face with both hands. He kissed me again.

I forgot about my foot when I slid forward onto his lap. He fell over sideways and took me with him.

"You're something else, you know that?" he said.

"You keep mentioning that. You're something yourself." My hair fell forward into my eyes. He fixed the problem by tucking it back.

"Maybe I'll ask someday. I wonder what you'd say?"

I was shy again, although how that could be, I can't imagine. I had no problem making my feelings known when it came to attacking his body. "That's kind of a dumb question, isn't it?"

His eyes shaded to insecure for a fleeting second. "It is?"

My shyness disappeared in an instant. "You have nothing to worry about," I promised him quietly.

His eyes brightened. "Hmm." He kissed me again, and this time we didn't stop to catch our breath. He was careful of my ankle, but nothing so paltry could keep me from him.

I was pretty sure that Mark hadn't exactly asked me to marry him, but that was okay. For now, barreling along in the direction we were headed together was enough.

Other Works

The Sedona O'Hala series (**Executive Lunch, Executive Retention, Executive Sick Days, Executive Dirt**) is a series of humorous cozy mysteries: Sedona solves a few crimes while fighting her way up the corporate ladder. Mostly she dangles from her fingertips, just trying to survive. You can find two free short stories in the Sedona series at Maria's blog.

Under Witch Moon is the first in an urban fantasy series: When dead bodies start turning up Adriel has no choice but to talk to White Feather, an undercover cop. Unfortunately, Adriel is a witch and White Feather isn't convinced she's innocent of wrongdoing. She's going to have to talk fast—and set spells even faster. **Under Witch Aura, Under Witch Curse** and **Ghost Shadow** complete the series.

Dragons of Wendal and **DragonKin** are cozy fantasies with a touch of romance.

Catch an Honest Thief is an adventurous caper across the New Mexico desert. Alexia is in search of treasure, survival and maybe love.

Soul of the Desert is an historical novel about an adopted child on the run from the mob.

If you're looking for short stories, you might enjoy the anthologies: **Tracking Magic** (Max Killian Investigations), **Sage** (Tales from a Magical Kingdom), **Black-Tie Bingo** or **Year of the Mountain Lion. Snitched, Snatched**, the inspiration for Dragons of Wendal, is still available as a short story in English and Spanish in one volume.

Maria's website: BearMountainBooks.com

www.ingramcontent.com/pod-product-compliance
Lightning Source LLC
Chambersburg PA
CBHW021149130626
46554CB00005B/1729